Enter the dark and seductive world of

JENNA BLACK

DEADLY
DESCENDANT

JENNA BLACK

Pocket Books

New York   London   Toronto   Sydney   New Delhi

Pocket Books
A Division of Simon & Schuster, Inc.
1230 Avenue of the Americas
New York, NY 10020

This book is a work of fiction. Names, characters, places, and incidents either are products of the author's imagination or are used fictitiously. Any resemblance to actual events or locales or persons, living or dead, is entirely coincidental.

Copyright © 2012 by Jenna Black

First Pocket Books paperback edition May 2012

POCKET and colophon are registered trademarks of Simon & Schuster, Inc.

For information about special discounts for bulk purchases, please contact Simon & Schuster Special Sales at 1-866-506-1949 or business@simonandschuster.com.

The Simon & Schuster Speakers Bureau can bring authors to your live event. For more information or to book an event, contact the Simon & Schuster Speakers Bureau at 1-866-248-3049 or visit our website at www.simonspeakers.com.

Designed by Jacquelynne Hudson

Manufactured in the United States of America

10 9 8 7 6 5 4 3 2 1

ISBN 978-1-4516-0680-5
ISBN 978-1-4516-0690-4 (ebook)

DEADLY
DESCENDANT

The Liberi Deorum

A long time ago, when the ancient gods were still around, they had children with mortals. Before the gods left Earth, they gave each of their children a seed from the Tree of Life. This seed made them immortal, and the Liberi thought they were gods themselves as a result. The only limitation they had—as far as they knew—was that they couldn't make their own children immortal, because the gods took the Tree of Life with them when they left. What the first Liberi didn't know until too late was that anyone with even a drop of divine blood—in other words, all of their children and descendants— could steal their immortality by killing them.

PROLOGUE

There's nothing like breaking things to lift a girl's spirits when she's had a lousy day. I'd been having a lot of lousy days lately.

I hefted a fat ballpoint pen, wondering if it was heavy enough to break one of the bottles I'd lined up on the opposite side of the clearing. Only one way to find out.

I sighted at a little eight-ounce Coke bottle, then pulled back my arm and threw the pen at it with all the strength I could muster. Pens aren't exactly aerodynamic, so my weapon's flight path was erratic at best. But seeing as I was a descendant of Artemis, goddess of the hunt, I had infallible aim. The pen tinked against the Coke bottle, making it waver on the fallen log I'd dragged into the clearing to hold my targets. Waver but not fall or break. Having infallible aim didn't mean I had the pitching arm of a Major League Baseball player.

Regular throwing practice was definitely making my arm stronger—when I'd first started, I never would have hit the bottle from this distance—but I was out here to break things, not just prove I could hit them. I bent over and dug into the tote bag I'd stuffed full of small, throwable household items. I pulled out a satisfyingly heavy ceramic coaster. Not exactly something you'd think of as a deadly weapon, but I was betting it would do the trick.

Instead of throwing overhand, this time I threw sidearm, thinking the coaster would fly more like a Frisbee. It wasn't the prettiest throw in the world, but it was accurate and hard. The bottle shattered into a satisfying spray of glass fragments, the force of the hit strong enough to break the coaster in two. Much more satisfying than the pen toss. If I'd been aiming at a person, I'd have done significant damage.

"I thought a petty thief had robbed the house, but now I see you were just gathering ammunition."

The voice came from behind me, and I couldn't help a little squeal of surprise as I whirled around to find Anderson Kane watching me.

Anderson was the leader of a small band of *Liberi*—immortal descendants of the ancient gods—who held to the lofty ideal that the *Liberi* should use their supernatural powers to help make the world a better place. I was the newest and most reluctant member of that band. We all lived together in Anderson's enormous mansion, although I had yet to acknowledge the place as home. I wasn't planning to give up my condo any-time soon, and I tried to spend the night there, in my own bed, at least once a week.

Anderson was also a god—not just the descendant of a god like the rest of his people but a real god, son of Thanatos and Alecto. Death and Vengeance, to their friends. He was also the only being in the universe—that I knew of, at least—who could destroy a *Liberi's* seed of immortality. Mortal descendants of the gods could *steal* a seed by killing a *Liberi,* but only Ander-son could actually *destroy* it, as I'd learned when I'd seen him reduce two *Liberi* to nothing more than a pile of empty clothes. I was one of only two people who knew his secret identity, and I hadn't been able to look at him the same way since I'd found out.

"Do you know how hard it is for me to find any time to myself in this place?" I grumbled at him, because even though he intimidated the hell out of me, I tried not to show it.

Anderson glanced at his watch. "I saw you storm out here about a half hour ago. I figured I'd given you enough time to do whatever brooding you needed to do."

I clamped my jaws shut to keep from saying any-thing I might regret. Anderson looked like such a normal, unprepossessing guy, everything about him "medium." Medium height, medium build, medium brown hair . . . You get the picture. But I'd seen him without his human disguise, and I knew beyond a doubt that I didn't want to piss him off.

"I'm not brooding," I ground out. "I'm doing target practice."

"Yes, I can see that. But I've noticed a strong correlation between you doing target practice and you being out of sorts about something. So tell me what's wrong."

The way he phrased that—like a command, not a question—rubbed me the wrong way, but then, just about everything was rubbing me the wrong way this afternoon.

"Nothing that matters to you," I said, sounding a little more sullen than I'd have liked. Have I mentioned it had been a really lousy day?

Anderson gave me one of his reproving looks. He was really good at them, and I decided I'd get rid of him sooner if I just told him what was eating me.

"There was a fire at my office building," I said, kicking at a patch of crabgrass. I was still nominally a private investigator. It said so on the door to my office. I'd had to put my work on hiatus when I'd first become *Liberi,* but now I was trying to resume at least part of my normal life. Which involved making money to live on. I might be getting free room and board at Anderson's mansion, but I was still paying rent and utilities on my condo, not to mention making car payments. I'd managed to work two whole jobs before today's setback. No, not setback, disaster.

"Some idiot left his space heater running when he went home for the night. Between the smoke damage and the dousing from the sprinkler system, my office is pretty much DOA," I continued. Insurance would reimburse me for the damages but not for the lost business or for the cost of the temporary office space I was going to have to find.

I kicked at the crabgrass again. Not that long ago, I'd been in a horrendous car accident. Well, it was an accident on my part, at least. Emmitt Cartwright, one of Anderson's *Liberi,* had strolled right into the middle of an ice-slicked road. He knew I was a mortal Descendant and therefore one of the only people in the world who could kill him. He'd used me to commit suicide, and by killing him, I'd inadvertently stolen his seed of immortality and turned life as I knew it on its ear.

The ripple effect of that accident was still causing me unexpected headaches. For example, I'd practically emptied my savings account to make the down payment on my new car, the old one having been totaled. Normally, that wouldn't have been a hardship, but now that I no longer had any money coming in, it was a different story. It sure looked like I was going to have to do something I'd vowed never to do: dip into my trust fund.

My adoptive parents had set up trust funds for me and their daughter, Steph, when we were kids. Steph had no qualms about living on that money, but I had steadfastly refused to touch it. It felt too much like charity, and as much as I loved them, I could never quite get over the feeling that I wasn't their "real" daughter. It was all right for their real daughter to use their money but not for me. Neurotic, maybe, but there you have it.

"Do you need some money?" Anderson asked.

"I'll be fine," I said, and it was true. I was going to have to swallow my pride, and I was going to feel like a hypocrite for touching that trust fund, but I wasn't facing financial ruin. All I had to do was get over my stupid hang-up. "I don't need charity."

There was a spark of something that might have been anger in Anderson's eyes, and I reminded myself who I was talking to. This was not someone I wanted to pick a fight with.

"I wasn't offering you charity," he said. "I was offering you a job."

That took me entirely by surprise. "Huh?"

He smiled faintly at the face I must have made. "I was trying to give you more time to acclimate before springing this on you, but it seems Fate had a different idea. One of the things I and my people do is help other *Liberi* and their families who are trying to escape the Olympians."

The Olympians are a group of *Liberi* descended from Greek gods. They do some truly awful things, slaughtering whole families of Descendants to protect their own immortality. Occasionally, they spare a small child and raise it as one of their own, indoctrinating it to their values of superiority, privilege, and cruelty. They had a whole flock of Descendant toadies, all vying for the privilege of being given a sacrificial *Liberi* from whom to steal the seed of immortality. Whenever the Olympians stumbled on *Liberi* who weren't descended from Greek gods or who refused to accept the natural order of things as dictated by the Olympians, they gave those *Liberi* to their pet Descendants to kill, and a new Olympian was born.

"Not everyone we help wants to join us," Anderson continued, then smiled ruefully. "And sometimes I'm not inclined to issue an invitation."

I frowned. "Then how is it you help them, exactly? Financially?"

He nodded. "That's one thing. But most important, we help them go into hiding, make sure the Olympians can never find them."

"You mean like a *Liberi* witness protection program?"

He grinned. "Exactly." The grin faded. "We've been doing this for years, and we've helped a lot of people. I think we do a damn good job, but we're not pros at this, and we've lost a couple of people."

"So what is it you want me to do?"

"I want you to go over the records for everyone we've hidden. See if you find any flaws in their cover, and then help us move them again with better cover if necessary. I'll pay you a retainer for as long as it takes to get all of the covers examined and patched."

The clanging sound in my head was the peal of warning bells. I had already been sucked into Anderson's merry band more deeply than I could ever have imagined. I was living in the freaking mansion, for Pete's sake! I'd spent too much time in foster care as a kid to allow myself to depend on anyone too much. The idea of fitting in somewhere, of being part of a family, of *belonging,* was my Holy Grail. But the Holy Grail wasn't real, and I knew better than to seek it. The last thing I needed was to let Anderson get even more hooks into me than he already had.

"Thanks for the offer," I said, "but I'd rather go it on my own. I haven't spent all this time building up my business just to abandon it at the first sign of trouble."

Anderson probably heard the falseness in my words. It wasn't commitment to my own business that made me refuse, but that was the most convenient excuse I could come up with off the cuff. Of course, I should have known better than to think Anderson would take no for an answer.

"Perhaps I wasn't completely clear about what I was asking," Anderson said. "People have gotten killed because we didn't do a good enough job of hiding them. I'm asking you to help me protect people who will be murdered—or worse—if their covers are blown. Surely, saving lives is more important than maintaining your independence."

Ah, the guilt trip. It was a highly effective tactic against me, and yet . . .

"Wait a minute. You want me to *examine your records* to see if these people are well enough hidden?"

"Yes."

Anderson was not an idiot, and I was sure he knew exactly what I was getting at. However, he didn't budge, giving me a look of polite, bland inquiry. Making me put it into words.

"Why the hell would you keep records on people you're trying to make disappear? It's like burying your treasure and then spray-painting a giant X on the spot."

"Only if the Olympians got hold of those records, and of course, we're very careful with them."

"But why?"

"You know why."

Of course I did. Anderson was capable of being a nice guy, but he was also a ruthless and manipulative son of a bitch when it served his purpose. "You want to make sure you can find them if you ever need them for something."

Hiding these *Liberi* fugitives gave Anderson a huge amount of power over them. If he needed something, and they refused him, he could hand them over to the Olympians. I didn't know if even he was ruthless enough to do such a thing, but it would make for a compelling threat.

"Nikki, you might not like how I go about things, but I am trying to keep these people safe, and I could sure use your help."

And I needed the money, unless I dipped into the trust fund. Which was the lesser of two evils: tapping the trust fund or letting Anderson draw me ever deeper into his world?

I was already being forced to live in the mansion because of the treaty Anderson had crafted with the Olympians. The Olympians had agreed that Anderson's *Liberi* and their families would be off-limits, and living in the mansion was what made someone "Anderson's *Liberi*." If I didn't live in the mansion, the Olympians would be free to continue their efforts to recruit me—efforts that included tactics like raping my sister. The Olympians had justified the attack by saying that Steph didn't count as family because we weren't blood relatives. Anderson had killed the bastard who hurt Steph, and Konstantin—the self-styled "king" of the Olympians—had sent a specious apology along with a promise to leave my adoptive family alone as long as I was one of Anderson's *Liberi*.

"Did you set the fire at my office to twist my arm into accepting this offer?" I asked, wondering at my ability to see Anderson as one of the good guys and yet still suspect him of something like that.

"No," he said, completely unoffended by the accusation. "You'll do it because you want to save lives, not because you need the money."

Anderson hadn't known me all that long, but he already had me pegged. If there weren't lives at stake, I'd have chosen taking money from the trust fund as the lesser of two evils in the end. I was already forced to depend on Anderson for room and board, thanks to his stupid treaty with the Olympians. To be forced to depend on him for my salary, too, was something I'd have greatly preferred to avoid.

But seriously, money aside, how could I justify using my abilities to track down deadbeat dads and people who skipped out on their bills when people's lives were potentially at risk? I knew I was being manipulated. But I also knew I couldn't live with myself if people got killed because of my selfish desire not to be subsumed.

"I want my old life back," I said sourly.

Anderson just gave me that knowing look of his.

ONE

Early January is not the best time to enjoy the outdoors in Arlington, but Anderson and his bitchy wife, Emma, were having a screaming argument in the house, and outside seemed the best place to be to avoid hearing it. I closed the front door behind me, and the shouting voices were muffled down to a low buzz. The winter air bit at my cheeks, and I stuffed my hands into the pockets of my jacket to keep them warm. Definitely not my favorite kind of weather, but the silence was sweet and soothing.

Figuring that I could handle the cold for a while, I sat on the picturesque porch swing and tried to pretend my life was my own. The illusion was hard to uphold when I lived in the mansion and spent my days working for Anderson, examining the covers he had built for the *Liberi* he had hidden.

He'd actually done a surprisingly good job, in large part thanks to Leo, our resident descendant of

Hermes, who had become a computer genius in order to better keep his finger on the pulse of the financial world. I hadn't found too many blatant holes in the covers so far, though I'd patched many small ones and still had a long way to go before I was finished.

My feet had gone numb, and I was beginning to think it was time to go in, when I noticed an unfamiliar car navigating the long driveway. I shivered in the freezing air as I watched the car approach, wondering who it could be. We didn't exactly get a lot of visitors at the mansion. That was sort of the point of the place. Whoever this was, someone was expecting them, since they had to be buzzed through the front gate.

I heard the door open behind me and turned to find Anderson stepping out to join me on the porch.

"Back inside, Nikki," he said, jerking his thumb at the house. "We're meeting in the formal living room."

I swallowed to contain my instinctive retort. I wasn't fond of being ordered around. A few weeks ago, when I'd thought Anderson was "just" a *Liberi,* I probably would have told him so. I wasn't a timid person, but I found I couldn't look at Anderson anymore without picturing him as the pillar of white fire he had turned into when he'd shed his disguise, and that image was more than enough to discourage my smart mouth.

I stifled my urge to protest and ducked back inside the mansion as Anderson waited on the porch for our mysterious visitors. The warm air flushed my cheeks, and they were probably red enough to look sunburned. Guess I'd been outside longer than I'd realized.

I made my way to the formal living room. I think the last time I'd set foot in there had been when Maggie gave me the grand tour of the house the night I'd moved in. It really was a *formal* living room, and Anderson's *Liberi* were a decidedly informal bunch.

The sofa and many of the chairs were already filled with other members of Anderson's household, with the notable exception of Emma. I guessed that meant her fight with Anderson was over—or at least on temporary hiatus. It was well nigh impossible to win a fight with Anderson, and Emma didn't take well to losing. Often, she flounced off in a huff afterward; other times, she'd go completely nonresponsive, staring off into space. She'd been Konstantin's prisoner for about a decade, until I'd found her and rescued her (with Anderson's help). When we'd first brought her back to the mansion, she'd been the next best thing to catatonic, and sometimes I harbored the guilty thought that I'd liked her better that way.

The woman was disturbed, no doubt about it, and there was only so much slack I was willing to cut her for the trauma she'd been through. I couldn't help wondering if some—if not all—of her "episodes" were faked, meant to guilt Anderson into being more agreeable. Sometimes it seemed to work. Other times, not so much.

I sat on a chair that, judging by the hardness of its seat and the carved knobs that dug into my back, was meant to be more ornamental than functional and leaned over toward Maggie. She was the closest thing I had to a friend among the *Liberi*.

"Any idea what's up?" I asked her.

She shrugged. "We have visitors, and I'm guessing it's Olympians, because Anderson gave us his 'my house, my rules' speech."

I made what I was sure was an ugly face. Anderson trotted out that phrase whenever he made an unpopular decision—like, for instance, when he invited me to live in the mansion. I was pretty sure that if it came down to a vote, I would be out on my ear. They were a close-knit bunch, Anderson's *Liberi,* and I was very much on the outside looking in.

"Sorry I missed it," I muttered, and Maggie laughed. She was a descendant of Zeus through Heracles, and she had the super strength to prove it. She was also by far the nicest of any of the *Liberi* I'd met. "Why would an Olympian be coming here?" I asked. I wouldn't quite say we were at war with the Olympians, but it was close. I suspected I knew what Anderson and Emma had been fighting about—her hatred for Konstantin and the Olympians was truly epic.

"I'm guessing we're about to find out," she said, jerking her chin toward the front, where Anderson was leading three people—two men flanking one woman—into the living room.

The woman was petite and fine-boned, like me, but that was where the resemblance ended. Her ash-blond hair was cut in a stylish bob, and though she wasn't classically beautiful, she was striking. I'd guess her age at around thirty—if she weren't *Liberi,* which meant she could be a thousand years old for all I knew.

Her posture was regally straight, with an aristocratic tilt to her chin that said she thought she was better than everyone around her. But then, she was an Olympian, and feeling superior to all non-Olympians was one of the membership requirements. The navy-blue skirt suit she wore looked like it cost about as much as your average compact car.

Beside the woman was a guy, maybe early twenties, with coarse-looking black curls and olive skin. He wasn't movie-star handsome, but he was roguishly cute, with a hint of dimples. He didn't have the woman's haughty demeanor, and he was dressed casually in jeans, a button-down shirt, and a slightly weathered sportcoat.

The other man had the look of hired muscle. Broad-shouldered, with buzz-cut hair and a square face, he was obviously wary of everyone in the room. The iridescent glyph on the side of his neck proclaimed him to be more than strictly human, but if I had to guess, I'd say he was a mortal Descendant, not a *Liberi* himself. At least, not yet.

Anderson invited the woman to sit in an armchair. When she crossed her legs, she made sure to flash the red soles of her Louboutins. Apparently, she wanted everyone to know that she was rich, because acting superior wasn't obnoxious enough. There weren't enough chairs for everyone, so our other two guests stood, the *Liberi* beside the woman's chair, the Descendant behind, looking menacing. As a Descendant, he could do what no one else could: kill a *Liberi,* thereby stealing his or her immortality and becoming *Liberi* himself. Well, no one else but Anderson, but that was far from common knowledge. His eyes suggested he was sizing us all up.

Across from me, Blake leaned forward and glared at the woman. He was a descendant of Eros and had once been a reluctant Olympian himself, until Anderson had offered him an alternative.

"You wouldn't be here if Anderson hadn't given you safe passage," he said. "Bringing your goon with you is an insult."

There was a glimmer of amusement in the woman's eyes. I doubted the insult had been unintentional, and Blake was giving her exactly the reaction she wanted. The goon didn't seem to mind being talked about that way, and the other guy deepened his dimples by smiling.

"How do you know the goon isn't mine?" he asked. His voice was pleasantly deep and mellow. "You could be taking Phoebe to task for something that is entirely my fault."

Blake looked back and forth between the two men and shook his head. "He's not your type, Cyrus." There was noticeably less hostility in his voice when he addressed Cyrus.

Cyrus laughed, looking over his shoulder and giving the goon a visual once-over. "Too true," he said, turning back to Blake. He leaned a hip against Phoebe's chair and propped his elbow on the top of it, his casual demeanor a striking contrast to the goon's menace and Phoebe's stiffness.

"This is supposed to be a peaceful meeting, Blake,"

Anderson chided. "Don't start a fight." He gave Blake a quelling look. Blake crossed his arms over his chest and leaned back in his seat.

Anderson turned his attention back to the two *Liberi*. "I believe you know everyone here except Nikki," he said, gesturing to me. "Nikki, this is Cyrus, Konstantin's son."

I might have blinked a bit in surprise, though now that I knew he was Konstantin's son, I could see the faint resemblance. Cyrus was much better-looking and didn't immediately set my nerves on edge as Konstantin had the one time I'd met him. His smile looked genuinely friendly, but looks can be deceiving.

"And this is Phoebe," Anderson continued.

"Also known as the Oracle," Blake said, and my eyes widened.

Blake had told me about the Oracle once before. She was a descendant of Apollo, and she had visions of the future. According to Blake, her visions were usually impossible to interpret until after the fact. It was thanks to some vision of hers that the Olympians had found out about me in the first place, and that automatically made her not one of my favorite people.

Phoebe looked me up and down, her lip faintly curled with disdain. Apparently, she wasn't impressed by what she saw. I can be sensitive about my looks sometimes, but I'd been looked down on by better snobs than Phoebe, and her disdain didn't bother me.

Phoebe dismissed me with a little sniff, turning her attention back to Anderson. "Let's not pretend a courtesy we don't feel," she said. "You don't like us, we don't like you, but at the moment, that's beside the point."

"Speak for yourself!" Cyrus said. "I like every-body." His visual once-over had been just as assessing as Phoebe's had been, but far less unpleasant. I was certain he wasn't a nice guy—otherwise, he wouldn't be an Olympian—but he put up a better front than any other Olympian I had met.

Phoebe gave him an annoyed glance. "We're here on business, remember?"

"I see no reason that should prevent us from being civil."

Either they were doing a good cop/bad cop routine, or Phoebe and Cyrus didn't much like each other. I put my money on the latter. The animosity between them seemed genuine.

"Why don't you tell us why you're here?" Anderson asked. I was sure he already knew, or he wouldn't have let the Olympians set foot in his territory.

Phoebe uncrossed her legs—I wondered if she'd crossed them in the first place just so she'd have the excuse to flash her Louboutins—and got down to business. "I had a vision."

"I'm shocked, *shocked* to hear that," Blake stage-whispered.

Phoebe spared him a curl of her lip, then pretended to ignore him. Cyrus sucked in his cheeks as if he was trying not to laugh.

"One that concerns both the Olympians and you people." There was a wealth of derision in the way she said that last part, and more than one of Anderson's

Liberi stiffened at the insult. A quelling look from Anderson forestalled any interruption, and Phoebe continued.

"If you've been reading the papers, you may have noticed that there have been a string of rather bizarre deaths in the area over the past three weeks."

Once upon a time, I'd been pretty good at keeping up with the news. Being up-to-date on current events struck me as a job requirement for a private investigator, but I'd been so distracted by my new life that I'd been slack about it lately.

"You're talking about the wild dog attacks, right?" asked Jack. He was a descendant of Loki, and making trouble was his religion. I wouldn't have expected him to be up on current affairs—that smacked almost of responsibility, a concept he usually disdained.

Phoebe inclined her head without speaking. Perhaps she didn't want to answer questions from "us people."

Jack let out an exaggerated sigh and rolled his eyes heavenward. "You've found me out!" he cried, jumping to his feet. "My evil plan is foiled!"

The air around him shimmered, and moments later, he disappeared, replaced by a massive black dog that looked like a cross between an Irish wolfhound and a pit bull. It barked loudly enough to rattle my teeth, then let out a fierce growl and bit the air.

It seemed I was the only one taken aback by Jack's little stunt. I'd had no idea he could do that. I made a mental note to look up Loki on the Internet when this meeting was over. Honestly, I should have spent some time researching everyone's divine ancestors by now, but I was still trying to adjust to my new reality. I had enough trouble worrying about my own ancestor and abilities without looking into others', at least for now. Maybe that was self-centered of me, but it helped protect my sanity.

Anderson shook his head in long-suffering patience. "Jack, sit. Stay. And shut up, while you're at it."

Jack gave him a doggie grin, complete with lolling tongue, then jumped back onto his chair, changing back into his human form in midair. I must have been staring at him in open amazement, because he turned to me and winked. I looked away quickly.

Phoebe was sneering again, and Cyrus's eyes twinkled with humor. He seemed to think pretty much everything was funny—rather like Jack, come to think of it. It made him seem less dangerous, and I realized that was the point. With his dimpled cheeks, Cyrus wouldn't be that good at overt menace, so camouflaging it to lull everyone into a false sense of security was probably a calculated strategy.

I put my speculation aside for the moment and looked at Phoebe. "What do wild dog attacks have to do with the *Liberi*?"

"They're not really wild dog attacks," she said, her every word dripping with condescension. Evidently, she didn't have a very high opinion of my intelligence.

"Yeah, I figured you wouldn't be here talking to us if they were," I said. "I was just trying to move this conversation along."

Phoebe glanced sidelong at Anderson, as if expecting him to chastise me for speaking out of turn. There was a moment of uncomfortable silence, and then Phoebe continued.

"In my vision, I saw a man with a jackal's head being dragged through an institutional-looking hallway under armed military escort. I believe that means there's a *Liberi* behind these attacks and that he's descended from Anubis."

The sum total of my knowledge about Anubis was that he was an Egyptian god with a jackal's head. Despite everything I'd seen and been through already, I always felt a little shock of incredulity when hearing about someone being descended from a god. A mental *Yeah, right* was still my natural reaction, although I'd feel stupid about it two seconds later.

"If I'm right," Phoebe continued, "we have to stop him before the mortals track him down. If the government gets its hands on a *Liberi* . . . Well, it would be bad. For all of us."

Blake snorted. "Notice how the fact that there's a *Liberi* out there killing people is completely irrelevant to this discussion. If the Olympians weren't worried about their own hides, they'd just sit back and enjoy the show."

"I don't see any sign that *you're* out there hunting the killer already," she retorted.

"Oh, we were supposed to know already that these wild dog attacks are actually the work of a *Liberi*?" He raised his eyebrows at her in a mockery of polite inquiry.

"You know now," Cyrus interjected, surprising me by taking the heat off of Phoebe. Not that I thought she appreciated it. "We don't have to have great and noble intentions, do we?"

"Maybe you ought to try it sometime," Blake said. The words were antagonistic, and yet there wasn't the same rancor in his voice when he spoke to Cyrus as there was when he spoke to Phoebe.

Cyrus shrugged. "I don't think it would suit me. To tell you the truth, I'm not sure it suits *you* all that well, either."

It wasn't Blake's fault he'd been an Olympian— before Anderson came along, the choice was join the Olympians or die—but I'd often thought his moral compass was a little short of due north. With his casual words, Cyrus seemed to have finally hit a nerve, and Blake clenched his jaw so hard I could see his bones outlined against his cheeks.

"So," Anderson put in before tensions could escalate, "do you have any idea what this *Liberi*'s powers are? How is he killing these people? And why is he doing it, especially here, of all places?"

Here in the *Liberi* capital of the world, he meant. Because the Olympians were headquartered here, the D.C. area had the highest number of *Liberi* per capita of anywhere in the world, by a wide margin. It was like the killer was just *daring* the Olympians to come after him and "harvest" his immortality.

"We're not sure how he's doing it," Phoebe answered. "Our best guess is that he can control any-thing canine and that when he wants to kill, he just summons all the stray dogs in the area and commands them to maul his victim. As for why . . ." She shook her head. "Either he doesn't know the kind of danger he's putting himself in, or he's just plain crazy. Serial killers don't necessarily need reasons—at least, not reasons that make sense to ordinary folk."

Phoebe turned to fix her eyes on me. "We will, of course, do our best to help find this *Liberi* and stop him. However, now that you have a descendant of Artemis in your fold, you probably are better equipped for the hunt than we are."

Although she was looking straight at me, she was obviously talking to Anderson. That didn't stop me from answering.

"You left out one strong possibility for why Dogboy would be wreaking havoc in D.C.," I said. "Like he knows perfectly well that this is the Olympian head-quarters, and he has a major grudge against Olympians. I mean, I can't imagine why, since you guys are all sweetness and light and everything, but I think the possibility bears examining."

The look Phoebe gave me was positively chilling— I seem to have a talent for pissing off Olympians.

"I can't imagine why someone who has a grudge against us would attack a bunch of mortals," she said. "That would be more likely to hurt *you* than *us*." She flashed Anderson a sly smile. "Perhaps it's someone who has a grudge against *you*? You have been around a while, and I'm sure you've made some enemies in your day."

I'd seen ample proof that Anderson had a temper,

and a scary one at that, but he showed no sign that Phoebe's insinuations had gotten under his skin.

"I'm not aware of any descendant of Anubis who might wish me ill," he said mildly, "though I suppose it's possible. I have, as you said, been around for a while. But then, so has Konstantin."

She conceded the point with a shrug. "I don't think it much matters why the killer is in D.C. He has to be stopped, before the mortals get their hands on him and our existence is exposed."

The overwhelming concern for human life was touching, to say the least. But despite her selfish motivations, she was right, and this guy had to be stopped. Assuming anything she'd told us was the truth, though I couldn't imagine what she'd have to gain by making this up.

Cyrus suddenly stood up straight for the first time, his gaze focused somewhere behind my left shoulder. I couldn't resist glancing behind me to see what he was looking at.

Emma stood in the hallway, just outside the living room. Her glossy black hair hung loose around her shoulders, making her skin look even paler and more delicate than usual. The ruby-red lipstick heightened the effect even more, though I already knew she wasn't as delicate as she looked.

Cyrus had stopped smiling, his expression turning solemn as he met Emma's gaze. Out of the corner of my eye, I saw Anderson stiffen ever so slightly, and I knew why. Konstantin and Alexis, his then right-hand man, had raped Emma while she was their prisoner. Anderson couldn't help wondering if any of the other Olympians had participated. Emma, apparently, refused to talk about it.

I think Cyrus saw and understood the speculation in Anderson's eyes, too, and he gave Emma a courtly half bow.

"What my father did to you was unnecessarily cruel," he said, and he sounded sincere enough. "He'll never apologize for it himself, so I'll do it on his behalf."

Phoebe made a sound of annoyance. "Oh, stop posturing, Cyrus. I never heard you complaining during the years she was our 'guest.'"

Emma stood silent and motionless in the hall; then she shivered and crossed her arms over her chest. I couldn't imagine the hell she'd gone through, and for the moment, I forgot her frequent bitchy spells and just felt sorry for her.

"I'd have complained if I'd thought it would make a difference," Cyrus said. His words seemed directed to Emma rather than Phoebe.

"Because you're such an all-around nice guy?" Blake needled. His tone made the barb sound almost friendly, like there was no real rancor behind it. If I had to guess, I'd say Blake actually *liked* Cyrus, despite the antagonistic potshots he'd been taking.

Cyrus finally pried his gaze away from Emma and glanced at Blake, his expression solemn. "Because I'm not my father."

Phoebe rolled her eyes and rose to her feet. "I think we're done here."

"I agree," Anderson said tightly. This talk of Emma's ordeal had clearly gotten to him. He stood up, his attention torn between Emma, who was now silently crying, and the Olympians, who were technically his guests—and whom he didn't trust for a moment.

"I'll show them to the door," Blake offered.

Anderson nodded his approval, then quickly crossed to Emma and gathered her into his arms.

Two

After briefly accepting Anderson's hug, Emma pulled away and gave him a quavering smile. She looked frail and broken, quite unlike the battle-ax I knew she was capable of being.

"Why don't you come sit down?" he asked her gently. "I'll fill you in on what you've missed."

But Emma shook her head. "I think I need to lie down for a little while."

Call me a cynic—or an insensitive bitch—but no matter how sorry I felt for Emma, I couldn't help being annoyed at what seemed a blatant attempt at manipulation. The pathetic way she was looking at him said she wanted him to come with her and comfort her. I didn't know how much of our meeting with the Olympians she'd overheard, but she had to know that we'd been discussing something important. There was no other reason Anderson would have let the Olympians cross his threshold. And yet she wasn't even interested enough to find out what was going on before she tried to draw him away.

Anderson stroked a tear from her cheek. "Are you sure? Maybe—"

"I'm sure," Emma interrupted. There was a slight edge in her voice, like she was really put out that Anderson might think there were more important things in the world than cuddling her when she cried. She put her nose in the air and made a tastefully dramatic exit just as Blake returned from seeing the Olympians out.

"You're not seriously considering teaming up with the Olympians, are you?" Blake asked Anderson the moment Emma was out of sight.

Anderson glanced at him but didn't say anything as he took his time crossing the room and sitting down. He was generally pretty easygoing and wasn't the type to bark out orders. Not the kind of guy who screams "alpha male" with every word he speaks and every move he makes. And yet he was an alpha male through and through, and I don't think he much liked Blake's tone.

Anderson sat back in his chair, making himself comfortable before he deigned to answer the question. "We're certainly not 'teaming up' with them. However, it's possible that just this once, their interests and ours are in line."

"If anything Phoebe said was true," Blake countered.

"Well, the part about the dog attacks was true," Jack said. "And you have to admit, that's not something you'd expect in the heart of the city. And the victims were all adult men. It's a rare pack of wild dogs that would attack an adult male."

"Since when have you become an expert in dog behavior?" Blake countered.

Jack grinned. "Wasn't it just this morning you called me a son of a bitch?"

I winced and groaned. "Ugh. That's bad even for you."

"Honey, I save my A material for people who are capable of appreciating my genius."

I knew he'd called me "honey" with the express purpose of irritating me, but that didn't stop the surge of indignation. I'd have dazzled him with my own witty repartee, except Jack was sitting there grinning at me, ready to pounce on my response. He loved being the center of attention, and I didn't want to play into his hands.

Lucky for me, Anderson intervened before I lost my ability to contain my retort. "Let's stay on topic, people. When Phoebe called me to request this meeting, I did a little fact checking, and there have indeed been three fatal dog attacks recently. Jack's right that it's all pretty bizarre. What kind of wild dog pack is randomly going to maul three adult men, all in different parts of the city, and with absolutely no witnesses?"

"No witnesses to the attacks," Jack added, "and no reported sightings of a pack of dogs large enough to do it."

We all chewed that one over for a while. It wasn't so ridiculous to think the attacks might be supernatural in nature. Once you allowed yourself to admit that the supernatural exists at all, of course.

"Just because a *Liberi* is probably behind the attacks doesn't mean anything else Phoebe said was true," Blake argued. "Like her explanation of why the Olympians care about someone who kills people."

"It's plausible that they would be concerned about the risk of exposure," Anderson said. "It's also plausible that there's something else behind their request for help."

"Like they're going to use this hunt to try to trap Nikki and force her to work for them," Blake suggested.

Konstantin had tried to recruit me for the Olympians when I'd first become *Liberi*. His recruitment techniques included such compelling persuasions as having his right-hand man kidnap and rape my sister—a fate I could supposedly have saved her from if only I'd agreed to join them. Of course, since it was their mission in life to wipe out every mortal Descendant in the world except for the chosen few they indoctrinated, if I'd joined them, they'd have made me hunt for who knows how many innocent men, women, and children whom they would slaughter. File that under "Not Gonna Happen."

"I'm not suggesting we go blundering into anything blindly," Anderson said. "I'd like us to start out by just doing a little more research." He turned to Leo, who was sneaking glances at a handheld every few seconds. Guess he was afraid the stock market would pull a fast one on him if he didn't keep an eye on it.

"See if you can get hold of the actual police reports. There might be information they haven't shared with the public that will help us figure out whether the attacks are supernatural or not."

"Sure thing, boss," Leo said. I'd known he was good with computers, but the confidence with which he agreed to go searching for police reports said he was hacker-level good.

"And Nikki," Anderson continued, "see what you can find out about the victims. See if you can find any link between them and the Olympians."

That was something I could do, something my years as a private investigator had prepared me for. Hunting for a supernatural serial killer, on the other hand, was so far outside my comfort zone it might as well have been brain surgery. I hoped to God we'd find out there was nothing supernatural whatsoever about these attacks so that I could get off the hook. It was a selfish attitude, no doubt about it, but I figured after the hell I'd been through lately, I was entitled to a little selfishness.

I stopped by the kitchen before going up to my suite. I needed a healthy dose of coffee before I got to work. By the time I'd brewed a pot, doctored it to my liking, and gotten to my suite, Leo had already emailed me several articles about the dog attacks, along with the police report on the first one.

I skimmed the news articles, although I seriously doubted they'd have a lot of important information compared with what I would find in the police reports.

Maybe I was just stalling because I wasn't looking forward to cracking open files that would have photos of dead, mauled bodies. I was a P.I., not a cop, and I was embarrassingly squeamish. I'd thrown up when we had to dissect a frog in high school, and even *thinking* about looking at the photos was making me a little queasy.

According to online reports, the attacks had each occurred on a Friday night, one attack per week over the last three weeks. The first had been in Anacostia, and the victim had been so badly mauled he had yet to be identified.

The second attack had occurred in Trinidad. The victim, Eddie Van Buren, was an unemployed former banker who'd been found near the National Arboretum. According to the article, Van Buren had been forty-three when he died, though the accompanying photo showed a man who couldn't be more than twenty-five. In the photo, he was handsome and athletic-looking, and I had to wonder if they'd chosen to use the old photo because falling on hard times had stolen his good looks.

The third attack had occurred in Ledroit Park, and the victim was Calvin Hodge, a criminal attorney. The picture in the paper showed a smiling middle-aged man with a neat black beard and a power suit.

It was impossible to imagine that a pack of wild dogs could cover that much territory in the heart of D.C. without being spotted by someone. It was also impossible that they would randomly decide to attack lone male victims on Friday nights exactly one week apart. The reporter who wrote the third article parroted the police's assertions that, despite the improbability of it all, these killings were all the result of wild dog attacks, but I could almost feel the reporter's skepticism.

Either the perpetrator was a serial killer who owned a pack of attack dogs, or Phoebe was right and there was a *Liberi* behind it. I had to put my money on option number two, no matter how much I didn't like it.

By the time I'd finished skimming the articles, copies of all three police reports were in my in-box. Leo worked fast. And I didn't want to know how he'd managed to get hold of confidential police reports within the space of an hour.

I chugged down the rest of my coffee before it got cold, staring at my in-box, trying to work up the courage to open the first file. I gave myself a mental kick in the ass, took a deep breath, and double-clicked on the first attachment. There were several pages of notes, but I skipped immediately to the photos, knowing I wouldn't be able to concentrate on the text until I'd gotten this part over with.

I managed to get through the first shot by almost convincing myself I was looking at special effects from some cheesy horror movie. I was less convinced when I peeked at the second one, and the third one made everything too real. I had to bolt to the bathroom, where I emptied out my coffee and my lunch. By the time I was finished, I was sweaty and shaking, my stomach still rumbling unhappily. I splashed cold water on my face and tried to keep my breathing slow and steady.

"Some kick-ass supernatural huntress *you* turned out to be," I muttered to my reflection.

The last thing in the world I wanted to do was go back to my computer and look at those photos again. What were the chances I'd spot something the police hadn't and that whatever I spotted would lead me to the killer? Even given my own brand-new supernatural abilities, those odds were pretty slim. But I knew I had to look. If it turned out there was something I should have seen and someone else died horribly because I'd been too much of a wimp to look at a few nasty photos, I'd never be able to live with myself.

It took several more tries before I could force myself to look at the photos for more than half a second at a time. My imagination was going to have a field day with these images if I let it.

"Mind over matter," I kept repeating to myself under my breath, then gripped the arms of my chair and forced myself to look.

It wasn't hard to tell why victim number one hadn't been identified yet. Saying he'd been "mauled" was an understatement. *Shredded* was more like it. The crime scene was under an overpass, and there was blood everywhere. Blood painted the sidewalk and the street, dripped down the walls on both sides, and spotted the ceiling. Bits and pieces of him were scattered willy-nilly, and I wouldn't have known these were human remains if it weren't for the head—skull, actually—that rested on its neck on the sidewalk, like it was rising out of the ground. Close-ups showed obvious teeth marks on the exposed bone.

I tried very hard to distance myself from what I was seeing, to look at it with dispassionate eyes and search for clues to who might have done this and where he might have gone, but I couldn't get past the horror. I hoped to God the poor man had been dead before most of the carnage occurred. I told myself he had to have been, otherwise someone would have heard the screams and seen something. Of course, residents of tough neighborhoods like Anacostia knew investigating sounds of violence was seriously bad for your health, as was volunteering information to the police.

Still shuddering in revulsion, I forced myself to look through all of the photos. If there was important evidence there, I failed to see it.

I combed over the written report, hoping I'd have an easier time coping with that. And I did, until I got to the part that said the victim's internal organs were missing. The report theorized that the victim had been killed by a pack of feral dogs and that the dogs had eaten the viscera.

Nausea roiled in my empty stomach, and my skin was clammy with sweat as I tried not to let my imagination paint too clear a picture of what the poor victim had been through. And what his family would go through, if and when the body was ever identified. The idea of having your loved one not only killed but eaten . . . I shuddered.

"I'm not cut out to be a cop," I muttered under my breath. There was a reason I'd chosen to be a private investigator instead of entering law enforcement. Numerous reasons, actually, but being exposed to violence on this level topped the list.

The next two reports were just as awful, the victims brutalized beyond recognition. By the time the third victim was found, the police were sure they were hunting a human suspect who used dogs as his deadly weapon, though they hadn't shared this conclusion with the press.

I spent several hours going over the police reports, and while they gave me a clearer picture of what had happened, I couldn't say they brought me any closer to finding the killer.

I closed down the files at around five o'clock, and as if he had a sixth sense, Anderson showed up on my doorstep at approximately 5:01.

"Ready to wrap up the case yet?" he asked me with a wry smile.

I was already jittery from my day's work. Being alone in a room with Anderson was not high on my list of things I wanted to do at the moment. Someday I would have to find a way to get over being creeped out by the knowledge that he was a freaking god, but I wasn't there yet.

I pushed back my chair and stood up, stretching out my stiff muscles and putting a little more distance between us as Anderson came to rest a hip on my desk.

"Not quite," I responded, hoping I didn't sound nervous. "You know, looking at crime-scene photos and police reports isn't exactly the same as chatting up nosy neighbors to see if they've seen the deadbeat dad around lately." I waved my hand vaguely at the computer. "This is not my area of expertise."

"Not yet," he agreed amiably. "But expertise or not, you're more likely to find the killer than the police are. They're going to be limited by their insistence on rational explanations."

I acknowledged that with a shrug. Since the police were convinced the killer had a pack of attack dogs, they were sure he was traveling in some kind of van or truck—a perfectly rational conclusion but one that could potentially skew their investigation. I didn't know exactly what the killer was doing, but I doubted it was what the police were thinking.

"What have you found?"

I moved to the other side of the room, Anderson following me. *There's no reason to be nervous around him,* I told myself. He was still the same guy he'd been before I learned his secret. True, I had seen him kill a couple of people, and that was bound to make me uncomfortable. But I'd known all along he had a ruthless streak, and it had never made me this edgy before.

I sat stiffly on the sofa, hoping Anderson would take the love seat. Of course, he didn't get my mental hint, instead taking a seat on the other end of the sofa and turning to face me.

He looked so unprepossessing it was hard to reconcile that image with what I knew was inside him. His medium brown hair was perpetually in need of a cut, his cheeks were perpetually peppered with five o'clock shadow—the kind that looks scruffy, not the kind that looks sexy—and he really needed to start buying no-iron shirts.

I cleared my throat, trying to focus on the here and now, not think about Anderson as a towering pillar of white light loping off in pursuit of his prey.

"The police are very confused," I said. "These definitely look like dog attacks. The bites indicate at least five or six medium-sized dogs. There are some paw prints here and there, though not as many as there should be with that many dogs, and the crime-scene techs haven't been able to find any dog hair, which is totally bizarre."

"Maybe the dogs were wearing gloves," Anderson suggested, completely deadpan.

The comment surprised a quick laugh out of me. "Or at least hairnets. Maybe the men were attacked by dogs in the food-service industry. That ought to narrow down the suspect pool."

Anderson smiled. "There. Now, that's more like the Nikki I know."

The comment killed my amusement. I guess I hadn't been acting as normal around him as I'd hoped. There was a long moment of awkward silence. I knew better than to race to fill that silence, but I couldn't help myself.

"What do you want me to say?" I asked. "I can't pretend I didn't see what I saw."

"But you don't have to tiptoe around me like I'm a keg of dynamite just waiting to blow. I'm dangerous to the bad guys, not to you."

I met his eyes in a challenging stare, too irritated by his statement to be cautious. "Are you forgetting that you threatened to kill me?"

He waved that off carelessly. "I had to give you incentive not to tell anyone about me. It's certainly not a threat I have any expectation of carrying out."

Oh, yeah, that made it *so* much better. "Look, I'll try to act more normal, but you're going to have to give me some time. I've had to absorb a hell of a lot of shocks in the last few weeks, and there's only so much I can take."

There was no mistaking the remorse that flashed through Anderson's eyes then. "Of course. I'm being an ass. Sorry."

All at once, he seemed more human to me than he had ever since I'd learned his true identity, and the knot in my gut loosened ever so slightly. I acknowledged his apology with a nod, then moved on.

"I guess my next logical course of action is to go examine the crime scenes myself," I said, thinking on the fly. "I didn't get anything out of looking at the photos, but maybe an idea will come to me when I'm on-site."

Anderson looked doubtful. "You really think there'll be any evidence left?"

"Probably not. But I'm not looking for evidence so much as clues. And if there's anything I've learned about my power, it's that I don't much understand how it works." My supernatural aim was something I could wrap my brain around, something I could pinpoint and control. My knack for finding people was much more elusive and hard to tap consciously. "Maybe looking at the crime scenes will give me nothing, but it can't hurt to try."

Anderson nodded. "Makes sense. But take Jamaal with you when you go. There's always a chance this is some kind of weird Olympian setup we don't understand. I don't want you going anywhere alone for the time being."

I was perfectly happy to take backup, but . . . "I'll take someone with me but not Jamaal."

Jamaal was a descendant of Kali, and he had some severe anger-management issues, especially where I was concerned. Not that I could blame him. I *had* killed his best friend, Emmitt, in a car accident. He probably didn't think I was an Olympian spy anymore, and he seemed to have accepted that I hadn't killed Emmitt on purpose, but I was still far from his favorite person.

"No, you'll take Jamaal," Anderson said firmly. "If you need the backup, you'll want someone who's good in a fight. Jamaal and Logan are the best for that, but Logan might draw unwanted attention in Anacostia."

"And Jamaal won't?" I asked incredulously. Sure, Jamaal was black, but he wouldn't exactly fit in with the gang-banger crowd.

"Maybe. But he looks a lot more intimidating."

Which I had to concede was true. Logan looked like an ordinary guy, despite being descended from a war god. Jamaal, on the other hand, looked like the kind of guy who could kill you with both hands tied behind his back. In fact, I was pretty sure he could. But

I still didn't like the idea of us spending so much time together, especially not without a referee.

Anderson met my mutinous gaze and smiled. "Think of it as a team-building exercise."

I'd have argued more, except I was sure this was an order, not a request. I didn't like taking orders, but Anderson was now officially my boss, so I didn't suppose I had much choice in the matter.

"You should give me hazard pay for this," I grumbled, and I meant for traveling with Jamaal, not hunting the killer.

"That can be arranged," Anderson said, though I'd meant it as a joke. "Chasing serial killers is definitely not in the job description I gave you."

I had a feeling that over time, I'd end up working on more and more stuff that wasn't in the job description if I let Anderson keep pushing me. But there was no way I was going to push back under the circumstances; I was just going to have to bite the bullet.

THREE

I found Jamaal out on the front porch, smoking one of those foul-smelling clove cigarettes he was so fond of. Anderson wouldn't let him light up in the house. I'm not a big fan of smoking, even if you were immortal and didn't have to worry about lung cancer, but I *am* a big fan of anything that helps keep Jamaal from going psycho, so as far as I was concerned, he could smoke five packs a day if it helped calm him. Still, my nose wrinkled whenever I caught the scent, and I tried to stay upwind.

"I'm going to go check out the crime scenes," I told him as the wind shifted and the cloud of smoke followed me like a homing pigeon. I waved my hand in front of my face and stepped to the side. "Anderson wants you to go with me in case the Olympians are lying in wait or something."

I refrained from rolling my eyes. Honestly, I didn't think this was an Olympian setup. If they'd wanted me that bad, they could have jumped me anytime in the last several weeks. I'd been cautious ever since I'd been dragged into the world of the *Liberi*, but it wasn't like I had a bodyguard with me twenty-four/ seven. Besides, one of the main reasons they'd wanted to "recruit" me had been to keep me from helping Anderson rescue Emma, and that horse had left the barn long ago.

Jamaal made a face and shook his head, the beads in his hair rattling and clicking. "You mean he wants us to make nice with each other," he said, stubbing out his cigarette in the ashtray he carried around with him.

The wind shifted again, and the cloud of smoke from Jamaal's last puff blew straight into my face, making my eyes burn. I stepped away, holding my breath until I was in the clear.

"That's how I interpreted it," I agreed. I didn't much enjoy the prospect of being shut up in a car with Jamaal. He'd dialed back on the hostility a lot, but I knew it was still there, lurking. He was learning to live with me, but I didn't think he'd ever forgive me for being the instrument of Emmitt's death.

Jamaal didn't look much happier with the situation than I was, but he'd learned his lesson about defying Anderson's orders, and he wasn't about to do it again anytime soon. He finished stubbing out his cigarette with a little more force than necessary, then laid the ashtray down on a low, glass-topped table.

"Fine. Let's go."

He headed down the stairs toward the garage, which was a separate outbuilding just past the circular drive. With his long legs and huge stride, he was practically halfway there before I even got moving. I hurried to catch up.

"Hold on a sec," I said. "I don't have my purse."

He didn't slow down. "What do you need a purse for? We're just going to look around, right?"

"Car keys, driver's license, wallet. You know. Stuff."

He reached into his front pocket and pulled out a set of keys. "I'm driving, so you don't need any of that shit."

Ah, the joys of living with supernatural alpha males.

"No, *I'm* driving," I said, still trailing along behind him. "I'm the one who knows where we're going, remember?"

He came to a stop so abruptly I almost crashed into him. "So give me directions," he said, glowering down at me. He had a very effective glower, and I had to fight my instinctive urge to take a step back. "I'm not cramming myself into that clown car you drive."

After I'd wrecked my last car, I'd decided to splurge and buy myself the Mini I'd been lusting over for a couple of years. I'd always driven sedate, nondescript sedans before—much more practical for my job than the zippy little Mini—but after the fistful of traumas I'd suffered, I'd decided to reward myself.

"Bullshit," I said. "You're just one of those guys who has a problem letting a woman drive."

I thought I saw the corner of his mouth twitch, like he might have been considering a smile, but Jamaal's smiles are as rare as four-leaf clovers. He hit the button on his key fob to open the garage door, then selected a key and held it out to me.

"Can you drive a stick?" he asked.

I had a feeling he already knew the answer. After all, I'd committed the ultimate sacrilege of getting my Mini with an automatic transmission. I was tempted to lie just to call his bluff—I wondered if he'd have a change of heart as soon as he learned I'd actually take him up on his offer—but decided to let it go.

"Fine," I grumbled, reaching for the passenger door of Jamaal's sleek black Saab. "You drive."

He nodded in satisfaction as he slid in behind the wheel.

About thirty minutes later, we arrived at the first crime scene in Anacostia. Naturally, it was dark by the time we got there. Anacostia is a neighborhood I'd avoid if possible during the daytime and categorically refuse to set foot in once the sun was down. I might not be eager to spend a whole lot of time in Jamaal's company, but I was reluctantly grateful to have him along as we walked from the dilapidated parking lot at Anacostia Park to the underpass where victim number one had met his demise.

There weren't a whole lot of people around, but those who *were* around stared at me like I was a zoo animal. Like, say, a dik-dik wandering through the lion enclosure.

The murder had occurred three weeks ago, so I wasn't expecting to find anything. I stood where our

John Doe had been killed, hoping to spot an important clue, and tried not to remember the crime-scene photos.

If the killer had been looking for the perfect place to kill someone in complete privacy in the heart of D.C., he'd done a good job of it. The road curved as it went through the underpass, limiting the line of sight, and the concrete walls would block sound effectively. Not that there seemed to be any houses or businesses within hearing distance right here by the park.

"See anything significant?" Jamaal asked me, and I had to shake my head. "Then can we get out of here? It reeks."

There was a certain eau-de-men's-room scent in the air. I looked around a little more, taking note of a couple of drains at the edge of the road, but nothing leapt out and yelled "Clue!" at me. I wished I had some idea of what I was doing. I was used to feeling like a more-than-competent professional, and this being-clueless crap sucked.

We made our way back to the parking lot, which was just around the bend in the road, and I silently cursed my mercurial power. I had no idea if I'd actually seen anything significant in that underpass, and I had to trust my subconscious to have absorbed whatever information might be there and disgorge it later, when and if it was relevant. Personally, I was a big fan of sure things, and anything subconscious was *not* a sure thing.

The parking lot had been practically deserted when we parked there, but, like chum in the water, Jamaal's

Saab had drawn some local predators. A handful of teenage punks, the oldest of whom was maybe sixteen, were circling the car, checking it out with greedy eyes. We'd probably been gone no more than ten minutes, but I got the feeling we were lucky the car was still there and in one piece.

When Jamaal and I stepped into view, the kids lost interest in the car and fixated on me. I'm short and fine-boned, and my delicate features make me look like an easy victim. The oldest of the kids straightened up from his slouch, his eyes locked on me in a way that made my skin crawl. I was afraid things were going to get ugly, and I wished I'd insisted on going back into the mansion for my purse, because I could have stuck a gun in it.

Beside me, Jamaal came to a stop, turning to glare at my admirers. There were five of them, and I pegged them as gang-bangers, probably armed despite their tender age. I worried that Jamaal's challenging stare would pique their leader's alpha-male instincts, but apparently, the kid was smarter than he looked. He only held Jamaal's gaze for about five seconds before something he saw there warned him off. I might have been imagining things, but I could have sworn the kid shuddered as he looked away. If he did, he recovered his composure quickly.

With a careless shrug, he beckoned to his pals and strutted down the sidewalk away from us. I turned to compliment Jamaal on his intimidation techniques, but the words died in my throat when I saw his face.

Jamaal is a naturally intimidating guy, and I'd been

on the receiving end of more than one of his death glares. He'd seemed to have backed off from the edge a bit lately—ever since Anderson had threatened to kick him out of the house if he didn't reel it in—but I saw now that the rage was still very much there. His chocolate-brown eyes were practically giving off sparks, and his lips had pulled back from his teeth in a feral snarl. He was leaning forward ever so slightly, his fists clenched at his sides, his breath coming in shallow pants. Now I knew why the kids had backed down so quickly: he looked like a maddened killer about to go on a rampage.

Anderson had told me once that Jamaal possessed some kind of death magic. Magic that would allow him to kill someone without even touching them. Magic that *wanted* to be used, that ate at Jamaal's self-control. I knew without a doubt that Jamaal was struggling for control right now, that the magic inside him wanted to be released, and that those gang-bangers could very well end up dead—even though they'd chosen to walk away—if I couldn't get Jamaal to cool it.

Unfortunately, I'd never had much luck in the past with cooling his ire, and I was afraid anything I said right now would draw his attention—and his death magic—to me. Of course, I was immortal, and the gang-bangers were not, so I had to risk it.

"Hey. We've got two more crime scenes to investigate," I said gently. "I don't know about you, but I've had enough of this neighborhood. What say we move on?"

For a moment, I thought he hadn't even heard me.

Then he blinked and shook his head sharply, like he was waking up from a dream. His fists unclenched, and he drew in a deep breath. He reached into his pocket and pulled out a cigarette and a lighter. His hands shook a little as he lit the cigarette and took a hasty drag. Wordlessly, he glanced down at me, and I read the question in his eyes.

I held up my hands. "Don't worry. I'm not going to tell Anderson you almost lost it."

He cocked his head, his brows drawing together in puzzlement. "Why not?"

Good question. I'd kept my mouth shut about one of Jamaal's little incidents before, and it had come back to bite both of us in the ass. You'd think I'd have learned my lesson. Except . . .

"Because you *didn't* lose it," I said. "Almost only counts in horseshoes and hand grenades, you know?"

He gave a short bark of something that vaguely resembled laughter before taking another long drag on his cigarette. "Some might argue I *am* a hand grenade," he said under his breath as he turned from me and unlocked the car, rounding the hood and heading for the driver's side. I hoped he would put out the cigarette before he got in, but I wasn't going to make an issue of it. He probably needed its calming effects more than I needed fresh air.

"More like an atom bomb," I replied, even though he'd clearly signaled the conversation was over and I knew his sense of humor wasn't exactly well honed.

He gave me a quelling look over the top of the car, but though he didn't laugh, he also didn't fly into a rage. For Jamaal, I figured that was a major break-through.

The scene of the second attack was a lot less unpleasant than the stinking underpass in Anacostia, though I doubted the victim had appreciated the upgrade. The neighborhood itself wasn't such great shakes, but the victim had been killed right against the fence that separated the neighborhood from the National Arboretum, an oasis of stately trees and well-manicured lawns. I wondered if he'd been trying to jump the fence to escape his attackers.

There were some houses across the street from the crime scene, their vinyl awnings and bent chain-link fences declaring them less than prime real estate. It was possible there was enough distance between the houses and the fence to keep anyone inside from hearing a disturbance late at night, at least if they were heavy sleepers. Possible but not likely. The cops had canvassed the neighborhood and gotten nothing, and I doubted I'd have any better success, even with Jamaal at my side.

There was still nothing that jumped out at me and yelled "I'm a clue!" so I had Jamaal take me to the third, most recent crime scene.

The third murder had taken place on the grounds of the McMillan Reservoir, which was, of course, closed for the night when we arrived. Jamaal parked on the street with a lovely view of a cemetery, and we walked to the barbed-wire-topped fence that surrounded a series of huge, empty fields, featuring regular circular depressions in the grass. I had no idea what the fields were about, but I made a wild guess that the rows of circular concrete structures that separated them were water towers of some sort. Our victim had been found just beside one of those vine-covered towers.

The crime-scene techs had found what they suspected was blood on the barbed wire atop the fence, so it looked like this victim had tried to escape by jumping a fence just like victim number two. Fat lot of good it had done him. The police were really scratching their heads over how the dogs had managed to follow him, since there were no breaks in the fence or tunnels underneath, and the gate was clear on the other side.

Come to think of it, I was scratching my head over that one, too.

"How did the dogs get past the fence?" I mused under my breath.

"Like this, I'll bet," Jamaal said. He took a quick glance around to make sure there were no witnesses, then walked through the fence like it was no more substantial than smoke. I touched the chain links, but for me, they were solid metal.

"How did you do that?" I asked, amazed. I was pretty sure I'd seen Jamaal walk through a locked door before, but we hadn't been on speaking terms at the time, so I hadn't ever asked him about it.

"It's a common ability among descendants of death gods. There's no way to keep Death out."

"Right," I said, nodding. "And Anubis is a death god."

As soon as the words left my mouth, I whirled

around, turning my back to the fence and facing the street.

"Wait a second. He's a descendant of Anubis . . . a death god . . . and there's a cemetery right on the other side of that street." Something went *click* in my head. "And didn't we pass a cemetery right before we got to the last crime scene?"

Jamaal nodded. "Mount Olivet, yeah."

There were a lot of cemeteries in the area, so it could have been a total coincidence. But then again, maybe not. I frowned as I thought about the scene in Anacostia.

"There weren't any cemeteries that I saw around the first crime scene," I said.

"The Congressional Cemetery is right across the river," Jamaal said.

"You sure know your cemeteries."

"Descendant of a death goddess, remember?"

Out of the corner of my eye, I saw a police car cruising down the street. It slowed as it went past us, and I figured we looked kind of suspicious loitering by the fence.

"Let's head back," I said to Jamaal, starting toward the car. "I think I've learned all I'm going to for now."

The police cruiser picked up its pace as soon as Jamaal and I crossed the street.

When we arrived back at the mansion after our excursion, we saw a white Mazda parked in the circular drive.

"That's your sister's car, isn't it?" Jamaal asked as he pulled into the garage.

"Yep."

Things were a little bit . . . strange between Steph and me these days. We'd always been close, ever since her parents had taken me in as a rebellious eleven-year-old troublemaker, but our relationship seemed to be undergoing an adjustment period since I'd become a *Liberi*. I'd always loved Steph, but it was becoming abundantly clear that I'd never had a whole lot of respect for her. She was the rich and beautiful socialite who lived the easy life, and I was the street-smart ugly duckling who understood how the world "really" worked. At least, that's how I used to see us.

Steph had gotten hurt—badly—because of me, and I was finally beginning to see just how strong a person she really was. But I'd been treating her like a child in need of protection for a long time, and I was having a hard time backing off and treating her like the responsible adult she was. Which meant I couldn't hide my disapproval of her relationship—whatever the hell it was—with Blake. That disapproval rubbed her the wrong way, big-time.

Jamaal stayed outside to smoke another cigarette, and I cautiously entered the house, hoping not to run into Steph and Blake. It was amazing how hard a time I had not editorializing whenever I saw them together.

Seriously, though, who could blame me? Blake was a descendant of Eros, and he had the power to arouse an overwhelming and unnatural lust in anyone, male or female, whenever he felt like it. I knew he wasn't doing that to Steph, but it made me uneasy that he *could*. And then there was that other major down-side to their relationship: according to Blake, he was such a supernaturally good lover that if he slept with a woman more than once, she'd never be satisfied with another man for the rest of her life. On the surface, it sounded like a ridiculous boast, and yet I knew he was dead serious.

Blake had enough of a conscience to keep out of Steph's bed—so far—but he *was* a guy, and I had a hard time believing he would go very long without sex. Which meant that someday, he was either going to misplace his conscience and sleep with Steph, or he was going to break her heart. Neither alternative was acceptable to me, but no matter how logically I argued with Steph, she refused to stop seeing him. Maybe she thought the sexual limitations were con-venient. After what she'd been through at Alexis's hands, maybe a relationship with no sex was all she could handle.

I made it up to my suite without encountering any-one and breathed a sigh of relief as I opened my door and stepped into my sitting room. Living in a house with eight other people didn't leave me with as much alone time as I was used to.

My first clue that something was up should have been that the lights were already on. I always turned them off when I left the room. But I was a little slow on the uptake, lost in thought, and I took a couple of steps in before I realized I wasn't going to get that blessed alone time after all.

Steph was curled up on my couch, drinking a cup

of coffee, and apparently waiting for me. I almost jumped out of my skin when I caught sight of her, but I managed to keep things down to a soft gasp and an adrenaline spike.

"Have fun on your date with Jamaal?" she asked with a little smile.

"If you call walking around a stinky underpass in Anacostia a date," I said, sitting down beside Steph and wondering what was up.

She laughed and took a sip of her coffee. "I've seen Jamaal, remember?"

My cheeks heated just a little, because yeah, I had to admit, Jamaal was a thing of beauty, and I would have had to be dead not to have noticed. But he's beautiful in the way that a leopard is beautiful—nice to look at, but you're a hell of a lot better off if there are some sturdy steel bars between you.

"Just because he's a hottie doesn't mean investigating crime scenes with him is romantic or anything. In case you haven't noticed, the guy's a psycho."

Steph had never seen Jamaal in action, but she knew about his previous vendetta against me, and she knew just how violent that vendetta had been. It should have been enough to quell even the slightest hint of attraction in me, but I had a long history of being attracted to the wrong men.

"Nikki . . ." Steph said in a warning tone, and I realized I might be protesting just a little too much.

"There's nothing going on between me and Jamaal," I said in what I hoped was a calm voice. "I'm not a moron."

Steph laughed. "You are where men are concerned."

"Says the woman who's dating a descendant of Eros."

That killed her amusement in a heartbeat. "Don't start."

I held up my hands in a gesture of surrender. "I'm not trying to start anything. Now, why don't you tell me why you're lying in wait for me? I know it's not because you want to talk about relationships."

Steph scrutinized me. She's two years older than me, which means she thinks she's older and wiser. Sometimes she can't resist dispensing advice, and I was afraid this was going to be one of those times.

I was more relieved than I liked to admit when she sighed and shook her head. "Actually," she said, reaching for a briefcase on the floor, "in a way, this *is* a bit about relationships. Just not the romantic kind."

"Huh?"

Steph popped open the briefcase, withdrew a manila folder, and handed it to me.

"What's this?" I asked, taking it cautiously from her hand, as if expecting it to bite.

"Your adoption papers," she said, and I quickly dropped the folder onto the coffee table.

Despite being a private investigator, I'd never had any interest in trying to locate my birth mother. The woman had abandoned me in a church when I was four, and I wanted nothing to do with her or with the baby brother she'd been carrying in her arms the last time I saw her. I knew my adoptive parents, the

Glasses, had a whole bunch of paperwork they'd kept for me, in case I ever changed my mind, but I'd never even given a passing thought to asking for it.

"What are *you* doing with my adoption papers?" I asked.

The Glasses were still on their around-the-world cruise and would be for another six weeks, so I knew they hadn't given the folder to Steph.

She gave me a chiding look that told me she thought I was being intentionally dense. Maybe I was.

"There's this thing called a key. You put it in the door, and, voilà, it opens. I thought you might try out this incredible invention yourself and get the file now that the mystery of your origins has become so much more interesting, but I got tired of waiting for you to make your move."

I looked at her askance. She knew perfectly well I had no intention of tracking down my birth mother. I didn't really think what I'd learned about myself changed anything. I wanted nothing to do with my birth mother. Even if I *wanted* to find her, I wasn't sure it was possible. She'd done a damned thorough job of abandoning me. The police were never even able to find out my last name, and all I could tell them was that my mom and I had been traveling by bus for a long time before she'd taken me to the church and left me there. It wasn't like she'd purposely put me up for adoption with a nice, neat paper trail.

"I'm really not interested," I told Steph, grabbing the folder and trying to give it back to her.

"Yes, you are," she said with total conviction.

"It's possible you got your divine blood through your mother, isn't it?"

The thought had already occurred to me. I'd even had a dream about the day she'd abandoned me, and in that dream, she'd suddenly developed a glyph on her forehead. But that had to be wishful thinking on my part. It was nice to think that my mom might have been a Descendant and might have been in trouble with the Olympians. If that were the case, I could tell myself she'd abandoned me in an attempt to sever our connection and protect me in case the Olympians caught up with her. But I'm not what you'd call a Pollyanna. It made a nice fantasy, but I was a big believer in Occam's Razor, and the simplest explanation for her abandonment was that she hadn't wanted me. I preferred to keep my faint hope that she'd abandoned me for a noble reason, and if I went looking for her and found her, I would most likely destroy that pleasant fantasy forever.

"It's possible, but I don't care," I said, still trying to get Steph to take the folder back. Of course, she wouldn't.

"I know you *do* care," she said gently. "You don't think I can see how badly you want to know why she left you?"

With a grunt of frustration, I threw the folder onto the coffee table. "I *don't* want to know," I insisted. "I want there to be a lovely, happy ending, where I go searching for her and find her and discover that she left me for my own good. But that isn't likely, and if she abandoned me because she didn't want me, then I'd really rather not know. So stop pushing me."

"I can't force you to do anything with the information," Steph said. "You can look for her or not. It's up to you. But I think you're wrong. I think you're the kind of person who'd rather know the truth than be left with a mystery. I know you've never been interested in looking for her before, but I think a big part of that was because you didn't think you had any hope of finding her. Well, now you do."

Maybe she was right, but I'd had enough crisis in my life lately. I didn't want to add to it by starting down this road, one that could so easily lead to a heaping helping of pain.

"I've got a lot of other stuff on my plate," I said. "I don't have time for any personal crap."

Steph gave me a long-suffering look. "Okay. Fine. Hang out in Denial Land a little longer. Eventually, curiosity is going to get the better of you, and you'll go looking for those answers. When you're ready, the file will be waiting for you."

She stood up, pointedly leaving the folder on my coffee table. I hurried to stand up, too, afraid she was angry with me again, but there was no anger in her eyes, only a hint of pity, which was just as bad, if not worse.

"I love you, you know?" she said. "And I know getting there sucked for you, but I'm glad you became part of our family. I hope you know that."

My throat felt suspiciously tight, and I found myself giving Steph a hug.

I'm not the most demonstrative person in the world, and I could feel her little start of surprise. But she hugged me back and seemed to accept that hug as a suitable alternative to the words that I couldn't force out of my throat.

When Steph was gone, I sat on my couch for longer than I care to admit, staring at the folder.

Did I want to find my birth mother? I'd told Steph categorically no, but I knew deep down inside that she was right, that there was a part of me that had always longed to know the truth. Even if it turned out to be painful and ugly.

But maybe now wasn't a good time to go poking around. I already had a supernatural murder case on my plate. One seemingly impossible task at a time seemed like enough.

I left the folder on the coffee table right where it was, the temptation out in the open and staring me in the face, daring me to go searching. I ignored it, instead popping open my laptop and looking for more information on the two identified murder victims.

It was hard not to keep glancing over at it from time to time, though.

FOUR

A few more hours of research on the two identified victims gave me approximately squat.

Different backgrounds, different ages, different socioeconomic status. The only thing I could find in common between them was that they were both white males, which was about all the police had been able to say about the first victim, anyway. It wasn't exactly a lot to go on, and I had the uneasy suspicion there would have to be another victim before I'd be able to make heads or tails of the case. If I ever could. A pillar of confidence I was not.

Tired and frustrated, I headed down to the kitchen to brew a pot of coffee. My plan was to ingest large quantities of caffeine and then continue researching the victims' lives until I found something or my vision went blurry, whichever came first.

My plans took an unexpected detour when I stepped into the kitchen and discovered I wasn't alone.

Anderson was sitting at the table in the breakfast nook, sipping from a cup of something hot and steaming. A quick glance at the coffee maker told me his beverage of choice was probably tea.

Before Anderson and I had had our little talk, I might have peeked into the room, seen him sitting there, and then beaten a hasty retreat. I was tempted even now to just grab a bottle of water from the fridge, but that smacked too much of cowardice. Besides, I was eventually going to have to get over my discomfort around him, seeing as I was living in the same house with him and he was my boss.

Anderson raised his mug to me in a silent salute, and I nodded. Then I began the ritual of making coffee, hyperaware that Anderson was nearby. I kept sneaking glances at him, and what I saw almost made me forget the whole god-of-death-and-vengeance thing.

He looked . . . sad. Almost lost. And I took a wild guess about just what the cause might be.

I doctored a cup of coffee, trying to talk myself out of starting a conversation with Anderson. Whatever was wrong was none of my business. Especially if it had something to do with Emma. Anderson wasn't my friend, not in any real sense of the word, so I had no moral obligation to try to make him feel better.

Logical arguments had no effect, and once my coffee was ready, I found myself walking toward the kitchen table instead of heading back to my suite and my work. I sat across from Anderson but didn't quite know what to say.

"Making any progress on the case?" he asked, then took a sip of his tea.

I shrugged. "Not a whole lot. The best lead I've got is that the murders seem to be happening close to cemeteries."

"I'll wager that's more than the police have."

He was no doubt right. Normal people wouldn't pick up on the proximity to cemeteries because they'd never dream it was significant. At least, not now—a few more murders with the same pattern might change that.

"It's more than nothing," I agreed, "but not as much as I'd hoped for."

Anderson nodded. "And how did you and Jamaal get along?"

Okay. I'd sat down to talk to Anderson because he looked like he needed a little human contact, but that didn't mean I wanted to have a deep, personal conversation, especially about myself. Or about Jamaal, for that matter. I remembered how Jamaal had almost lost it when those gang-bangers had challenged him, and I knew that Anderson would expect me to tell him what had happened. That didn't mean I was about to do it.

"We're both still alive, and no body parts are missing," I said with a hint of a grin. Maybe if I kept it light, we'd quickly move on to another subject, and I'd stop feeling uncomfortable. "It's an improvement."

I decided that only a moron would ask Anderson probing questions; I then decided that sometimes I *was* a moron, like right now. As a bonus, it would be a handy change of subject.

"Did you and Emma have a fight?" I asked. I was pretty sure I already knew the answer, because only Emma seemed able to put that particular shade of misery on his face. Blake had once described Emma as "high-maintenance." From what I'd seen, that was a charitable assessment.

Anderson smiled faintly. "Is it that obvious?"

I didn't bother to answer. "Are you okay?" I asked instead.

He shrugged. "We're going through a rough patch. It's not the first time. And I can hardly blame her after what she's been through."

Thanks to Konstantin, Emma had spent the better part of ten years chained at the bottom of a pond, unable to free herself but also unable to escape through death. If that wasn't an ordeal that would warp a person beyond recognition, I didn't know what was.

"Give her some time," I said, though I didn't for a moment think time was going to fix whatever was going on between the two of them. "She's doing a lot better now than she was when we first brought her home."

Being a raging bitch was better than being catatonic, right?

Anderson nodded. "She's doing better, but the scars . . ." His voice trailed off, and he looked haunted. "She's always been volatile, but she's a powder keg right now. One wrong word, and . . ."

Yeah, that about summed it up. But from what I'd gathered from the rest of the *Liberi,* that wasn't anything new for her.

"Maybe you need to learn not to speak," I suggested.

Anderson's smile was faint but nice to see.

The smile disappeared moments later, when Emma bulled into the room. Her eyes scanned the kitchen—obviously looking for Anderson—but when she saw me sitting there, she did a double take, like it was a total shock that the two of them might not be alone in the room. Maybe she forgot there were eight people living in the mansion besides herself.

Emma was disgustingly beautiful, with glossy black hair that would have done a shampoo-commercial actress proud and the figure and face to go with it. She was kind of like Steph, in that she instantly brought out my inner insecurities, making me feel plain and dowdy in comparison.

The look she gave me was anything but friendly as she stalked over to the coffee pot and helped herself to a cup, her movements jerky with anger. Apparently, she was eager to resume her fight with Anderson, and I was in the way.

I wanted to get up and flee the room, but the pleading look Anderson shot me kept me rooted to my chair. I knew without being told that he was hoping my presence would curb Emma's enthusiasm for their fight, but I also knew it wasn't going to work. Emma had never shown any sign that it bothered her to fight in front of the rest of us.

Why did I stay anyway? I guess I'm a glutton for punishment.

Emma brought her cup of coffee to the table, fixing me with a glare that made me shiver inside. There was a spark of madness in her gaze, and I really didn't want it to remain fixed on me.

"I see you're consoling my dear husband after our little quarrel," Emma said with a curl of her lip. "How kind of you."

Yikes. Guess I should have run when I had the chance. I held up my cup of coffee and tried to look nonchalant.

"I'm just drinking a cup of coffee. My laptop and I needed a little time apart." I decided that it wasn't too late to get out from between the happy couple, so I pushed my chair back from the table.

Emma was still staring daggers at me. Her expression reminded me a little too much of how Jamaal had looked when he'd lost his mind in rage, and I wondered exactly how unstable she was. I'd thought of her as annoying ever since she'd started talking again, but I'd never considered her dangerous.

The look in her eyes now said that had been a mistake.

"Nikki has every right to be here," Anderson said quietly, and I tried not to wince. I was now officially stuck in the middle, and I wanted to kick myself for not getting out when the getting was good.

"I'm going to go back to work now," I announced, eyeing the doorway longingly. Unfortunately, Emma had positioned herself in front of it, and considering the sparks in her eyes, I didn't think getting close to her was a good idea.

"Oh, no," Emma said with a hard smile. "Please don't let me interrupt your little tête-à-tête. I know you and my husband get along *famously*."

Double yikes. If I didn't know better, I could have sworn she sounded jealous. But why the hell would a woman like her be jealous of someone like me? It wasn't like there was anything going on between Anderson and me. I liked him and all, but there was nothing romantic about it.

Anderson heaved a sigh. "Please, Emma. Don't be childish."

She snorted. "Says the man who runs away from conflict as if it might kill him."

I took a couple of steps toward the door, hoping maybe Emma would move out of the way and let me go. She stood her ground, and I came to an indecisive stop.

"We've had a year's worth of conflict in the past week alone," Anderson countered, sounding tired. "Leave it be for a while, why don't you?"

"Leave it be?" she cried, her voice rising. "How can you possibly ask me to leave it be? Especially when you run straight into the arms of your new girlfriend here."

O-kay. Crazy as it seemed, I'd have to say that really was jealousy in Emma's voice. Which made no sense.

"Listen," I said, hoping I didn't sound as desperately uncomfortable as I was, "I'm going to get out of your hair. You two hash things out in private, okay?"

Neither one of them looked at me, locked in their own staring match. I'd had enough, so despite my reluctance to go anywhere near Emma when she looked like she was about to explode, I walked toward the doorway, giving her as wide a berth as I could.

Just as I thought I was home free and that she would let me pass unmolested, Emma reached out and grabbed the top of my arm in a brutally tight grip, yanking me toward her so hard that half my coffee sloshed out of the mug onto the floor.

"You listen here," she growled at me, baring her teeth.

"Emma!" Anderson said sharply, and I heard the sound of his chair scraping hastily back. "What are you doing?"

Emma gave me a little shake. "You stay away from my husband. Am I making myself perfectly clear?"

Yeah, she was making it perfectly clear that she was insane. Why did the nut cases always seem to focus on me?

I fought the urge to wince at the tightness of her grip. Maybe humoring the crazy would have been my best move, but I didn't think things through before I spoke.

"Your husband is my boss," I said in what I thought was an admirably calm voice. "Are you really going to fly into a rage every time I speak to him? Because you have to know there's nothing going on between us."

Her grip on my arm became even tighter, which I hadn't thought was possible, and this time, I couldn't suppress a gasp of pain.

"Emma," Anderson said. "Let go of her. *Now.* You can fight with me all you want, but leave my people out of it."

I had a feeling he was only making things worse by sticking up for me, and the blackness I saw in Emma's eyes confirmed it. I was beginning to wish we'd left her at the bottom of that pond, though I felt guilty for the thought the moment it crossed my mind.

"Stay away from him," Emma repeated, then let go of my arm and shoved me out the door.

FIVE

Predictably, Emma's and Anderson's raised voices echoed down the hall as I made my escape. The whole incident had completely creeped me out.

Why the hell was Emma jealous of me? I could think of no logical reason, and no matter how closely I scrutinized my own actions, I couldn't think of anything I'd done that could give Emma the impression I was after her husband.

But what really had me worried was that her hostility toward me seemed to be escalating. If I wasn't doing anything to fan the flames—and I was sure I wasn't—I worried that nothing I *did* do or say would calm them. I didn't get the feeling that Anderson's people were huge fans of Emma, but she was Anderson's wife and had been with them way longer than I had. Life in the mansion could get very, very difficult for me if I couldn't find some way to patch things up.

With those cheerful thoughts in mind, I retreated to my suite to work on the clearer, more manageable task of catching a serial killer. However, fatigue was making me loopy, and my brain seemed determined to obsess over the situation with Emma. I wasn't getting anything useful done, so I forced myself to turn off the computer and crawl into bed.

Eventually, I drifted off to sleep. I slept late enough that there was no one in the kitchen when I cautiously poked my head in the next morning. Someone had cleaned up the coffee I'd spilled. I'd bet anything it wasn't Emma. I hurried through making a fresh pot of coffee, wanting to get out of the kitchen quickly. This was one of those times when I really missed living in my condo. It was like the tension of the argument had soaked into the walls, and I was glad to escape back to my room. Maybe I should buy myself a coffee maker to keep in the suite.

When the caffeine hit my system and woke up my still-sluggish brain cells, I realized I'd really needed that sleep. It seemed my subconscious mind had been hard at work mulling over the issue of how to catch the killer while I was sleeping, and I now had the inklings of a plan. Maybe not the safest or sanest plan in the world but a plan nonetheless.

My first impulse was to go haring off on my own the moment I had some idea what to do. For most of my adult life, I'd been an independent operator, doing what I wanted, when I wanted. That was one of the big perks of starting my own business and not joining someone else's P.I. firm.

I wasn't an independent operator anymore. I was part of a team—a concept I was still getting used to—and I had a boss to answer to. I knew better than to think Anderson would be okay with me making unilateral plans of action. Not only that, but for once in my life, I had some serious backup available, which was a nice luxury. Nonetheless, it chafed a bit, because talking to Anderson before acting smacked of asking permission, something I'd never been too good at.

I found Anderson ensconced in his study, the one room in his wing of the mansion that the rest of us *Liberi* were actually allowed to enter without special dispensation. He was sitting at his desk, his brow furrowed as he stared at a piece of paper in front of him. I had a feeling he wasn't really seeing that paper, that he was actually lost in thought, but he didn't jump when I rapped on the door. He merely turned his chair toward me and raised his eyebrows in inquiry.

I made a show of looking up and down the hall before stepping cautiously into the room. "Is Emma around?" I asked. "Do I need to get us a chaperone?"

As attempts at humor go, it wasn't my best. The corners of Anderson's mouth tightened, and he dropped his gaze like he was embarrassed.

"I'm really sorry about that," he said softly, and I wanted to kick myself for being a smartass. Marital troubles weren't funny, not to the people involved. As a private investigator, I'd seen more than ample evidence of the fact.

I sighed and invited myself in, dropping into one of the chairs in front of Anderson's desk like a good little employee.

"You don't have to apologize," I assured him. "I'm sorry about the dumb joke. Sometimes I joke when I'm uncomfortable."

Anderson leaned back in his chair. "I'm sorry that Emma and I have made you uncomfortable. What the Olympians did to her seems to have brought out every insecurity she's ever had. She's having a hard time coping, and I'm not making things any easier by fighting with her."

I didn't think Anderson had anything to apologize for. From what I could tell, he was acting perfectly reasonable. It was Emma who was the loose cannon, but even with my low relationship IQ, I knew better than to say that.

"She wants me to declare war on the Olympians," Anderson said. "She can hardly think of anything but revenge."

"To tell you the truth, I've been kind of expecting you to declare war myself. I thought the only reason you weren't fighting them was that they had Emma."

He shook his head. "That was just one reason. I hate Konstantin, and I hate the Olympians, and I hate everything they stand for."

Was it my imagination, or were there literal sparks coming from his eyes?

"But there are a lot more of them than there are of us," Anderson continued. "And with their stable of brainwashed Descendants, they have far more deadly weapons than we do. If I start a war, then it's highly likely all my people will end up dead. It's not a chance I'm willing to take. Now, if I could get Konstantin somewhere nice and private where there were no witnesses, that would be another matter altogether."

His smile was fierce and chilling, and I was glad that menace was not directed at me. Then the smile faded and the menace with it. "I know Emma understands my reasons deep down, and I know she'll come to her senses as her psyche heals. But for now, she's not thinking straight."

Personally, I didn't think Emma was the one who wasn't thinking straight. I'm no shrink, but I felt pretty convinced that her trauma had caused permanent damage, that she would never go back to being the wife Anderson remembered. Assuming that wife had ever existed in the first place.

"But you didn't come here to talk about me and Emma," Anderson said. "What can I do for you?"

"I have an idea for how we might—and I emphasize *might*—catch our killer."

"I'm intrigued. Tell me more."

"You know how I told you last night the murders all occurred near cemeteries?"

He nodded.

"They've also all occurred on Friday nights."

"Hmm," Anderson said, his eyes narrowing. "I'm beginning to see where you might be going with this." And based on the way he was looking at me, he didn't like it.

Still, I forged on. "Seeing as this is Friday, I have a strong suspicion our killer will strike again tonight and that the attack will be somewhere near a cemetery."

Anderson nodded. "Probably true. But do you know how many cemeteries there are in the area?"

"A shitload," I agreed. "But when you look at a map, you can see that each attack occurred north of the attack before." I had brought my big map of the D.C. area with me, and I unfolded it on Anderson's desk, the sites of the three murders numbered and circled. They formed more of a triangle than a straight line, but I still felt there was a definite direction of movement. A pattern I could exploit.

"I've highlighted the cemeteries in yellow," I pointed out, "and I think if his pattern holds true, he'll hit near the Rock Creek Cemetery tonight." I pointed helpfully at the cemetery in question.

Anderson looked skeptical. "That seems like an awful lot of conjecture."

I couldn't help grinning. "Conjecture seems to be a big part of my power." My gut was telling me this wasn't all in my head, that there really was a pattern to the murders. I couldn't say I completely trusted my gut, but it had certainly steered me in the right direction many times before.

"Even if you're right, Rock Creek is huge. And if you have to include anything within walking distance in your search, the chances of you running into the killer are really low."

I grabbed the map and started wrestling it back

into its tidy brochure size. "My chances are better if I go hang around the cemetery than if I sit here doing nothing. I checked the weather and the lunar calendar, and I should have plenty of moon action tonight." My powers were stronger in the moon-light, though it was difficult to pinpoint exactly what effect the moonlight had. The best explanation I had was that it made my hunches stronger and more accurate.

Anderson looked anything but convinced, and I couldn't say I blamed him. If I were an ordinary human being, or even an ordinary *Liberi,* my chances of finding the killer with so little information would be almost nil. But I wasn't an ordinary human being, not anymore.

"Look, it may still be a long shot," I said, "but what do we have to lose by trying?"

Anderson thought about it a little more, then came to a decision. "All right. We'll go stake out the cem-etery tonight."

"We?" I'd known he wouldn't let me go alone, and with his ability to kill *Liberi,* Anderson seemed like a logical choice to go with me, but something about the way he said it told me he didn't mean just him and me. "Who's *we?*"

"All of us," Anderson said, and my jaw dropped. "We can cover a lot more ground if we all go together and then split up."

"But I'm the only one who's got a realistic shot at finding him. Maybe."

"Your shot at finding him doesn't get any worse if

the rest of us are there looking, too, and our chances of actually *catching* him are a lot better. We don't know what he can do, and I'm not sure what it'll take to subdue him."

It was then that I realized the very important question I had so far failed to ask, had failed even to contemplate. "What are we going to do with him if and when we catch him?"

Anderson was the only one of us who could actually kill a *Liberi,* but I knew without asking that he wouldn't do it. For reasons I didn't understand—and was too fond of being alive to want to delve into— Anderson didn't want anyone to know who and what he actually was. Even Emma didn't know, and I doubted her finding out the truth would make their marriage any smoother. What Anderson saw in her— other than beauty—was beyond me.

"First, we'll question him and see how much of what the Olympians told us was the truth. There's nothing he can say to excuse what he's done, but if the Olympians are hiding something, I think it's important we find out what it is."

I had to agree, though given the ferocity of the killer's attacks, I wasn't sure how much reliable information we could get out of him. He seemed several eggs short of a dozen to me.

"Okay, so we question him," I said. "If we can. Then what?"

Anderson looked at me warily, and I knew I wasn't going to like whatever was coming next. "Then we hand him over to the Olympians."

I was right: I didn't like it.

"No way in hell I'm handing *anyone* over to those sons of bitches," I said in what I hoped was a calm voice.

I thought my statement might piss Anderson off, but there was no sign of it.

"What do you suggest we do instead?"

And that, of course, was the problem. Dogboy couldn't be allowed to run around ripping innocent bystanders to shreds, and Anderson wouldn't tip his hand by killing him.

"We can lock him up," I said weakly, though I already knew the suggestion sucked. We had some rooms in the basement that were basically prison cells, but it wasn't like we were equipped to be the killer's eternal prison guards.

"It's really hard to keep a death god descendant locked up. Most of them can walk through walls and doors."

I sighed. "And fences," I murmured, remembering Jamaal's demonstration at the reservoir.

"If we can't contain him, then we have to kill him. And we're not equipped to do that."

He gave me a meaningful look, and I swallowed my desire to argue. "So we hand him over to the Olympians, and they have one of their pet Descendants kill him, and now they have a new *Liberi* under their thumb."

"I'll admit it's not an ideal solution," Anderson said. "But it's the best we've got."

Anger burned in my chest, and I fought to hold

it back. That *wasn't* the best solution we had, and we both knew it. Death-by-Anderson was not a pleasant fate, and I hated the thought of putting anyone through it, but better that than to hand the Olympians a new *Liberi* on a silver platter. Not to mention that from what I'd heard, the Olympians weren't exactly into clean kills themselves.

"Why won't you—"

"Do not go there!" Anderson warned, and the steel in his voice told me in no uncertain terms that it wasn't open to discussion.

I bit my tongue, but it was hard. Generally, I liked Anderson. When I was able to see him as something other than my boss or a god, he seemed like a genuinely nice guy, and I respected his mission to make the world a better place. If it weren't for him, every descendant of a Greek deity in this mansion—me, Maggie, Blake, Emma, and Leo—would have been forced either to join the Olympians or forfeit our immortality to one of the Olympians' pet Descendants. Those descended from other pantheons—Jack, Jamaal, and Logan—would have been killed, their immortality "harvested" for someone the Olympians considered more worthy. And let's not even talk about all the hidden *Liberi* and their Descendant families Anderson had helped.

Anderson was one of the good guys, but right now, I thought he was being a coward.

I didn't say that out loud, of course, but I didn't make any particular effort to keep my opinion from showing on my face.

Anderson and I stared at each other in a silent battle of wills. Ordinarily, I'd bet on myself anytime, but to my shame, I looked away first. I could never unlearn what I'd found out about him, and I wasn't sure I'd ever be able to stand up to him the way I thought I should again.

Six

We headed out toward the Rock Creek Cemetery at about ten o'clock. To my surprise, when Anderson had said we were all going, he'd really meant all. Even Emma joined us, though it was clear she'd rather have stayed home and let us do all the work. She had little interest in fighting evil—unless that evil was Konstantin.

It was way earlier than any of the previous attacks had occurred, but there was always hope—however faint—that we might be able to find and capture Dog-boy before he struck. Anderson had assigned us to teams of two, with Leo, our immortal accountant and nonfighter, tacked on to one of the teams as a third wheel. I'd argued against him coming, but he was another warm body, and it was theoretically possible he could be helpful. Maybe he could capture our killer and bore him to death with talk of managed futures.

Anderson teamed me up with Jamaal again, but I

didn't mind quite so much. Jamaal had been perfectly civil to me on our mission the day before; and besides, if you have to prowl a cemetery in the middle of the night, having a super-intimidating death goddess descendant by your side is the way to go.

As Anderson had said, the Rock Creek Cemetery was huge. As if that wasn't enough death to choke anyone, there was also the National Cemetery right across from its southeastern border. Both cemeteries were surrounded by spiky iron fences, but it wouldn't be particularly hard for a determined trespasser to get over them.

Each team was assigned a section to patrol. Something about the stretch of Rock Creek Road that ran between the two cemeteries called to me, so Jamaal and I took that as the focus of our surveillance. We'd determined that my supernatural aim made me the most likely to take the killer down without too much of a struggle, so my .38 Special was tucked in my coat pocket. It was about as creepy a section of road as I could imagine, with the National Cemetery and its regular pattern of small rectangular headstones on one side and the Rock Creek Cemetery with its more varied headstones and mausoleums on the other. The streetlights made a feeble attempt to light the darkness, but there were enough pools of deep shadow to make *anyone* uncomfortable.

The night wasn't particularly cold, although there was a chill wind that made me long for a cup of hot chocolate in front of a crackling fire. Jamaal wasn't much of a talker, so our first hour of surveillance went by with nary a word between us to break the eerie silence. There was occasional traffic on the street, but the later it got, the longer the gaps between cars, and the sense of isolation made the hairs on the back of my neck stand up. We weren't actually *in* a cemetery, but my lizard brain didn't much appreciate the distinction.

After the first hour, Jamaal broke out the clove cigarettes. He smoked with quiet intensity. Usually, the cigarettes seemed to be good at helping take the edge off, but he still seemed kind of agitated when he stubbed the butt out. I wasn't entirely surprised to see him light another about five minutes later.

"What do you think the significance of the cemeteries is?" I asked Jamaal when I couldn't stand the silence anymore. "Why does the killer attack near them?"

He blew out a steady stream of smoke before answering. "They may call to him. Maybe he feels most at home among the dead."

"Could it have anything to do with his death magic? I mean, do you think it's, I don't know, powered by the cemeteries or something?"

He shook his head, making the beads at the ends of his braids click and rattle. "I don't know any more about this guy or how his power works than you do." There was an edge to his voice, like maybe my questions were getting on his nerves. He took another deep drag on his cigarette. "I'm descended from Kali, not Anubis."

"Yeah, but they're both death gods, and—"

"And death gods all look the same to you?"

I came to an abrupt halt and stared at him. Was he really suggesting there was something racist about my questions? I noticed the fingers of his free hand were twitching slightly. I didn't think that meant anything good.

I held up my hands innocently. "Whoa. Remember, I've only been a *Liberi* for a few weeks," I said, keeping my voice calm instead of snapping at him as I was tempted to do. "I don't know as much about the gods or about magic as the rest of you, and I never will if I don't ask questions. I didn't mean to offend you, if that's what I did."

Jamaal's eyes glittered in the darkness, and my pulse began a slow and steady rise. If he was going to lose his grip on his temper, I was in deep shit. We were smack dab in the middle of the stretch of road between the two cemeteries, with no possibility of anyone hearing if I yelled for help. Not that I *would* yell for help against Jamaal if it was possible civilians might come to my aid.

Before I had a chance to get too worked up, Jamaal closed his eyes and sucked in a deep breath. He held it for a moment, then let it out slowly. When his eyes opened again, his hand had stopped twitching, and he no longer looked like he was irrationally pissed off at me.

"Sorry," he said softly, hanging his head. "I'm getting the feeling hanging around the cemeteries for so long isn't such a great idea for me. It's making me . . . edgy." He took one last long draw on his cigarette, then used the glowing butt to light another.

I was pretty sure he was feeling ashamed of his weakness, but I had to wonder how much of it was his fault. Did being around so many dead people make his death magic long to come out and play? He had trouble controlling it under the best of circumstances.

I took my life in my hands and decided to try a little humor to lighten the mood. "And this is different from the norm how, exactly?"

He gave me a rueful smile, and my pulse blipped from something other than fear. Jamaal with a smile on his face was enough to make any red-blooded woman swoon.

"I'm sure there's room for one more grave in there," he said, jerking his thumb toward the Rock Creek Cemetery.

I blinked. "Wait a minute. Did you just make a joke?" Jamaal had the sense of humor of an angry bear.

"Who says I was joking? Now, let's keep moving. And save the Q and A for sometime I'm not surrounded by the dead."

We resumed our pattern, walking up one side of the road, then crossing when we got to the end and taking the other side on the way back. The moon was close enough to full to give us some light, but the place still felt oppressively dark. And Jamaal's body language was getting progressively more tense. Despite his chain-smoking, I saw no sign that the clove cigarettes were helping the situation.

"Are you okay?" I asked tentatively, afraid the question would set him off.

His Adam's apple bobbed, and he rattled his beads

again. "I'm sick of all this useless wandering around. I want to *do* something."

No doubt about it, he wasn't in as much control as he had been just a few minutes ago. If I didn't think it would make him blow up, I'd have suggested he head back to the car and take a break for a while. There was a light sheen of sweat on his face despite the bracing wind, and he'd picked up his pace, covering so much ground with his long strides I could barely keep up. I could practically feel the . . . *something* . . . within him that was struggling to burst out.

"We should be *hunting* the killer," Jamaal continued, "not just hoping to stumble on him by pure luck."

"We're hunting the best we can with so little information to go on," I reminded him. "And there's a luck factor to—"

"Goddammit, Nikki! Shut up!" He was panting now, both hands clenched into fists. He looked as feral as he had the day before during our brief confrontation with the kids.

I'd have obliged him, except I'd been quiet for most of our watch, and that hadn't stopped his control from decaying.

"How can I help?" I asked instead. He was as twitchy as an addict desperate for a fix, and I suspected he was about as unpredictable. He was also infinitely more dangerous.

A growl rose from his throat. "You can't."

And then he disappeared into thin air.

I had a sense of motion off to my left, and though I looked in that direction, I couldn't see anything. I heard Jamaal's braids rattling, and I used the sound to track his motion as he either leapt over or went straight through the fence and into the cemetery.

"Jamaal!" I called, but he didn't answer, and the sound of clicking braids faded. "Dammit!"

I didn't know where he was going. Maybe even *he* didn't know where he was going. With my subconscious tracking skills, I could probably follow him, but I wasn't exactly sure I wanted to catch him. Whatever progress he'd made toward becoming sane and rational seemed to have fled him completely, and the effect had obviously grown worse the longer we'd been near the cemeteries. I hoped to God it would fade once we got him out of here. Assuming we could.

I might not have known where Jamaal was or where he was going, but what I did know was that I was standing in the dark all alone with a cemetery on both sides of me. Immortal or not, this was *not* a situation in which I felt even remotely comfortable. I dug my phone out of my coat pocket. I hated to tattle on Jamaal and tell Anderson he'd wigged out on me, but I didn't see that I had much choice.

I'd just turned on the phone when I heard the sound of running feet behind me. My first thought was that it was Jamaal coming back, and I wasn't sure if that was a good thing or a bad thing. I shoved the phone back into my pocket, wanting both hands free to defend myself if Jamaal had gone completely berserk, but when I whirled around, the running figure I saw was not Jamaal.

He was approaching from Allison Street, which

led to one of the residential areas near the cemeteries, and he was running full speed, arms pumping like mad, coattails flapping behind him. He tried to turn the other way on Rock Creek Church—away from the cemeteries—but something spooked him, and he let out a strangled cry. Then he was running between the cemeteries. Straight toward me.

I got a quick look at him when he passed under one of the streetlights. A tall, well-built white male with dark hair and a matching beard and mustache. His eyes were wide with terror, and I knew he was running for his life. I even had a guess what he was running from, only there was no one else in sight. No dogs, either. Just this one guy, running.

I reached into my other coat pocket, drawing out the extremely illegal concealed weapon I was carrying. Too bad I didn't see anything to shoot at. I took a step toward our would-be victim, thinking I was going to feel like an idiot if he was just some asshole on a bad drug trip.

"Where are they?" I called to him, making sure not to point my gun straight at him.

His eyes went even wider, and I had the feeling he hadn't even seen me until I'd spoken.

"Help me!" he cried desperately as he pumped his legs even harder. Then he came to an abrupt stop, practically falling on his ass as he ground his shoes into the grassy earth that bounded the cemetery.

Just like I saw nothing to explain why he was running, I saw nothing to explain why he'd stopped. Until he screamed, that is.

A shadowy shape coalesced out of the darkness, leaping through the air. The shape was little more than a blot in the darkness until it crashed into the victim, when it became a medium-sized dog that looked like a small wolf. A coyote, maybe. It clamped its jaws around the guy's arm, and even a solid blow to its muzzle didn't dislodge it.

Another shape flew through the air at him, and I fired at it. The creature went insubstantial again in midair, and my bullet passed harmlessly through where it had been. The other, however, had a firm grip on the victim's arm, snarling and shaking its head as he screamed in pain and terror.

I took aim at the creature . . . coyote . . . whatever the hell it was. Despite knowing my aim was infallible, I hesitated before pulling the trigger, afraid to shoot at something that was so close to the victim, but I figured I didn't have much of a choice. I couldn't see any more of them coming, but I *knew* they were there, that we would soon be overwhelmed.

I squeezed the trigger, and this time, the coyote stayed nice and solid. The bullet hit it square in the head, and the man was finally able to shake it off his arm. The coyote landed limply on the pavement, but I saw no sign of blood except for that on its muzzle.

The man climbed to his feet, breath sawing in and out of his lungs as blood soaked the arm of his coat. I hurried to help him, knowing he had to be in dire pain. I kept a careful eye on the coyote as I slipped past it. Its eyes were closed, its tongue extended through bloodied teeth.

It wasn't a coyote, I realized. It was a jackal.

I couldn't remember ever seeing one in person before, but I'd watched enough nature shows to know one when I saw it. I supposed it made sense for a descendant of a jackal-headed god to have a pack of them at his beck and call.

By the time I reached the man and put my arm around his waist to help support him, the jackal had become insubstantial again, just a vaguely dog-shaped shadow against the grass.

"What the hell?" the dazed victim murmured as the shadow lost its shape and dissipated into the darkness of the night.

I didn't have time to contemplate the latest dose of weirdness before something slammed into the guy's back, knocking him to the ground despite my arm around him. When he fell, there was a jackal on his back, its jaws clamped on his shoulder. I pointed the gun, but even with supernatural aim, I had no shot. Anything that hit the jackal would hit the man, too.

Another jackal coalesced out of the air in midleap, landing at the victim's feet and grabbing hold of an ankle. The one on the guy's back could have torn his throat out by now if it wanted to, but it settled for sinking its fangs into the flesh of his shoulder. His screams were swallowed by the emptiness of the night and the silence of the dead.

Two more jackals appeared and dove at the victim, jaws snapping and releasing as the first two maintained their grip, holding the victim down so the rest of the pack could attack with impunity. I still had no shot at the one on the guy's back, but I took aim at the one holding his leg. My bullet hit it square in the head, knocking it back, but it was a Pyrrhic victory, because another immediately took its place. Shooting the jackals was like chopping the heads off the Hydra, so I whirled around, looking for the *Liberi* who controlled them.

He was standing about twenty yards away, leaning against a lamppost, watching the action. He looked like a homeless dude, with lank, greasy hair, filthy sweats, and tattered Windbreaker. He was so skinny it was a wonder the light breeze didn't blow him away. His breath steamed in the night air as he stared at the jackal I'd just killed, his expression one of rage, madness, and, it appeared, raw grief.

I took aim at his head. Because he was *Liberi,* I couldn't kill him. However, I could incapacitate him, and hopefully if he lost consciousness, the jackals would go *poof*.

The jackal I'd shot disappeared, and the *Liberi*'s eyes snapped to mine. The feral smile that shaped his lips gave me about half a second's warning, but it wasn't enough. I tried to dodge and shoot at the same time, but the jackal slammed into me so hard even my supernatural aim couldn't compensate.

The gun fired into the ground as the jackal grabbed hold of my arm with crushingly strong jaws. White-hot pain drew a scream from my throat, but I kept my head enough to transfer the gun to my left hand. Gritting my teeth as my eyes watered and I fought desperately to stay on my feet, I fired at the jackal from point-blank range. It let go, but another one was instantly on me.

I knew the jackals couldn't kill me. I was *Liberi,* immortal. I'd seen Jamaal recover from being decapitated. None of that logic did anything to quell the primal panic that coursed through my blood as I fell.

Another jackal came at me, its jaw clamping down on my left wrist, shaking me until the gun fell from my limp fingers. I slammed my other fist into the side of its head. My body was fighting on autopilot, the pain and terror overwhelming conscious thought. The jackals were everywhere, winking in and out of their solid forms as they darted in for attacks.

I was sure I was about to find out exactly what it felt like for a *Liberi* to die. The magic of the *Liberi* meant that I would revive, but logic is no match for panic. The jackals were going to rip me into bloody shreds, devour me, and they were going to take their time about it.

But all at once, they disappeared.

I lifted my head and saw their master give me a mocking salute before he, too, faded into the night.

Seconds later, a collection of shadows drew together, and Jamaal emerged from their depths. It looked for a moment like he was going to take off in pursuit of the killer, but it was pretty damn hard to follow someone who was invisible. And as big and powerful as Jamaal is, I don't know if he'd have had any better success against the phantom jackals than I had.

I was bleeding from bites on both of my arms and one of my legs. I was pretty sure I'd broken a finger or two punching a jackal in its hard skull. It would all heal in a matter of hours, but goddamn, did it ever hurt.

The poor man I'd been trying to help was in considerably worse shape. He lay facedown on the grass, blood seeping from about a dozen wounds. I could tell he was still alive, because his back occasionally rose and fell with a breath, but I didn't think he would stay alive much longer if he didn't get immediate medical attention.

I forced myself into a sitting position, the pain almost making me black out, then scooted nearer to the victim. I got a better look at him and wished I hadn't. There was a lot of blood, and so many wounds I didn't know which one I should try to put pressure on first. I glanced up at Jamaal, meaning to snap at him to get over here and help me, but the words died in my throat when I saw him.

He was not himself. Literally. I mean, yes, it was *Jamaal* standing there, but not the Jamaal I knew. The small crescent-moon glyph in the center of his forehead was glowing with a golden light, as were his eyes. His expression was of a man in a trance, seeing nothing of the world around him. He took one slow step toward the bleeding man, then another. His hand rose as if guided by an invisible puppet string, reaching out toward the victim.

I hadn't the faintest idea what to do or say. Jamaal wasn't easy to reason with even when he wasn't out of his mind, and I wasn't sure he knew I was there at the moment, his attention entirely focused on the victim. I wanted to at least put myself between the two, but my own pain was making me light-headed and wobbly.

The victim's eyes flew open suddenly, but, as with Jamaal, there was no sign of human intelligence in them. Jamaal's reaching hand tightened, fingers curling into a fist. He was still about five feet away from the victim, not within touching range, but I knew he was doing *something*. Something not good.

The victim's eyes stayed open, but even so, I could see the moment his life slipped away. I couldn't have told you what was different about him. His eyes were no more vacant than they had been from the moment he'd first opened them, but he was dead.

I looked at Jamaal in horror. The glow in his eyes and his glyph faded, and for one moment, I saw an expression of clarity on his face, like he'd come back from wherever he'd been. Then his eyes rolled up into his head, and his knees went out from under him.

SEVEN

I wanted to sit there on the grass and take some time to gather myself, try to make sense of what I'd seen. But I was badly wounded, sitting by the side of the road with one dead man and another unconscious one, and I didn't have the luxury. It was dark, but not dark enough to hide the carnage if someone drove by, and though traffic was sparse, it wasn't nonexistent. I suspected we were far enough away from the residential area that no one had heard the shots, but I couldn't be sure of that.

With shaking hands, I pulled out my cell phone and speed-dialed Anderson. He answered on the first ring.

"Have you found him? We heard gunfire." He was slightly out of breath, and I realized he was running. I cursed the cemetery for being so big, for forcing us to spread out so much.

"N-need help," I managed to stammer out, my whole body now racked with shivers. I didn't know if I was reacting to my own wounds or if I was having a well-deserved panic attack, but I was having trouble getting words out of my mouth and breath into my lungs.

"Nikki? Are you okay? What happened?"

I tried to spit out an explanation, I really did. But what came out was a gasp, followed by something that sounded suspiciously like a sob. My throat was so tight I could barely breathe, and I was shaking so hard it was a miracle I hadn't dropped the phone.

"We're coming, Nikki," Anderson said. "Hang on. Are you still on Rock Creek Church?"

I managed a hiccuped affirmative that, amazingly, he was able to understand.

"Just hang on. We'll be there soon."

He hung up on me, which was just as well, considering I was practically incapable of speech.

I'd always thought of myself as something of a tough chick. I'd spent years in foster care, getting passed from one family to another like an unwanted present that kept getting regifted. I'd been a loner, a rebel, a troublemaker. But becoming *Liberi* had taught me in a very short time just how far I was from being the tough chick I'd imagined. Girls like me weren't supposed to sit by the side of the road and have hysterics after a fight. No matter how horrifying the attack. No matter that they were bleeding from multiple and very painful wounds. No matter that the guy they'd tried to save was dead or that one of the good guys had killed him while in some kind of altered state.

In the distance, a pair of headlights approached, and I knew there was no way whoever was in that car was going to miss the carnage. The strip of grass we were on wasn't wide enough for us to huddle outside the range of the headlights, and there was nothing to hide behind—even if I could have moved both the dead guy and Jamaal. Not to mention the splatters of blood everywhere.

I was coming close to panic again, frozen where I was, my brain trying to think of what to do and coming up empty. That was when a large black dog came galloping through the cemetery, leapt over the iron fence like it was only an inch high, and landed on the grass beside me. Another burst of adrenaline flooded my system, but before I had a chance to react, the dog shimmered, and suddenly, it was Jack kneeling there in the grass beside me—stark naked, though I was too fuzzy-minded to take much note of it.

The headlights were coming closer, and we were sitting ducks, nowhere to hide. Without a word, Jack grabbed my arm, his hand fortunately not landing on one of the bite wounds, jerking me to the ground beside the dead guy. I tried to voice a protest, but Jack ignored me, forcing my hand against the dead guy's mauled shoulder and holding it there with an iron grip while reaching for Jamaal with his other hand.

I tried to pull away, shuddering with revulsion, but

Jack turned and hissed at me. "Hold still! Just until the car passes."

I didn't want to. My hand was sticky with the dead guy's blood, and my stomach wanted to rebel at the thought of what I was touching. The car was slowing down as it approached us, and I figured adding a naked guy to this scenario wasn't doing much to improve the visuals. I cringed when the headlights hit us, hoping the driver would go shrieking off in terror at warp speed, giving us time to do . . . something . . . before he called the cops. Instead, the car cruised slowly past us. I had the brief impression of a man's face, taking a good look at us through the driver's-side window, then turning to face front with a grimace.

The car picked up speed as it passed, but there was no squeal of tires as the driver put pedal to metal, and it didn't look to me like he was going more than a little faster than the speed limit.

Jack let go of me, and I jerked away from the dead guy. My head swam at the sudden movement, and I closed my eyes to avoid passing out.

"What the hell was that about?" I snarled at Jack.

"What good is a trickster if he has no illusion magic?" Jack responded, sounding smug. Apparently, the blood and gore didn't bother him nearly as much as they did me.

I forced my eyes open, and though my head still swam, it wasn't quite as bad. Jack was sitting on the bloody grass between the victim and Jamaal, showing no sign of self-consciousness. I kept my eyes pinned on his face as I realized something.

"I've seen you change forms before. You don't have to be naked to do it." When he'd changed in the living room, his clothes had changed right along with him.

He grinned at me and stretched out his legs to give me a better view. "I don't technically have to, but it's more fun this way. You should see the look on your face."

If my gun had been in easy reach, I might have shot him. "Some poor bastard just got mauled to death by jackals, Jamaal is lying there unconscious, I'm bleeding, and you think this is a good time to yank my chain?"

He met my eyes as the humor left his. It was the first time in my memory I could remember seeing Jack look serious. His expression was strangely chilling, maybe only because it looked wrong on a face that was always smiling.

"I'm a descendant of Loki," he said in a tone that suggested I'd ticked him off. "Deal with it."

Loki, who was a trickster and who didn't much care about the feelings of those around him.

"That may be true," I said. "But that doesn't mean you *are* Loki. You could show a little compassion every once in a while."

The grin was back. "Why would I want to do a silly thing like that?"

I guessed appealing to his better nature was a lost cause. Which I should have known before I opened my mouth. Tricksters aren't known for being nice. I shook my head.

"You're an asshole," I told Jack, who was not the least bothered by it.

Down the street a bit, I could see a couple of people turn the corner at a run. They were far enough away that I couldn't tell who they were yet. I supposed I should be grateful that Jack had gotten there as quickly as he had. If I'd been in trouble, the others would have been too late to help me. Assuming Jack wouldn't have sat on the sidelines eating popcorn if I *had* been in trouble.

"Put some damn clothes on," I snapped at him, only to realize that in the brief moment I'd looked away, he'd somehow managed to clothe himself.

The rest of the *Liberi* converged on us in the next couple of minutes. I was still light-headed and woozy, and the bite wounds hurt like a son of a bitch. I didn't feel like reliving what had just happened multiple times, so I waited until everyone was there before I gave them the play-by-play.

I debated whether to tell everyone about how Jamaal had wigged out and then ended up killing the victim, but he was still lying there unconscious, and I figured I had to explain. I hoped I wasn't condemning Jamaal to a fate worse than death by telling Anderson what had happened. But I knew it hadn't really been Jamaal who killed the victim; it had been his death magic, which had taken him over completely, possessed him like a demon. I hoped Anderson would understand that.

There was silence among the gathered *Liberi* as they contemplated everything I'd said. Anderson knelt by Jamaal's side and lightly tapped his cheeks, trying to wake him up, but he was still out cold. Another car passed by, and Jack did his thing, reaching down to touch me and the dead guy and Jamaal. I noticed more than one *Liberi* grimace and look away, and, as before, the car went right on by the bloody murder scene without stopping.

"Do I want to know what you're making people see?" I asked Jack.

"No," several people answered at once, and I realized that I was probably the only one who hadn't seen the illusion. I bit my tongue to resist asking him why I couldn't see it. I wasn't particularly in the mood to start up a conversation with him.

"We'd better get back to the house," Anderson said, standing up and brushing dead grass off the knees of his jeans. Somehow he'd managed not to get any blood on him. "The killer isn't going to come back here tonight."

"What about Jamaal?" I asked.

Anderson gave me a neutral look. "I'm not making any decisions until he wakes up and gives me his side of the story. Maybe he had a good reason for what he did."

But Anderson hadn't seen him, hadn't seen the absolute lack of humanity in his face. I wondered if Jamaal would even remember anything when he woke up—assuming the death magic hadn't pushed him over the edge permanently.

Anderson moved around to Jamaal's feet and

squatted, glancing up at Logan. "Help me carry him, will you?"

I didn't know how much Jamaal weighed, except that it was a lot. It probably would be easier to use a fireman's carry, but we had a considerable walk to get to where we'd parked, and I figured the guys were going to have to take turns, so maybe two at a time would be more efficient in the end.

Logan was just starting to bend down when Maggie grabbed his shoulder and tugged him back.

"I can carry him," she said, then bent and slid one arm under Jamaal's shoulders and one under his knees, lifting him like he weighed no more than a toddler. "See? Light as a feather."

Maggie had told me once that although the guys all knew about her supernatural strength, testosterone poisoning made them really uncomfortable with letting her carry stuff. I could see she was right by the way the guys shifted uncomfortably on their feet. Maggie smiled tightly, and I knew it bothered her that they were threatened by her strength.

I forced myself to stand up, though it seemed to take a massive amount of effort, and putting weight on my wounded leg made a reluctant whimper rise in my throat.

"I guess I should carry *you* instead," Anderson said, and before I had a chance to protest, he'd swept me off my feet. I instinctively put an arm around his neck to hold on.

"I can walk," I insisted like an idiot.

"Yeah, if we don't mind it taking three hours to get back to the cars," Anderson retorted.

In my peripheral vision, I saw Jack bend down and feel around the dead guy's pocket until he found a wallet, which he promptly transferred into his own back pocket.

"You're stealing his wallet?" I asked, my voice a little shrill with my indignation.

Jack shrugged. "It'll have ID and credit cards, which might help us find out more about him and maybe figure out why he was targeted."

I didn't think that had anything to do with it. He could have just glanced at the ID to find out who the poor guy was, then left it at the scene.

Anderson turned away before I had a chance to tell Jack what an asshole he was—for the second time in the last ten minutes—and we started down the road toward where we'd parked.

"The best way to handle Jack is not to engage with him," Anderson told me.

Jack said something under his breath that I think it was good I couldn't hear.

Anderson carried me gently, but I felt every footstep reverberate through my body, bringing stabs of pain from my wounds. I gritted my teeth and held on, trying not to make any undignified noises or start crying.

Emma was watching me with narrowed eyes, and I realized she wasn't at all happy about Anderson carrying me. It made me want to snuggle in closer to him just to piss her off, but I hurt too much to indulge in mind games. Instead, I closed my eyes and prayed for my supernatural healing to hurry up and do its job.

I think I passed out for part of the trip back to the cars, because we seemed to get there faster than I expected. Obviously, neither Jamaal nor I was in any shape to drive, so we had to shuffle passengers and drivers around a bit. I ended up stretched across the backseat of Anderson's car, which I didn't think was the smartest seating arrangement in the world, seeing as Emma was still glaring daggers at me. Anderson must have noticed—she had a few daggers in her arsenal to spare for him, too—but he ignored it.

I *know* I passed out for a while during the car ride, and based on the stony silence and bitter expressions I woke up to, it was probably just as well. Anderson was staring straight ahead, all his concentration fixed on the road in front of him, while Emma stared out the side window, her arms crossed over her chest. I hoped it wasn't me they'd been fighting about. I thought they had enough issues without Emma's irrational jealousy thrown into the mix.

The ride was long enough that I expected to be feeling somewhat better by the time we arrived back at the mansion, but everything still hurt, and I was still weak. In fact, I seemed to be even weaker, although that was probably because I'd let myself forget just how miserable I'd felt the last time I tried to stand.

Anderson wound up carrying me again, and I could tell Emma was just thrilled about it. Here I was, making friends and influencing people without even having to *do* anything.

Jamaal was still pretty out of it, although he was technically conscious. Maggie's arm was around him, and he leaned on her heavily as he walked. I really wanted to know what the hell had happened back there in the cemetery, but I knew I wasn't getting an explanation anytime soon. Jamaal looked like a stiff wind would knock him down, and he was shivering even though it wasn't all that cold. By the time we got through the front door to the main stairway, he was completely spent, and Maggie had to carry him up the stairs. That he didn't protest showed just how out of it he was.

Anderson took me up to my own room. I didn't want him to lay me on my nice, clean bed when I was covered in blood, so I directed him to take me to the bathroom so I could get cleaned up first. When he put me down, I had to grab hold of the sink to keep from falling.

"I feel like shit," I grumbled, wishing my supernatural healing would do its thing a little faster.

Anderson's brow furrowed as he looked at me. "You're looking rather pale."

He had to help me get my ruined coat off, and that's when we first got a close look at one of the bites. My stomach lurched, and I had to tighten my grip on the sink to stay upright.

The jackals' fangs had left a series of deep puncture wounds, and they didn't appear to have healed at all, even though it had probably been almost an hour since the attack. The flesh around the punctures was red and swollen, and if I hadn't known better, I would have sworn I had a raging infection.

"Why isn't it healing?" I asked Anderson, wondering if I shouldn't have just skipped the cleanup and collapsed into bed.

"I don't know," Anderson said grimly. He reached up and touched my forehead, and I realized for the first time that I was sweating. Anderson looked even more grim. "Feels like you have a fever, too."

"But that's impossible. Isn't it?"

"I would have thought so." There was no missing the worry in his eyes, and that didn't do much to comfort me. "Lets get the wounds cleaned up and put you to bed. Maybe there's some irritant in the jackals' saliva that's keeping you from healing."

An "irritant" probably wouldn't have given me a fever, but I felt too awful to argue.

"I'm going to need some help," I said, though I knew it was obvious that I wasn't up to cleaning and dressing the wounds myself. "I think Emma and I would both be happier if you sent Maggie in to help me instead of doing it yourself."

Anger flashed in Anderson's eyes. "Emma wouldn't be so shallow as to be jealous of you in the state you're in."

Ah, denial. I'd seen the way she'd looked at me while he was carrying me, and I knew without a doubt that she was, indeed, jealous. Ridiculous it might be, but then, feelings often were. But that was not an argument for right now.

"Then forget about Emma," I said. "*I'm* not much of an exhibitionist, so I'd really rather Maggie help me than you. No offense."

"None taken," Anderson said, though I wasn't sure that was true. He reached over and closed the lid of the toilet, then helped me traverse the few feet between it and the sink so I could sit down. Instead of leaving me there and going to get Maggie, he actually called her on his cell phone. The idea that he was worried enough not to leave me alone for the five minutes it would take to go find her was not at all comforting.

My head started to throb, as if the wounds themselves didn't hurt enough. When Maggie arrived, Anderson had a whispered conversation with her right outside the bathroom door. I couldn't hear a word they said, but I didn't think it boded well for me.

Things got a little fuzzy then, so I only vaguely remember Maggie helping me out of my clothes and cleaning my wounds. She had to use water at first, because the *Liberi* didn't have things like alcohol or peroxide sitting around—who needed them when your body repaired itself in a matter of hours?—but somebody must have been sent out to raid a drugstore, because the peroxide came eventually.

By the time I was laid out in bed, my wounds all bandaged, I was sweating and shivering at the same time, and all my joints ached. I'd never been this sick in my life, and I spent some time complaining to myself about how life wasn't fair. Here I was immortal, invulnerable, and I was sick and hurting and scared I was going to die anyway.

My sleep that night was sporadic at best, interspersed with nightmares that would have made me sit up and scream if I'd had the energy.

Eight

I was no better in the morning. In fact, if anything, I was worse.

I was burning up and freezing cold by turns, aching down to my bones while the bite wounds continued to throb. I made the mistake of checking under one of the bandages, and the sight brought bile into the back of my throat.

Not only were the wounds not closed, they were seeping with pus, the redness and swelling spreading. When Maggie came in to check on me and change the bandages, it hurt so much I couldn't stop myself from crying like a baby. And the worst part was there was no sign cleaning the wounds or changing the bandages was doing any good.

Whatever was wrong with me, I knew it was bad when Anderson brought Steph in to visit me. I was sure he'd brought her because he thought I was going to die, and based on how much she cried despite efforts to put on a brave face, she thought the same. She sat by the side of my bed, holding my hand as I drifted in and out of sleep.

I wasn't even vaguely inclined to eat anything, and though Maggie had left a glass of water by my bedside when she'd put me to bed last night, it was still full. Steph urged me to drink, and I knew she was right and I ought to. Considering how much the fever was making me sweat, I had to be pretty dehydrated. With her holding my head up off the pillow, I lifted the glass to my lips, but I couldn't muster the will to swallow.

"It's no use," I told Steph, handing her back the glass. "I'll just puke it back up if I drink it."

In actuality, it wasn't that I felt nauseated. I just didn't want to drink. I couldn't have explained why if you'd asked me, but just the thought of taking a sip made my throat close up.

I have some vague memory of Steph trying again to get me to drink, more determined this time. I think I ended up shoving her away, making her spill the water all over herself, but I wasn't sure if that was real or just one of the nasty dreams I kept having.

The next time I woke up, Steph was gone. I was as miserable as ever, and I tried to turn over in the vain hope that I could find a more comfortable position. That was when I discovered the restraints fastened to my wrists and ankles.

Another nightmare, I told myself as I tugged weakly at the restraints. The movement made all the aches and pains flare up, and I discovered the skin around the restraints was red and raw, as if I'd been struggling against them. If I had, I didn't remember. But the fact that it hurt so much told me this wasn't a nightmare after all.

I tried to call out for help, but my mouth and throat were so dry I couldn't get any sound out. Instead, I closed my eyes and willed myself back into unconsciousness.

When I woke up again, it was dark out. There was a nightlight on in my room—someone must have brought it in from the bathroom. It took me a moment or two to assess my situation, to realize I was still deathly ill and in restraints, but when I did, panic seized me, and I started struggling as if my life depended on it.

My rational mind knew I couldn't fight free, that fighting the restraints was only causing me more pain, but I couldn't help it. I had to get loose, had to be free. I couldn't stand being in that bed for another moment, never mind that I wouldn't be able to walk two steps without collapsing.

"Nikki, please calm down," Anderson's soft voice said from beside my bed, but I couldn't seem to stop myself from thrashing.

I tried to talk, but it came out as an incoherent screech.

"She's probably delusional just now," said a voice I didn't recognize.

The sound of an unfamiliar voice reached my panicky core in a way that Anderson's soothing had not, and I stopped struggling as I strained my eyes in the darkness to see who was there. Someone turned on the bedside lamp, and when I got over being blinded, I blinked a few times and saw a stranger hovering over me.

She was a plump brunette with a round face and hard blue eyes, maybe around forty. An iridescent caduceus glyph marked her cheek, and I gathered that meant she was some kind of healer. I didn't think any kind of healer was going to do me much good. Whatever was wrong with me was impossible, so it was hard to believe someone could magically cure it.

"Why am I tied up?" I croaked.

"Because you've been hallucinating," the healer said, sitting down on the side of my bed. "You tried to get out of bed a few times, and it didn't go so well."

I didn't remember any of that, but Anderson wasn't contradicting her, so I guessed it was true. I didn't want her there, didn't want a stranger so close to me, especially not when I was so vulnerable. I glanced over her shoulder at Anderson, who was standing with his arms crossed over his chest and a tight, unhappy expression on his face.

"Get her away from me," I said, scooting over as much as the restraints would allow. The panic tried to rise again, but I fought it with everything I had. I didn't need any more raw spots on my wrists and ankles.

"Nikki, this is Erin," he said, ignoring my polite request, surprise, surprise. "She's a descendant of Apollo . . . and she's a healer."

I recognized her from the files I'd been examining for Anderson before hunting a serial killer became my top priority. I made a mental note to myself to put her file at the top of my list, seeing as she'd compromised her cover identity by coming here.

Erin reached for me, and I let out a screech of warning, thrashing wildly, my heart pounding and my breaths coming in gasps. I was conscious of everything I was doing, but it felt like my body was not my own, like the sickness was driving me. I wanted to stop thrashing around, if only because of how much it hurt, but everything within me rebelled at the thought of this woman touching me.

I won't repeat the names I called her as she inexorably planted her hands on both sides of my face, holding me down with the weight of her forearms on my chest. The touch of her fingers on my skin made me scream, and I think I even tried to bite her.

Anything to get her off me.

But between the restraints and the weakness, I was no match for her, and she held me with little difficulty as her hands began to glow white.

That glow sent me into another paroxysm of sheer, unadulterated panic. My throat was hoarse from screaming, and if I'd been any stronger, I'd probably have broken bones in my wrists and ankles in my attempts to escape.

Erin said nothing as she sat there with her glowing hands on my face, her eyes closed. I was vaguely aware of Anderson saying soothing things, but I couldn't make out the words, and I was incapable of being soothed, anyway.

Eventually, the glow died down, and Erin dropped her hands from my face.

"Well?" Anderson asked before she had a chance to speak.

"She has rabies," Erin said simply, the words sucking all of the air out of my lungs.

One of my foster mothers had had a rabies scare when she'd been bitten by a stray dog. She'd gotten the preventive treatment and was just fine, but everyone in that family had learned more about rabies than we ever wanted to know. Like that it was fatal once the symptoms started to show.

"Can't be." I gasped. "Not long enough." The words didn't make much sense, but Erin seemed to know what I was trying to say.

"If you were a mortal who'd been bitten by a rabid animal, no, you wouldn't be showing symptoms yet. But this isn't normal rabies—that wouldn't affect a *Liberi*. There's something different about this strain. I've never seen anything like it, but if I had to guess, I'd say the virus itself is supernatural in nature."

"What can we do?" Anderson asked, beating me to the question.

Erin gave us both an apologetic look. "Even in humans, rabies isn't curable at this stage. There's nothing I can do for her."

"There has to be something!" Anderson insisted, and I'd have been touched by the depth of his concern if I weren't fighting the realization that I was going to die.

"I'm sorry," Erin said. "There's nothing."

"If I die from this," I whispered, "do I get to come back?" A *Liberi* could come back from death by decapitation. Surely a little rabies wouldn't keep me down . . .

Erin shook her head. "Let's hope not. Your body will still be infected when you die, so even if it heals the damage, you won't be in any better shape."

I shuddered and had to fight a scream. It would be like what Emma had gone through for ten years in the water—coming to life only to find yourself back in the same situation that had killed you in the first place, a fate worse than death.

"What if we killed the virus?" Anderson asked, and I could tell by the look on his face that he had an idea, but I wasn't getting my hopes up. "If she could come back to a body that was virus-free, she'd be fine, right?"

Erin nodded cautiously. "I suppose so. But I don't know how you'd go about killing the virus. *I* can't do it, and there's no medicine on earth that can do it either."

"What if after she . . . dies . . . we burn the body?"

I must have made some kind of panicked noise, because Anderson nudged Erin out of the way and sat beside me, taking my hand and giving it a firm squeeze.

"You can come back from that," he assured me in a soothing croon. "If your body is entirely destroyed, then you'll just generate a new one. I know *Liberi* who have done it. The immortal seed isn't a physical object, isn't something that can be destroyed, and it's the seed that brings us back when we die."

"It might work," Erin said. "Burning the body

would kill the virus cells. If your body has to regenerate from scratch, there's no reason it would regenerate the virus, too. At least, no reason that I can think of. But having never seen anything like this before, I can't make any promises."

Anderson reached out and brushed my hair out of the tear tracks on my cheek. "It's the best chance we have."

"I don't like this plan," I whispered. A sudden chill seized me, and I shivered so hard I practically bit my tongue. My eyes were burning fiercely, but there wasn't enough moisture in my body to produce any more tears.

"I don't much like it, either," Anderson replied, fingers absently stroking my hair like he thought the gesture could soothe me. It couldn't. Nothing could.

"We can just let nature take its course, if you prefer," Erin said, not sounding as sympathetic as Anderson. "Die, come back, be miserable, then die again, lather, rinse, repeat."

Anderson glared at her. There was something about the way they looked at each other, some kind of invisible sparks, that told me they'd been a couple once. I'd seen enough love-gone-sour looks in my days as a P.I. to recognize it when I saw it.

"Your work is done here, I think," he said. "You can go."

Erin laughed. "What do you think I am? Your servant?"

"No. I think you're a healer who's outlived her usefulness in this situation."

Erin's eyes narrowed. "Don't think this gets you out of anything. You owe me, whether I could cure her or not. I took an enormous risk coming here, and—"

"Yes, yes, I owe you," Anderson said impatiently. "That was the deal. Now, please go instead of terrorizing your patient just to get to me."

She laughed hard at that one, shaking her head. "You have an inflated opinion of your importance to me." She dabbed at imaginary tears of mirth in her eyes, and then her expression hardened. "You mean nothing to me," she said, an obvious lie. "And you'll pay handsomely for this visit."

"Get out."

Still looking mighty pleased with herself, she turned and headed out the door, not looking back.

"Your taste in women sucks," I told Anderson. Maybe not the most sensitive observation in the world, but it was true.

Anderson gave me a small smile, one that looked pretty damned forced to my eyes. "She came by her hard feelings honestly. I left her for Emma many years ago."

Boy, Emma must have been overjoyed that Anderson had called his old girlfriend to come take care of his new girlfriend, or whatever the hell she thought I was. She was probably going to throw a party when she found out I was going to die.

"Her bedside manner could use some work," Anderson said, "but she *did* come out of hiding to help you. It was a big risk for her."

Somehow I didn't think Erin had taken that big

risk out of the goodness of her heart. Anderson had made it perfectly clear when he hired me to look over his records that he wanted to keep track of the people he'd helped—even though keeping track of them was detrimental to their covers—so he could press them into service as needed. I seriously doubted Anderson had given Erin much of a choice when he'd requested her help.

"If she hadn't identified the virus, we'd have had no idea what to do to help you."

I swallowed hard, which was quite a feat with my parched mouth and throat. "Letting me die and burning my body isn't exactly the kind of help I was hoping for."

"I know."

Anderson was still stroking my hair, and I was beginning to find the gesture a bit irritating. My skin felt overly sensitive, and even the light brush of his fingers felt like the scrape of sandpaper. I could only imagine what Emma would think if she saw.

I turned my head away from his touch, hoping that would make him stop. Instead, he reached out and cupped my other cheek, turning my face back toward him. I was too weak to resist as he held both hands to my face and leaned down to plant a kiss on my forehead. I was too stunned to say anything, but I hoped that kiss meant he was about to let go of me and give me some space.

"I'm sorry," he whispered against my skin.

I didn't comprehend what he was about to do until the very last instant, which I'm sure was what he intended. Just as the metaphorical light bulb went on over my head, Anderson's hands tightened around my head. I felt him begin to wrench my head around, and then there was nothing.

I had a vague feeling that time had passed when I next regained consciousness, but I didn't know how much, and I couldn't even have said what made me feel that way. I tried to open my eyes, but nothing seemed to happen. I was in complete and utter darkness, and though my brain was sending signals to my eyes that they should blink a few times in case there really was some light somewhere and I just needed to clear them, I couldn't actually feel my eyes doing anything.

I tried to suck in a deep breath to calm myself, but that didn't work, either. My body remained in absolute stillness, and I couldn't even feel the beating of my heart. I tried again for the deep breath, but it was no use.

I felt like I had a body—you know, like you know your foot is there even when it's not moving or touching anything. But I seemed to be utterly paralyzed, my heart not beating, my lungs not working, my limbs ignoring my increasingly frantic orders to move.

I'm dead, I told myself, remembering the feel of Anderson's hands on my face. He must have thought giving me a quick death was a mercy compared with whatever the mutant disease had planned for me.

My nonexistent lungs demanded oxygen, but no amount of trying would persuade my body to take in air. Terror coursed through my blood, though with no heartbeat, it seemed that should be impossible. I shouldn't have been able to feel any of this, but telling myself that didn't stave off the desperate need to breathe. I was suffocating, and there was nothing I could do about it.

But I was already dead, wasn't I? That meant I *couldn't* suffocate. Anderson was probably even now planning the bonfire in which he would burn my earthly body. God, I *hoped* he was doing it now. The sooner he burned the body, the sooner the magic of the *Liberi* would cause it to regenerate.

Unless all of that had been a comforting fiction, meant to give me hope when no hope was left.

I'd thought the symptoms of the illness had made me miserable, but that was a walk in the park compared with being dead. Maggie had told me once that dying was a horrible experience, even for the *Liberi* who knew they would come back.

She was right. More than right.

There was nothing to see, nothing to hear, nothing to smell. Nothing to feel, except for that frantic need to breathe, like a fish gasping in the bottom of a boat. Only I couldn't even gasp.

At first, I kept mentally talking to myself, trying to keep myself calm, or at least as calm as possible. As miserable as I was, this was temporary. This, too, shall pass and all that.

That worked for a while, though I couldn't have told you how long, because I had no sense of time. I was still terrified, would have screamed and thrashed and cried if I could have, but I wasn't out of my mind. Not yet.

But there was only so long I could hold on before the panic took on a life of its own.

Suffocating. Paralyzed. Alone.

What if Anderson and Erin were wrong? What if I couldn't come back from this? What if what I was feeling now was all there was, all there would ever be, until the end of time? I couldn't escape death by dying, so there was no reason to believe this would ever end.

Time passed, and every second felt like a year. A year of unadulterated terror.

This was hell, I eventually decided.

This was my punishment for all my years of youthful rebellion, for all the times I'd been an ungrateful bitch to those who'd tried to take care of me.

With no way to move, no way to make any sound, no way to cry, there was no outlet for the terror, and it just festered inside me, growing more and more powerful, until fear was all I knew.

I was going slowly mad, screaming endlessly inside, praying for an end I was convinced would never come.

NINE

I jackknifed into a sitting position, dragging in a breath so huge it was a wonder my lungs didn't explode. I immediately sucked in another, the air rasping through my throat.

My heart was back online, that was for sure, my pulse racing, adrenaline flooding my system as my hands rose to my throat and I tried to take about three breaths at once.

"Easy," said a feminine voice, and in a moment, Maggie was sitting on the bed beside me, holding my wrists, keeping them away from my throat. I think I'd been about to tear open my trachea to get the air in faster. "You're back now, and it's going to be all right."

I was not convinced. I didn't know how long I'd been dead, but it had felt like forever and a day. I had so much residual panic stored up it was a wonder I stayed conscious.

I burst into tears, frantic sobs that made my chest

hurt and my nose clog up. Maggie put her arms around me, rocking me and murmuring soothing nonsense like I was a baby in need of comfort. It shows just what bad shape I was in that it never even occurred to me to object.

It took a long time before rational thought returned. I gently extricated myself from Maggie's hug, then fell back limply onto the bed, utterly exhausted.

I felt like I was in recovery from the world's worst case of flu, and I was frankly surprised I'd been able to scrape up enough energy to sit up in the first place. Amazing what existential panic can do. I closed my eyes and concentrated on breathing, loving the feel of oxygen flowing into my lungs even though my throat and chest hurt from my previous attempts to hyperventilate.

The good news was that there were no aches and pains in my joints and no throbbing in my arms and legs where I'd been bitten.

"It worked," I said in a small voice, barely able to comprehend what had just happened. I'd died. My body had been burned. And yet here I was, alive again.

"It did," Maggie confirmed, and I opened my eyes to see that hers were all shiny.

"Why are you crying?"

She smiled through the tears. "Because we didn't know if it would or not." She reached up and dabbed at her eyes. "When you're immortal, you get used to thinking that your immortal friends will never die. It's one of the perks, especially when you've outlived anyone you ever knew from your mortal days." There was a wealth of sadness in those words. I couldn't imagine what it was like to see everyone you loved die. One day, I, too, would know the feeling, but I shoved the thought aside.

"I didn't like the idea of losing you," Maggie concluded.

I was touched by her care, which brought a few tears to my eyes, too. We hadn't known each other for very long, but I had the distinct impression she'd been starved for female company before I came along.

"How long have I been . . . gone?"

"Four days."

My heart gave a thud in my chest. "Four days? Jamaal came back in a few hours!"

"Jamaal didn't have to generate a whole new body from scratch. It's time-consuming. Now, stop asking questions and get a little rest. When the others find out you're back, they're going to storm the room and won't give you a moment of peace. Especially Steph."

I didn't want to rest, not after what I'd been through. But I was running on fumes, the supernatural effort to come back to life having stolen every drop of my energy. The power of suggestion was too much, and I found my eyes drifting closed despite myself.

Maggie wasn't wrong about the storming-my-room thing. It seemed like practically everyone in the house came by to welcome me back. The whole thing felt pretty surreal. I mean, I'd only known these people a handful of weeks, and I didn't think most of them liked me all that much. Why should they, when they'd all been together for years, and I'd only come into their midst by killing one of their friends? Maybe they were just freaked out by the idea of a mutated supernatural rabies virus so powerful it could kill *Liberi* and they wanted to assure themselves I was still alive.

Steph, naturally, was beside herself. She'd always been more comfortable with tears than I was, and she cried plenty of them when she came to see me.

"I couldn't believe you would come back," she told me. "No matter how much everyone assured me you would, it seemed impossible."

I probably would have felt the same way in her shoes, despite having personally seen Jamaal come back from the dead twice. That didn't make me squirm any less at the tears. I never knew quite what to do with them.

"What was it like, being dead?" she asked. "Were you . . . aware?"

I fought down a shudder. I'd have given anything not to have been aware. But Steph's question told me that no one had mentioned to her how unpleasant dying was. If she didn't know, I saw no reason to enlighten her. Not to mention that the last thing in the world I wanted to do was talk about it.

Another shudder rippled through me as I wondered if I'd experienced death as regular humans did. Would my sister and my adoptive parents find themselves in the same state someday, with no hope of it ever ending? The Glasses were Christians, their faith low-key but there nonetheless. They believed in the afterlife, but if what I'd experienced was the true afterlife, I wouldn't wish it on my worst enemy.

It was a thought too terrible to contemplate, and I added it to my ever-expanding list of taboo subjects. I shook my head at Steph, silently lying to her. I would never, ever tell her what had happened to me when I'd died. If I had indeed experienced the fate that awaited all mortals, I didn't want Steph to know anything about it. Not until she had to.

By the time Anderson came to see me, it was nearly dinnertime, and I'd been wondering to myself if he was too chicken to face me after having killed me. He'd done the right thing, and I knew that. I'd have died anyway, and who knew how long the disease would have made me suffer before putting me out of my misery?

Actually, *not* putting me out of my misery, just condemning me to a whole other level of misery. I'd still have been dead, still would have had to spend four days in Limbo, or wherever the hell I'd been. But it would have been nice if the choice had been mine, rather than his.

I still wasn't close to full strength, but I'd at least found the energy to get up and take a shower. I hadn't bothered getting dressed, though, so I was sitting around in plaid flannel pajama bottoms with a utilitarian camisole when Anderson came in. My hair was still wet from the shower—blow-drying it would have taken way more energy than I had—and I glanced down at the cami to make sure there weren't any embarrassingly revealing wet spots. Either that, or I was glancing down to avoid Anderson's eyes—take your pick.

I was sitting cross-legged on the bed, feeling bone-tired, as if I'd just finished running a marathon. I would have lain down, except I was afraid I might fall asleep again. Besides, I didn't much like the idea of closing my eyes and triggering memories of the smothering darkness. Hell, if I had my way, I'd never sleep again.

Anderson came to sit on the edge of the bed, resting his back against one of the massive wooden posts. "How are you feeling?"

I found my courage and looked up to meet his eyes. There was an uncomfortable amount of understanding and compassion in his gaze, and it pissed me off. He didn't get to be Mr. Nice Guy after he'd broken my freaking neck.

"Like someone who's been dead for four days," I said with a stubborn lift of my chin. Even saying the words sent a chill through me, and I fought off memory as fiercely as I could. I was going to have to come to terms with what I'd been through someday, but I planned to put that off for as long as possible.

Anderson didn't flinch from the anger in my voice. "There wasn't any other way to save you."

"You could have warned me!" I snapped. "Or, hell, I don't know, *asked* me before making a unilateral decision."

He cocked his head. "Would your decision have been different from mine?"

"That's not the point!"

"I didn't think knowing about it in advance was going to make it any easier. I did what I thought was best for you at the moment." His calm, reasonable voice scraped against my nerves, though it was silly of me to expect wailing and gnashing of teeth.

My first instinct was to lay into him some more, but I took a deep breath and went in search of my self-control. I knew Anderson too well to think I'd convince him what he'd done was wrong. To tell you the truth, I wasn't entirely sure *I* was convinced it was wrong—just that I didn't like it.

"How's Jamaal?" I asked instead, hoping Anderson would let me change the subject. Jamaal was the only one who hadn't come to see me, and I hoped that didn't mean Anderson had evicted him for his lack of self-control at the cemetery.

"He's . . . struggling."

"Meaning what?"

"Meaning I never should have sent him to spend several hours in a cemetery." Anderson might not have felt particularly guilty about breaking my neck, but the look on his face said that this he felt guilty about. "It gave the death magic too much power, until Jamaal couldn't control it, no matter how hard he tried."

I was still mad at Anderson for what he'd done, but I didn't see that he had any reason to feel bad about sending Jamaal to the cemetery with me. "Did you know that was going to happen?"

Anderson shook his head. "I've never known that to happen before, but Jamaal is the only descendant of Kali I've ever spent any significant time with."

"If you didn't know he'd react that way, then you couldn't have known it was a bad idea to send him to the cemetery. If you're going to beat yourself up about something, at least do it about something you could have changed. Like, say, breaking my neck."

He gave me a reproachful look but failed to pick up the gauntlet I'd thrown down again. "I *should* have known. Should have at least considered the possibility. He was stabilizing, but now . . ." His voice trailed off, and the look in his eyes was troubled.

I sighed. "If you're going to toss blame around, toss some my way. I noticed that Jamaal was acting strange, but I didn't do anything. Hell, throw some blame Jamaal's way, too, because he *knew* something was wrong long before his control snapped. He could have fessed up and gotten out of there before things went to hell."

A small smile played around the corners of Anderson's mouth. "Oh, I'm not taking all the blame, don't worry. I'm not holding you responsible, because you aren't experienced enough to have guessed what his loss of control meant. Also, you never in a million years would have been able to talk him into leaving. He *is* an alpha male, you know."

"I've noticed."

"You're right that Jamaal should have recognized he was having a problem and how dangerous the problem was. He's been spending his time in the basement ever since, though I'm inclined to release him now that you're back with us."

In one of the makeshift prison cells, he meant. Not that those cells could hold Jamaal, unless he allowed himself to be held. At least Anderson hadn't imposed a

more draconian penalty, as he had the last time Jamaal
had lost it.

I wasn't able to stifle a yawn. Amazing what dying
and then coming back to life can do for your energy
level.

"You should get some more rest," Anderson said as
he rose to his feet. "You'll feel much better tomorrow,
as long as you don't overtax yourself tonight."

"What about the case?"

Anderson had already turned for the door on
the assumption that the conversation was over, but I
wasn't about to let him go that easily.

"We can talk some more tomorrow," he said.

"What have you found out about the victim?
I assume you had Leo do some digging while I was
gone."

He turned back toward me with a quelling look.
"We'll talk about it tomorrow."

"Today is Wednesday, right?"

He nodded cautiously, as if afraid of agreeing
with me.

"That means we have two days before the killer
strikes again. We don't have time to wait until I'm all
better."

"You're in no shape to work right now."

Another yawn forced its way up my throat, no
matter how hard I tried to stop it. Not the best way to
convince Anderson I was fit for duty.

I could have argued with him some more, could
have tried to insist he let me work. But in the end, I
didn't need his permission. The data I needed was no

doubt either on my laptop or at least available from it. All I needed was for Anderson to go away, and then I could do what I pleased.

"Fine," I said with a huff, pulling back the covers and sliding into bed. "I'll sleep. But I'm getting to work the moment the sun rises tomorrow, so make sure Leo sends me anything he's dug up."

Anderson raised an eyebrow. I doubt he was used to being given orders. But he didn't call me on it, instead issuing a murmured "good night" and slipping out of the room. I suspected he might be hovering outside the bedroom door waiting to make sure I did as I was told, so I lay down and turned off the light. I even closed my eyes, in case he did a Columbo and came back into the room for "one more thing." And that was a mistake.

When I next awoke, it was after midnight. Someone had left a plastic-wrapped sandwich, a bag of chips, and a bottle of water on my bedside table. I guessed that was my dinner, though whoever had left it probably hadn't counted on it sitting there that long before I got to it. I was ravenous, and I couldn't die of food poisoning, so I stuffed down the sandwich and the bag of chips in about sixty seconds.

I opened the bottle of water and washed down the remaining salty goodness of the chips, then slid out of bed and gave a tentative stretch. I still felt weak, and despite the six hours or so of sleep I'd just gotten, I had the feeling if I let myself fall back into bed, I'd be out for the rest of the night. Still, I felt a whole lot better than I had for a while, and I was all too aware of the clock ticking. If I couldn't track down the killer before Friday night, someone else was going to die horribly.

What we were going to do if and when I tracked down the killer was a whole other question. How do you capture someone who's immortal and has a pack of rabid phantom jackals at his beck and call? Sure, I was back from the dead, but I was not at all up for another face-to-face with those damn jackals.

I told myself not to think about that part, then made my way into my sitting room. I debated going downstairs to get a cup of coffee while my laptop was booting up but decided against it. I was definitely still pretty washed out, and while I was sure I could make it down the stairs, making it back up afterward might be a challenge.

Despite his distaste for being given orders by a worker bee like me, Anderson had obviously talked to Leo, because there were a bunch of new emails waiting in my in-box. The first one I opened purported to be about the latest victim, and though I honestly wasn't sure what I could hope to learn, my instincts told me it was important.

My mind wasn't exactly firing on all cylinders. I had read all the way through Leo's dossier, learning more than I wanted to know about the victim's life, before something finally struck me. I minimized the email so that only the victim's picture was visible, then fished through the rest of my emails and brought up pictures of the previous two identified victims.

One of them was lean and athletic-looking, and had olive skin with dark hair and a beard and mustache.

Just like the latest victim. The other was clean-shaven, although he did have olive skin. I also remembered that he was the one whose picture in the newspaper was obviously at least a decade out of date.

I searched Google for a more recent photo and found one in no time. And wouldn't you know it, he had the black beard and mustache, too. He wasn't as athletic-looking as the other two, but he was certainly lean—to the point of looking unhealthy.

I only had three victims to go on, since the first was still unidentified, but the resemblance couldn't be a coincidence. Lean, dark hair, olive skin, beard and mustache . . . all three bore more than a passing resemblance to Konstantin.

And that meant Phoebe was lying when she told us the Olympians had no idea why the killer was hunting in D.C.

The attacks were personal—and aimed at Konstantin.

And that meant Konstantin knew damn well who the killer was.

TEN

I sat back in my chair and stared at the three photos on my computer screen, wondering if I could be making something out of nothing.

No, I didn't think so.

Who was this guy? What did he have against Konstantin? And why had Phoebe and Cyrus lied about it? The obvious conclusion was that they were hiding something—no doubt on Konstantin's orders—but I had no clue what.

I didn't have answers to any of these questions, and I knew that the next logical step was to have a heart-to-heart with Konstantin. Maybe now that the jig was up, he'd be more forthcoming about what was going on. He might not care how many people Dog-boy killed, but he *did* want him stopped. I couldn't help wondering if Phoebe's "vision" had been any more truthful than anything else she'd told us. Was Konstantin really trying to keep the killer from being captured by the government, or was he just using us to clean up his mess?

I wanted to question Konstantin right away, but I knew better than to think that was an option. I wasn't getting an interview with him at nearly two in the morning. Not that I believed I was capable of getting the truth out of Konstantin, anyway. I had no leverage over him, no way to make him talk to me if he didn't want to—which I already knew he wouldn't.

Anderson, however, might be able to manage it. He planned to kill Konstantin someday, and they both knew it. Unless Konstantin was clinically insane, he had to be at least somewhat afraid of Anderson, even if he'd never admit it.

I briefly debated venturing into Anderson's wing to wake him up and get him on it right away, but there was no point in it. Anderson wasn't going to be able to get hold of Konstantin at this hour any more than I could. Besides, waking Anderson meant waking Emma, and that struck me as a bad idea.

I knew I should go back to bed and get some more sleep. I was far from fully recovered. But as drained as my body felt, I no longer felt sleepy, and I was afraid that if I lay down and closed my eyes without instantly falling asleep, I'd end up lying there remembering the suffocating darkness of death.

Even letting my mind brush against the memory made me shudder.

I didn't think there was much else I could do to help the case along at this point, but I needed to keep my mind occupied. I decided to brave the rigors of the stairs after all. Despite the old-fashioned formality of the mansion, there was a fairly comfortable den/media room on the first floor, and I figured I could either find something bearable to watch on cable or I could pop in a movie. Something mindless enough not to require much energy but engaging enough to absorb my attention and keep me from thinking.

I stopped by the kitchen first to make some coffee, then found myself having to sit down to rest before I could manage the trek from the kitchen to the den. Anderson had told me I should feel much better tomorrow, but at my current rate of recovery, I doubted I'd be at a hundred percent. Of course, my refusal to crawl back into bed and sleep the rest of the night probably wasn't helping, but there was no way I was climbing all the way back to my room on the third floor now.

Carrying a travel mug of coffee, because with my shaky legs I was afraid I'd spill with a regular mug, I made my slow and steady way to the den. I didn't bother turning lights on as I went, so I noticed the flickering glow emanating from the den as soon as I stepped into the hallway. There was a faint murmur of voices in the background, but it was the TV, rather than a bunch of people. Either someone had forgotten to turn the TV off before going to bed, or I wasn't the only one up at this ungodly hour.

I was doing exactly what Anderson had warned me not to do: overtaxing myself. My legs felt like overcooked spaghetti, and there was no way they were carrying me back up to my room, no matter how much

I didn't want company. Putting my hand against the wall for a little extra support, I continued down the hall until I could see into the den.

The den was about as masculine as you could imagine, with a pool table dominating one half of the room while a huge flat-screen TV with all the fixings dominated the other. A dartboard hung on one wall—well away from the precious TV—and the furniture was dark wood and leather. The only obviously feminine touch in the room was on the built-in bookshelves, where Maggie kept her collection of romance novels. In a relatively good-natured battle of wills, Maggie liked to pull out the books with the most lurid covers—classics from the seventies and eighties were a favorite—and prop them on the shelves facing out. Whenever she left the room, someone always tucked the books back into their places, spines out.

The guys had been remiss in their duties, because there was a nice collection of covers facing out, including a couple of more modern erotic romances, which featured naked guys discreetly blocking their best features from view. It made me smile. Maybe she'd finally worn the guys down. Or maybe everyone had better things to do than fight the battle of the sexes.

I didn't see anyone in the room at first. The program on the TV was a nature show about penguins, but the sound was so low I couldn't make out what the narrator was saying.

Fighting the fatigue, which was getting worse with each step I took, I set my sights on the couch, planning to collapse there. It wasn't until I'd put my hand on the back of the couch and started to move around it that I realized I wasn't alone after all.

Jamaal was slouched so low the top of his head hadn't shown over the back of the couch. Considering he was about six foot three, that was a lot of slouching. He was wearing a wife-beater and a pair of faded jeans, his bare feet propped on the coffee table. He was facing the TV, but there was a blank look in his eyes that said he wasn't actually watching it. He was spaced out enough that he didn't even seem to have heard me enter.

"Jamaal?" I said softly, hoping I wouldn't startle him. Startling a man who can crush you like an ant isn't good for your health.

He blinked as if coming back to himself, then turned his head slightly toward me. He made a soft grunting sound, put his feet on the floor, and pushed himself up into a normal seated position. If I'd been sitting like that, my back would have been hurting, but he seemed fine.

"What are you doing up?" he asked, his voice gravelly like he'd been sleeping. That was when I noticed the whiskey bottle on the floor by the side of the couch. I didn't know how much had been in it when he started, but it was almost empty now.

"I was going to ask you the same thing," I said, then let myself collapse onto the far seat of the couch before I ended up doing it involuntarily. My head spun for a moment, and I had to close my eyes. I was still holding the travel mug of coffee, but I didn't feel particularly inclined to drink it.

"You should be sleeping," Jamaal said, ignoring my question entirely. "I know how . . . draining it is to die."

I shivered and opened my eyes, to hell with the dizziness. Seeing the room spinning around me was better than seeing the darkness behind my eyes, a darkness that reminded me too much of the complete sensory deprivation of death.

Jamaal had three times surrendered himself to death to win back the right to stay in the mansion after Anderson had kicked him out. Perhaps the first time, he hadn't known exactly what he was getting himself into, but he knew after that—and he'd done it anyway. I didn't think I could ever voluntarily allow myself to die again. Not that the first time had been particularly voluntary.

"How could you . . . ?" The words died in my throat as horror threatened to choke me. I wanted to burn the memories from my head, but I was stuck with them, and I wasn't entirely sure they weren't going to drive me mad. "You knew what it was going to be like, and yet . . ."

Jeez, I couldn't even get a full sentence out. I'd come down here hoping *not* to think about death. I guess it was just my bad luck that Jamaal was the one I bumped into.

"It'll get better," Jamaal said, and maybe I was already crazy, but I could have sworn I heard something like compassion in his voice. "I've found that the memory fades with time. It feels almost like a bad dream now."

I nodded and swallowed hard, hoping like hell he was right. I'd barely brushed on the subject, and yet my pulse was racing, my skin clammy. If I wasn't careful, this was going to devolve into a full-scale panic attack.

There was a rustling sound, accompanied by the telltale clicking of beads, and to my shock, I realized that Jamaal was scooting closer to me on the couch. His proximity did an admirable job of distracting me from the panic. He took the travel mug from my unresisting fingers, popped the lid off, and poured in most of the remaining whiskey. Then he put the lid back on and handed it to me.

"Booze makes it all better?" I asked with a nervous laugh. He was still sitting intimately close. I could smell the faint hint of whiskey on his breath, along with the faded remnants of clove cigarettes.

"No. But sometimes it helps."

I didn't know what to say to that, so instead, I took a sip. The coffee was only lukewarm by then, and the whiskey was pretty overpowering, but I didn't care. Beside me, Jamaal raised the bottle to his lips and drained the last little bit. He didn't strike me as being particularly drunk. Just . . . mellow. Which is not a word I'd ever have associated with him before.

"I'm sorry," he said, staring at the empty bottle like it was the most fascinating thing in the world. "I fucked up. Again." He let out a sigh and set the bottle down on the coffee table. Then he didn't quite seem to know what to do with his hands. "If I hadn't lost my shit, I'd have been there when the jackals attacked. Maybe you wouldn't have gotten bit."

I took another sip of coffee, mulling over his words. "I think if you'd been there, we'd both have ended up with mutant rabies. It's not like either of us would have known how important it was to avoid being bitten."

He shrugged. "I dunno. I think if I'd been there, it would have been me they went after. No offense, but you don't look like much of a threat."

I reached out and patted his knee before I thought about it. "Yeah, well, I don't think I'd want to be around you if you came down with super-rabies," I said as my cheeks heated with a blush. I was not the touchy-feely sort, but this was not the first time I'd found myself touching Jamaal when I shouldn't.

He gave a snort of something that resembled laughter, blessedly ignoring my faux-pas. The hint of laughter faded between one breath and the next.

"I still shouldn't have run off like that."

I wasn't about to disagree, despite my doubts about how useful he'd have been.

"Why *did* you run off?"

He shook his head, the gesture accompanied by the almost musical clicking of his beads. "I knew I was losing it. I didn't trust myself not to . . ." Another shake of his head. "I don't know what I thought I might do, just that it would be bad. I meant to run back toward the cars, but somehow that wasn't what I ended up doing. I went right into the heart of the cemetery, where the call of the magic was even stronger."

I could hear a wealth of remorse and self-loathing

in his voice. He'd done some pretty shitty things to me in the past, things I could easily hold against him even though I felt a little too much kinship with him to condemn him. But this I was pretty sure wasn't his fault.

"Why did you come back?"

"I heard the gunshots. I meant to come back and help you, maybe save whoever the killer was after."

"And ended up killing the victim instead." Despite all of my empathy for him, there was still a hint of accusation in my voice. I knew he hadn't exactly been present when he killed the guy, but still . . .

"He would have been dead in a few minutes anyway," Jamaal said.

"You don't know that. Modern medicine can do miraculous things."

"I *do* know that," he said more firmly. "Believe me, Nikki, I know death when I see it. Comes with the territory. The poor bastard wouldn't have lived long enough for modern medicine to reach him. Look what happened to you."

"So that makes it all right for you to kill him?" I asked with a definite edge in my voice. He'd sounded pretty damned guilty about having abandoned me, but it didn't seem like he felt bad about having killed a guy. Maybe I was being judgmental, but it seemed to me he should feel at least a little sorry.

"I wasn't in control. I couldn't have stopped myself if I tried."

"But you didn't try, did you?"

"No." He met my eyes, and there was both a challenge and a plea in his gaze. I noticed irrelevantly that he had absurdly long, thick lashes. "When it gets to a certain point, trying to stop it just makes things worse. I was already well past that point."

I felt tempted to poke at him some more but managed to shut myself up. He wasn't showing a lot of overt remorse, but he wasn't sitting here at two in the morning drinking whiskey and staring at a nature show because of his callous indifference to what he'd done. I remembered Anderson telling me that he was "struggling," and I had to admit, he didn't look like himself. Despite the alcohol, there was a tightness to his jaw and an almost haunted look in his eyes. I very much doubted he liked the feeling of being out of control, and I couldn't blame him.

I wondered what he'd been like before he'd become *Liberi* and realized with a bit of a jolt that I knew next to nothing about him, despite having lived in the same house with him for a few weeks. I didn't know how he'd become *Liberi*—he had to have killed someone to do it, and I had no idea who or whether he'd known what he was doing. I didn't even know how old he was. Anderson had made a comment once about how Jamaal had only had "a couple of decades" to learn to control his death magic, but I had to wonder how good a sense of time Anderson had, seeing as he'd been around for thousands of years.

"So that's my sob story," Jamaal said into a silence that was becoming uncomfortable. He seemed to have muted the TV without me even noticing. "Now, why don't you tell me why you're down here talking to me instead of in your room fast asleep?"

"Let me get this straight. You're actually initiating conversation with me? Has hell frozen over?" Just because he didn't seem to hate my guts anymore didn't mean we were friends, and Jamaal was far from the talkative type. There was something of a dreamlike feeling to this whole conversation, and if I didn't feel so physically and emotionally drained, I might have thought I really was up in my bed fast asleep. But there was nothing dreamlike about my exhaustion.

Jamaal ignored my half-assed teasing. "Remember, I know exactly how shitty you feel right now. You should be sleeping it off, so I figure you're down here because something's wrong."

"Why do you care?" I asked, sounding pretty peevish even to my own ears. Getting bitten by jackals, killed, and brought back to life didn't put me in the perkiest of moods.

Jamaal once would have met my flare of temper with one of his own. I'm sure I would have deserved it if he'd done the same now, but he didn't.

"Because you're likely the only one who can lead us to this guy so we can stop him. Unless we spooked him last Friday, which I doubt, he'll be up to his old tricks again in about forty-eight hours. And if you push yourself too hard and are falling over with fatigue, you're not going to do anyone any good."

His words stung a little with their cold logic. It didn't make a whole lot of sense, but I wished Jamaal cared about *me,* not about my special abilities. I guess it was a hint of neediness, left over from my years of foster care. I was luckier than the average foster kid, having found a permanent home at the age of eleven, but the warmth and love I'd found with the Glasses couldn't completely undo the damage from the foster-care merry-go-round.

I grimaced and rubbed my eyes, tired down to the marrow of my bones. Yeah, coming downstairs had been a stupid decision. I could feel how my body was fighting me, telling me to stop being a moron and get some sleep. But I knew that the moment I closed my eyes, my mind would take me back to the darkness, and I wasn't brave enough to face it.

When I stopped rubbing my eyes, I was embarrassed to find that my fingertips were wet. God, I was such a wuss.

"You'll fall asleep faster than you think," Jamaal said, his voice conspicuously gentle, something I wouldn't have thought him capable of.

I blinked a couple of times, still trying to fight off tears. "Huh?"

"You're down here drinking coffee because you're afraid to close your eyes, right?" I didn't want to admit the truth, but Jamaal wasn't waiting for my confirmation, anyway. "That's how I felt the first time. But your body will take over, and you'll fall asleep before you can make yourself too miserable."

I hoped he was telling the truth, rather than a comforting lie. "I guess I'll have to find out whether it works the same for me. It's not like I can stay awake forever."

I was not looking forward to dragging myself back

upstairs and was halfway tempted to simply curl up on the sofa. Instead, I put down my barely touched spiked coffee and used the arm of the sofa to help lever myself up to my feet.

I got so light-headed I almost fell back down, and I realized I might end up sleeping on the couch after all. I honestly didn't think I could make it to the third floor without collapsing. But Jamaal shocked the hell out of me by rising to his feet and sweeping me off mine.

I gave an undignified bleat as my feet left the floor. "What are you doing?" I gasped.

He carried me like I weighed about twenty pounds. "What does it look like I'm doing?"

I didn't know what to do with my right arm, which was positioned awkwardly between our bodies. I should have put it around Jamaal's neck, but that felt way too intimate.

"You don't need to carry me," I said weakly as he made his way to the grand staircase in the foyer.

Jamaal ignored my words, which he had to know were more wishful thinking than fact. I'd have been lucky to make it to the base of the stairs on my own, much less to actually climb them.

Tentatively, I slipped my arm around his neck, because it just felt too awkward not to, like I was afraid to touch him or something. The beads at the ends of his braids tickled my arm, and I was hyper-aware of the warmth of his body, the beat of his heart. He'd hated my guts for most of the time he'd known me, and any sane woman would have locked her libido in a safe and then buried the safe, but I couldn't help the highly inappropriate little flutter in my belly.

It didn't matter that he sometimes bore a disturbing resemblance to a raving lunatic; Jamaal was hot, hot, hot. And there was something about him that called to me, that always had, even when he'd been half-mad with hatred. Something that told me that he and I were a lot alike, that we'd both gotten a raw deal in life, that we both felt terribly alone, and that we lashed out at those around us because that felt safer than letting someone get close.

In short, we were both totally screwed up.

There was no particular tenderness in the way Jamaal carried me. He was just helping me because it was the practical thing to do. I'd certainly seen no sign that he'd ever noticed me as a woman. But that didn't stop my pulse from tripping or my skin from tingling.

Steph had once told me she thought my tendency to fall for inappropriate or unavailable men had something to do with my quite understandable fear of abandonment. As long as I fell for men I knew from the beginning could never work out, I never had to risk having someone walk out on me unexpectedly. She made this diagnosis on the basis of having been a psych major in college, but though I always told her she was seeing things that didn't exist, I had the secret suspicion that she was right. And if I ended up pining for Jamaal, it would just be more of the same.

He carried me all the way to my bedroom in silence, not setting me down until we'd reached the bed. I felt almost unbearably awkward, having no idea what to say to him at a moment like this.

I finally settled for a mumbled thanks as I tucked my legs under the covers and lay down with a sigh of relief. Instead of leaving, Jamaal sat on the edge of my bed.

"Go ahead and close your eyes," he said, looking at his clasped hands, rather than at me.

I wondered what was going on, why he hadn't left yet, but my eyelids had grown heavy, and asking questions seemed like too much effort. Despite a shiver of dread, my eyes slid closed.

The moment my eyes closed, the darkness descended on me, pressing on my chest, smothering me, making my pulse race.

"Just focus on the sound of my voice," Jamaal said, so softly I had to strain to hear him.

And then he started to sing just as softly.

His voice was a rich, low baritone, so warm I wanted to wrap myself up in it. I didn't recognize the language he was singing in or the melody, but if I'd had to guess, I'd have said the song was a lullaby of some sort. It had a lilting, soothing quality that wrapped me in a cocoon of warmth and somnolence.

There was no room in my head for anything but the sweet sound of Jamaal's voice, no room for thoughts of death and darkness. I focused on that sound, losing myself to it, letting my muscles relax one by one.

When sleep pressed around the edges of my consciousness, I wanted to hold it off just a little while, wanted to preserve this moment when I felt so serene and peaceful. But my exhausted body had other ideas, and I faded away before the song was finished.

It echoed in my dreams that night, keeping the nightmares at bay.

ELEVEN

When I next awakened, the sun was high in the sky, the light pouring through my windows telling me I'd slept until almost noon. I yawned and stretched, then pushed myself into a sitting position and waited to see if the effort made me dizzy.

When a minute passed without any hint that I might be about to collapse, I slid out of bed and cautiously stood up. My head felt fine, and there was no telltale quivering in my knees.

I showered and dressed and even blow-dried my hair, and still I felt pretty much normal. Maybe a little weak but not enough to interfere with my day. Sleep had obviously done me a world of good.

I smiled when I remembered the sound of Jamaal's voice singing me to sleep, feeling somewhat bemused by the gesture. Clearly, there were sides of him other than the bitter, angry, dangerous man I thought I knew. Sides I had no business being intrigued by, I warned myself.

Whatever redeeming qualities he had, Jamaal was bad news.

My mood faltered as I made my way down the stairs toward the kitchen in search of a late breakfast. Sleeping till almost noon might have done wonders for my physical woes, but it meant there were now only about thirty-six hours before the killer was likely to strike again. I had to tell Anderson what I'd found out about the victims and their resemblance to Konstantin and then hope that Anderson could pry the killer's identity from his archenemy's lips. And that learning the killer's identity would help us find him. Oh, yeah, and that we could actually *stop* him if we *did* find him.

"One step at a time," I muttered to myself, picking up my pace as the sense of urgency increased. I'd have skipped breakfast entirely, except I was hungry enough to eat a whole elephant, and I feared if I ignored my body's needs, I'd end up weak and sick and useless again.

The scent of what I guessed was pizza wafted on the air as I neared the kitchen, and I figured that meant some of Anderson's *Liberi* were having lunch. However, when I stepped into the kitchen, there was only one *Liberi* in sight: Emma.

She sat at the kitchen table, a slice of pepperoni pizza drooping in her hand, her eyes glazed and vacant. I expected her to blink and come to herself the moment I came into view, but she didn't. I took a couple of tentative steps closer, but she still didn't blink or move.

"Emma?" I queried, just in case she was lost in

thought and hadn't noticed me, but she didn't react. She might be present in body, but her mind was taking a break, wandering off to wherever it went when she entered this fugue state. It had been happening less and less often as she continued to recover from her ordeal as Konstantin's prisoner, but obviously, she still had a ways to go.

Most of the time, I couldn't stand her. She was jealous and possessive, bossy as hell, and sulky when she didn't get her way. But when I saw her like this, I still felt a twinge of pity. No matter how much of a bitch she was and no matter how miserable she made Anderson, she didn't deserve what had happened to her.

Not that I thought for a moment she'd appreciate my compassion.

The pizza box was still laid out on the kitchen counter, so I helped myself to a slice. It was ice-cold, fresh from the fridge, and if Emma hadn't been sitting there, I'd probably have nuked it. However, I preferred to be gone when she snapped out of it, so I merely grabbed a paper towel to serve as a napkin and munched on the cold pizza—breakfast of champions!—as I made a quick getaway.

It showed how little I wanted to face Emma that I left the kitchen without even getting any coffee.

Still stuffing my face, I headed back upstairs, hoping Anderson would be in his study. I got lucky for once and found him right where I wanted him. Unfortunately, the sight of his usually pristine workspace brought me to a jerking halt.

Papers and books lay strewn on the floor, along with a smattering of pens, a stapler, and enough paper clips to supply a high school or two. One of his guest chairs was lying on its side, and broken glass from an overturned lamp peppered the carpet.

Anderson sat at his desk, his head bowed as his fingers pinched the bridge of his nose. Everything except his computer had been swept off the desk, but based on how scattered it all was—and on the damage to the chair and the lamp—I didn't think it was Anderson who'd done the sweeping.

Putting this scene together with Emma sitting vacantly in the kitchen, I figured the two of them had just had one of their epic battles. Ordinarily, I'd have had the good sense to retreat, but the urgency was still riding me. I rolled the stale pizza crust in the paper towel and cleared my throat.

Anderson slowly raised his head. I tried not to gasp when I saw the angry red furrows that crossed his cheek, but I was too shocked to mask my reaction entirely. He frowned and looked around the room as if noticing the damage for the first time.

"This isn't a good time, Nikki," he said, sounding as exhausted as I'd felt the day before.

"Yeah, I can see that. But I'm afraid this can't wait."

He muttered something I presumed was a curse under his breath, then shoved himself to his feet, practically sending his desk chair rolling into the wall. With swift, jerky movements, he circled his desk and picked up the fallen guest chair, setting it upright with enough of a bang he was lucky it didn't break. Then he stalked back behind his desk and sat down, clasping his hands in front of him and spearing me with a look that made me want to tuck my tail between my legs and run.

"What is it?" he snapped impatiently when I hesitated.

I didn't like finding myself caught in the crossfire of a domestic dispute, and the awkwardness had made me hesitant at first. However, I can only be tactful so long when someone's being an asshole.

"If whatever you and Emma are fighting about is more important than catching the killer, then tell me to go away. Otherwise, I'd appreciate a little more common courtesy and a little less misplaced hostility."

He glared at me a moment longer; then the tension suddenly drained out of his shoulders, and he laughed weakly. "I think I liked it better when you were intimidated by me."

I snorted as I pulled back the chair and sat down. "Yeah, I'll bet." If he thought my snappish response meant he no longer intimidated me, then I was happy to nurture the illusion.

"I apologize for my manners. It's been a lousy morning."

I swept the room with a quick look. "No kidding?"

He frowned at my attempt at humor. "Keep the commentary to yourself."

I pondered the possibility of telling him that Emma was sitting in the kitchen having an out-of-body experience but rejected the idea because it smacked of getting in the middle again. But Anderson interpreted my silence as a different kind of commentary altogether.

"Don't judge her," he said as he reached up to rub the healing scratches on his cheek. "She's having a really hard time readjusting to normal life, and I'm afraid I'm not making it any easier for her. Every time she does something out of character, I get furious at what those Olympian bastards did to her. Then she thinks I'm angry with *her,* and . . . she doesn't take it well. None of this is her fault, and I wish I knew how to help her."

Maybe I was reading into the situation, but it seemed to me Anderson was trying to convince *himself* more than me. Emma had suffered atrociously, but I didn't think her suffering justified all of her behavior. No matter *what* she'd been through, surely she bore some responsibility for her actions. But Anderson was never going to see it that way, and he was perfectly happy to make excuses for her.

"Now, what did you need? You said it was important."

I told him about the similarities among our killer's victims and watched the shift in his face as the harried husband became the leader of a band of *Liberi* once more.

"That son of a bitch," Anderson said when I was done, shaking his head in disgust. Then he sighed. "Well, we suspected Phoebe wasn't telling us everything, so I guess I shouldn't be surprised."

"Do you think Konstantin will tell us the whole truth now that we've partially figured it out?"

Anderson laughed. "You don't know him very well."

"And I don't want to. But if he can tell us who the killer is . . ."

"He won't. It's just not his way."

"But—"

"Phoebe, on the other hand, I might be able to talk into being practical."

My mouth snapped closed on the protest I'd been about to raise. Of our two Olympian visitors, I would have thought Cyrus was the more likely to give us straight answers. "Not Cyrus?"

Anderson shook his head. "There's a reason Alexis was Konstantin's right-hand man instead of Cyrus. I don't know how many of his own children Konstantin has killed over the years, but it's a lot. He can't ever bring himself to trust them, no matter how loyal they are. He wouldn't share any sensitive secrets with Cyrus."

I probably shouldn't have been surprised that a man who had no qualms about slaughtering whole families would be willing to kill his own kids. It would forever be beyond my comprehension how someone could be so cold-blooded.

"And you really think *Phoebe* knows something?"

"She's in love with him. Has been for decades, God only knows why. He treats her like garbage. But if anyone knows what he's hiding, it'll be her. And since I presume he's sicced us on the killer because he knows he's in danger, Phoebe might decide she has to confide in us for his own good."

There was more uncertainty in this scenario than I felt comfortable with, especially when the clock was ticking so loudly in my mind.

"I'm going to invite her back to the house for a debriefing this afternoon," Anderson said. "I'll want you there, and I'll want Blake."

I raised an eyebrow. "Me I understand, but why Blake?"

Anderson's smile was cold enough to make me shiver. "Because Phoebe won't set foot in this house without her goon, and I need someone who can keep the goon occupied from a distance if things get antagonistic."

My nose crinkled with distaste as I figured out what Anderson meant. "You're going to ask Blake to seduce the goon?" I knew that Blake didn't have any qualms about using his power against men, despite his clear preference for women, nor was he hesitant to use sex as a weapon, but still . . .

"When you're fighting Olympians, sometimes you have to get dirty."

"We're supposed to be the good guys, remember?" I said with more than a hint of disgust in my voice. I'd probably have been okay with just conking the goon on the head but not with subjecting him to what amounted to rape, even if it never went that far.

For a moment, I thought Anderson was going to bite my head off for being a wuss. There was certainly a dangerous spark in his eye. But the spark faded quickly enough, and he reached up to scrub a hand through his already unkempt hair.

"It'll be a last resort," he promised me. "Only if we can't get Phoebe to talk without . . . shaking her up. In which case, we have to make sure the goon doesn't kill anyone."

Anderson may have reined in his anger, but my own blood pressure was starting to rise. "You mean only if you decide she needs to be tortured?" None of this was what I had in mind when I pictured the "good guys."

"If you don't like it, then suggest something better. I don't know how else to get the information we need, unless I can guilt her into talking for Konstantin's own good, which I'd say is about a fifty-fifty shot. So, what would you have me do instead?"

Of course, he had me on that one. I didn't know whether anything Phoebe told us could possibly lead us to the killer before he struck again, but I was pretty damn sure we weren't going to find him if we didn't get more info. I'd been able to predict which cemetery he'd show up at last time, but if he realized that running into another *Liberi* out for a casual stroll in the cemetery at night was more than a freaky coincidence, he might change his pattern.

No matter how hard I looked, I couldn't find a moral high ground. If we weren't willing to press Phoebe for details, then we were most likely condemning some other poor bastard to die a horrible death, to put his family through untold misery. I could only imagine what it felt like to have a loved one not only killed but torn to shreds and partially eaten, as the previous victims had been.

"Time's a-wasting, Nikki," Anderson said. "Let's hear your suggestion."

But I couldn't come up with one. "I hate this," I said instead, feeling sick to my stomach.

"Let's not sweat it too much yet. It's possible Phoebe will cooperate, and then none of this will matter."

But it *would* matter, whether it came to pass or not. Because I knew that given the choice, I was willing to stand by and let the evil happen, and that revelation scared the ever-living crap out of me. I *liked* being a bleeding heart. It proved that my difficult childhood hadn't destroyed my ability to empathize with others and that empathy made me feel less isolated. My willingness to go along with Anderson's plan suggested that I might be starting down the road to losing that empathy, and I didn't like what that said about me or what it portended for the future.

I offered to help Anderson clean up the mess in his office, but he declined, which was probably just as well. My feelings were a bit too jumbled to survive prolonged contact with him, at least for the moment.

I really wanted a cup of coffee but wasn't willing to risk running into Emma, so I went back to my room instead. I didn't have any plans for what to do with the rest of my day as I waited for word from Anderson that Phoebe was on her way, but when I stepped into my sitting room, I found myself glancing over toward the coffee table, where the manila folder containing my adoption records had been sitting unopened since Steph had brought it to me.

My intention wasn't to start delving into my past. But I did a double take when I saw that the folder was lying open on the table. I knew for a fact that *I* hadn't opened it. Steph had probably done it when I was ill, hoping to draw me to it.

Mouth dry, I approached the table cautiously, as if I thought the folder were about to fly up and bite me.

There was a substantial stack of papers in the file, and the one on top appeared to be a chronological list of all of the families I'd fostered with. I told myself to shut the file and have done with it, but instead, I found myself sitting down and picking up the list. There were two more sheets stapled to the first, and I was amazed to see how many different homes I'd had in the seven years before the Glasses had taken me in. I'd never bothered to count before.

Two and a quarter pages of names and addresses. Some of the families I'd stayed with so briefly that I didn't even remember the names, couldn't conjure up a picture of my foster parents' faces. In the beginning, I'd gotten my hopes up each time I was moved that *this* would be my permanent home, that I would find the stability and love I so desperately craved. Then the disappointments mounted up, and all hints of optimism faded.

I'd brought it on myself, of course. After my mother's abandonment, I'd become a total hellion, bound and determined to make everyone else as miserable as I was. I'd lied, I'd cheated at school, I'd shoplifted—if it got me into trouble, I did it. And then, each time a family gave up on me, I felt validated in my conviction that no one loved me, that every home was temporary, that security and stability were myths.

Maybe I *should* start researching my past, if only to find all of the foster parents I'd tormented and apologize for the hell I'd put them through. Sure, there were some apathetic losers in the bunch, ones who returned me like defective merchandise and didn't give a shit about anything but their own inconvenience, but I was sure I'd driven some of my foster mothers into tears of despair. Despair they didn't deserve.

How the Glasses had seen past all that I had no idea. If I'd been in their shoes, I'd have sent me away in a heartbeat. But they were better people than I, and I loved them so much for what they'd done for me that my throat ached with it.

My body had gone on automatic pilot the moment I'd set eyes on the folder, and I hadn't even bothered to close my door. When someone knocked softly on it, I jumped and hastily slammed the folder closed, as if I'd been looking at porn or something. When I looked up to see Jamaal standing in my doorway, I felt something akin to panic stir in my chest. I couldn't deal with him right now, not when seeing the history of my childhood had scraped my nerves raw.

He came in without waiting for an invitation, closing the door behind him. I meant to tell him to go away and leave me alone, but I couldn't seem to force myself to talk.

Jamaal didn't say anything as he dropped into the love seat. At least he was leaving the sofa to me, giving me some space. But something about the way he looked at me was too knowing.

"You looked at this, didn't you?" I asked as I dropped the folder back onto the coffee table, wishing I'd never laid eyes on the damn thing.

He'd changed the beads at the ends of his braids, I noticed. They'd been white last night, but today they were all in shades of brown and amber. A bright white T-shirt—so new it still had fold lines on it—made his skin look darker than usual. There was an artful tear across one knee of his jeans, and he wore unlaced combat boots.

"It was lying here open," he said, no hint of apology in his voice. "I was curious."

"It was none of your business!" I said between gritted teeth, surprising myself as much as Jamaal.

He tilted his head like a curious dog. "I really didn't mean anything by it. I thought it might be your file on the case when I first saw it."

I sucked in a deep breath and told myself to get a grip. There was no reason to be ashamed of my background, and there was certainly no reason for me to snarl at Jamaal. Not after he'd been so nice to me last night.

"What are you doing here?" I asked, too stubborn to apologize.

"Checking on you."

"As you can see, I'm fine. And why do you need to check on me, anyway? You hate my guts."

God, could I sound any more like a whiny child? But knowing he'd seen the file had catapulted me straight into ultradefensive mode, and I wished he'd just go away.

"I do?" he asked with another of those head tilts.

It was true he hadn't been acting like he hated me anymore. His feelings for me had certainly run to hatred when I'd first come to the mansion, but the more he came to accept that I wasn't an Olympian spy—and the more control he gained over himself—the milder his opinion had seemed. That didn't mean he *liked* me, though. He'd certainly never been anything remotely like friendly toward me before.

"Just leave me alone, okay? I'm not feeling real chatty right now."

He settled deeper into the love seat, studying me. I refused to let myself squirm under his gaze.

"I spent almost fifteen years trying to track down my parents," he said, and something inside me shifted.

The knot that had been steadily tightening in my stomach relaxed. Not all the way but enough that I could take a full breath, that I could let go of some of the almost unbearable tension.

Jamaal wasn't looking at me anymore. He was tugging at a loose string at the torn knee of his jeans, studying it with the intensity of a surgeon at work, which told me just how uncomfortable his own admission had made him.

I spoke carefully, afraid I'd spook him. "Did you find them?"

He shook his head, still fidgeting with the string. "I found my father's grave, but I never did find my mother."

A lump formed in my throat. His voice was perfectly calm and level, but I heard the pain in it nonetheless. I'd always felt a certain amount of kinship with Jamaal, had never been able to condemn him for the things he'd done. I'd sometimes worried that I was seeing similarities that didn't exist, that I was making excuses for him based on my own experiences, when his own actually bore no resemblance to mine. But now I wondered if some hidden part of me had known all along that Jamaal and I had a lot in common.

"I'm sorry," I said, though the words were lame and useless.

One corner of his mouth tipped up in a bitter smile. "I'm not. If I'd found them, I probably would have killed them, and I'd have regretted it eventually . . ." he said. "Guess that sounds terrible. But it took me years to get the death magic even slightly under control. When I was searching for my parents, I didn't know how to fight it yet, and it didn't take much to set me off."

I tried my best not to be judgmental. I had no idea what Jamaal had been through, had no idea what it felt like to have this malevolent force residing within me, eating at my self-control. Still, as angry as I was at my mother for abandoning me, I couldn't imagine *killing* her if I ever found her.

"And you think your parents would have set you off?" I asked, because the question seemed relatively neutral.

"My father, almost certainly. My mother . . ." He thought about that a moment, then let out a grunt of disgust. "She'd have started defending my father, and that might well have pissed me off more than I could handle. I shouldn't have started looking for them in the first place."

Obviously, he hadn't been abandoned as a small child. He knew his parents—enough to despise them.

I'd been lost in my own funk when Jamaal had appeared in my doorway, but curiosity was quickly getting the better of me, kicking my family woes to the background as I tried to figure out how to keep Jamaal talking. Talking wasn't generally one of his strong suits.

"How did you get separated from them?" I asked, hoping the question wasn't too direct.

Jamaal's eyes met mine and locked on. "I'll tell you, if you tell me what happened to you."

The quid pro quo surprised me a bit. He made it sound like I was secretive about my past, which I wasn't. Sure, I'd gotten a little touchy about him looking at the file, but that was because I didn't like having my privacy invaded. And because looking at the file myself had put me on edge.

Of course, while I might not make a big secret of my past, I didn't exactly volunteer information about it, either. Everyone in this house knew I was adopted, but that was about it.

Maybe I made a big secret of it after all and had just never noticed. I wasn't always a pillar of self-awareness.

"My mother abandoned me in a church when I was four," I said. "I don't know who my father was or why he wasn't in our lives. And my mom made damned sure no one would be able to identify me or tie me to her when she dumped me." It was about as bare-bones a version of the story as I could tell, but as the words left my mouth, I realized that I had never told even that much before.

My usual response to questions about my childhood? I'd say I was adopted and then change the subject. So this was progress for me.

I thought Jamaal might press for details, but he settled for giving me a knowing look. Then he fulfilled his part of the bargain, doing a much more thorough job of it.

"My mother was a slave," he said, and I stared at him in shock. Obviously, he'd been dealing with his death magic for longer than the "couple of decades" Anderson had said. "My father was a white man. Her *owner*." He bared his teeth at the word, and I couldn't blame him.

"My father was married to a woman named Matilda, and she couldn't have children. When I was born, Matilda had no idea I was her husband's son, and I became the child she'd always wanted but could never have. She and my father both doted on me, spoiled me way more than my mother could. They treated me like a member of the family, not a slave. I honestly didn't understand that I *was* a slave. I loved them, and I thought they loved me.

"Then, when I was eight, Matilda found out her husband was my father. I think he confessed in a moment of guilt. She totally lost it. Couldn't stand the sight of me or my mother anymore. She told my father he had to choose between us and her. And he chose her.

"My father sold my mother and me, and our lives went straight to hell. Neither one of us realized how good we'd had it at my father's house. We'd been blissfully ignorant of what life was like for the average slave.

"I was sold again when I was ten, separated from my mother. I never saw her again. And I have no idea what happened to her. But I bet she died still making excuses for my father, for what he did to us. She never once blamed him for giving in to Matilda's demands. And the stupid bitch felt *sorry* for Matilda!"

There was anger on Jamaal's face—fury, even. But even more prominent was the deep, abiding hurt. He'd been betrayed by everyone he loved. Even his mother's sympathy for Matilda was a betrayal, since it was Matilda who'd caused them to be sent away.

I had no idea what to say. Jamaal's story made my own hellish childhood seem practically ideal. Was it any surprise that he and anger were such great friends? He'd probably have been a powder keg even without the addition of the death magic.

There was a long, awkward silence as I floundered for something to say. Maybe if it had been someone other than Jamaal sitting there, I might even have been able to find something. But let's face it, he was capable of scrambling my wits at the best of times, and this wasn't the best of times. Still, I had to say *something,* couldn't just sit there like a moron.

"I can't even imagine . . ." I started, but couldn't figure out where to go from there.

What was the matter with me? I wasn't the type to get all tongue-tied like this.

But you're also not the type to have personal conversations, I reminded myself. Steph had told me once that I tended to avoid intimacy, and I didn't think she was off base.

I cleared my throat. "I can't for the life of me think of anything to say," I told him, deciding to settle for complete honesty. "Why did you decide to tell me this?"

His shoulders rose in a hint of a shrug. "I was wrong about you. I know you're not an Olympian, and I know you didn't kill Emmitt on purpose. I treated you like shit, and then I left you alone to face a madman with a pack of rabid jackals. I owe you more than a little. If you need any help tracking down your birth mother . . ."

The offer made my eyes sting even as my emotional barriers flung themselves into place. "You don't have to do penance."

"Maybe I'm just using your search as a way to relive my own, preferably with a different outcome."

"I haven't even decided for sure whether I want to go looking or not."

Jamaal pushed himself to his feet, and I suspected he was giving me a condescending look, though I didn't have the courage to check.

"Well, when you decide to go looking, let me know."

He said that like he was sure he knew which decision I was going to make. I didn't like him making assumptions and might have told him so, except he was already on his way to the door.

"By the way," he said before he left, "you're the only one I've told. Everyone else thinks I'm only about fifty. I don't want sympathy or pity, and Anderson won't be happy if he finds out how much I haven't told him, so I hope you'll keep a lid on it."

I was too choked up—and too confused by everything I was feeling—to do more than nod.

TWELVE

Phoebe waited until it was almost dark before she finally hauled her ass over to the mansion to talk to Anderson. He asked Blake and me to wait in his study, because he'd suggested to Phoebe on the phone that he would be meeting with her alone. I guess the rest of us hadn't made a very favorable impression the last time she'd dropped by.

Blake and I had both sat in chairs against the wall on the near side of the room, where the open door would block Phoebe's view until she was fully inside. The choice was not coincidental. Her eyes widened in surprise when she saw us, but she wasn't the only one with a surprise in store for her.

Phoebe's goon—whom no one had ever bothered to introduce—we had expected, but Blake was obviously as surprised as I was when Cyrus followed the goon in.

Blake raised his eyebrows. "Who invited *you*?"

The words were confrontational, but his tone didn't quite match.

Cyrus grinned. "I invited myself," he said as Anderson closed the study door behind him. Cyrus's grin faded. "Though perhaps that was a miscalculation."

Phoebe turned to Anderson with a narrow-eyed stare that was probably meant to be intimidating. It's hard for petite blondes to be intimidating.

"What are *they* doing here?" Phoebe asked with a curl of her lip. "You told me—"

"I know what I told you," Anderson interrupted. "But we really need to sit down and have a serious conversation. One that involves you telling the truth."

Phoebe bristled, and it looked for all the world like she was genuinely offended. "I don't know what you're talking about. And if you haven't invited me here to share intel, then this conversation is over."

"Oh, we'll share intel. Nikki, will you do the honors?" he asked without taking his eyes off of Phoebe. I hoped Blake was ready to step in at a moment's notice, because the tension level in the room had risen to dangerous levels in no time flat. Phoebe was steaming, the goon looked ready to leap into action, and Cyrus looked tense and wary. Interestingly, his attention was mostly focused on Blake, and I had a feeling Cyrus knew exactly why Blake was in the room.

I grabbed the photos I'd printed of the three victims who'd been identified, then held them up one at a time so that Phoebe could see them. I could tell she didn't want to give up her staring match with Anderson, but curiosity got the better of her. She tried to hide her reaction, but the sudden tension in her shoulders told me that she grasped immediately the significance of the photos. And the sudden, sharp look Cyrus gave her suggested that Anderson had been right, and Cyrus didn't know whatever it was his father was hiding.

"These are three of the four victims of 'wild dog attacks,'" I said, sure I had their full attention. "You might notice there are certain similarities in their appearance."

"As in, they all look kind of like Konstantin," Anderson finished for me with more than a touch of steel in his voice.

Phoebe blinked a couple of times, and I could almost see the thoughts flitting through her head. Should she pretend ignorance? Stonewall? Make up a total fabrication that would throw us off the trail?

Apparently, she liked option D best: retreat.

"We're done here," she said, striding toward the door, although Anderson stood in her way.

Anderson didn't move. Phoebe's goon smiled, like he was really looking forward to a little action. He reached into his jacket, where, no doubt, he had a shoulder holster.

"Don't!" Cyrus warned, reaching out to grab the goon's arm, but he was too late.

Blake did his thing, and suddenly both men froze, their eyes locking on each other as their pupils went dark and unfocused. Phoebe turned to bark an order at them, but then she saw the looks on their faces and quickly whirled on Blake.

"Stop that!" she commanded, but there was a hint of fear in her voice that stole all the power from her command.

Blake grinned like he was having a great time. "Make me."

"Real mature," I couldn't help grumbling under my breath. So far, Blake was being relatively restrained. The lust was plain to see, but it wasn't so strong that Cyrus and the goon couldn't resist it. Yet. But resisting it took all of their concentration, making it impossible for them to make any hostile moves.

Phoebe turned back to Anderson, her eyes flashing with fury, which I suspected was a cover for more fear. I had yet to meet anyone who wasn't freaked out by Blake's power, and she was obviously no exception.

"Call him off!"

Anderson just laughed at her as he stepped around her and relieved her goon of his gun.

I could tell Phoebe was thinking of making a run for the door while Anderson was busy, so I moved over to block her way. It looked like she was considering going through me, but she thought better of it and settled for growling. "Get out of my way."

"You came to us for help because you knew Konstantin was in trouble," Anderson said to Phoebe's back. "Helping Konstantin isn't high on my list of priorities, but presumably, it is on yours. I'm willing to do everything in my power to stop this killer, *despite* the fact that it will help Konstantin. But to do that, I need to know the truth. Even if Konstantin doesn't want you to tell me, you know it's in his best interests."

For a moment, there was a hint of uncertainty on Phoebe's face, and I thought Anderson might have found the perfect persuasion. Then the steel returned to her eyes.

Phoebe turned back toward Anderson, and there was not a drop of give in her voice. "I've told you everything I know, and I don't appreciate the strong-arm tactics."

Anderson laughed. "Lady, I haven't even *begun* the strong-arm tactics yet." The look on his face hardened. "I've got three questions for you," he said, counting them off on his fingers. "One: who is the killer? Two: what does he have against Konstantin? And three: why did Konstantin *really* ask for our help?"

Phoebe sneered at him. "First: I don't know. Second: I don't know. And third: I already told you."

Anderson clucked his tongue. "Are you sure that's your best answer? Because things could get ugly here if you don't start telling the truth."

"Surely I must be mistaken," Phoebe said, drawing herself up to her full height. "You couldn't possibly be threatening me."

He laughed again. "Really? Because I'm pretty sure that's what I'm doing." The humor bled from his face, replaced by something cold and implacable. "You lied to me. Gave me incomplete information so that I'd throw my people into danger without knowing the risks. That pisses me off."

"Konstantin—"

"Can come talk to me in person if my tactics bother him. Now, start talking, whether to save Konstantin's ass or your own, I don't care which."

Phoebe's face had paled, and though she was trying to put on a brave front, she wasn't doing a very convincing job of it. "You wouldn't dare," she said, but it sounded more like a question than a statement.

Anderson bared his teeth in a savage grin. "Which would be more fun, do you think? Having a three-way with Cyrus and your talking ape?" We all looked at the goon, who was sweating with the effort of resisting Blake's magic. Cyrus was sweating, too, and he managed to look furious and seriously horny at the same time. On some silent command from Blake, their attention turned from each other to Phoebe. "Or talking to the hand?"

Anderson held his palm up for display, and a strangled gasp of dismay left Phoebe's throat. I guess she'd seen Anderson's Hand of Doom in action before. I couldn't blame her for wanting no part of it.

"Or you could just tell the truth," Anderson continued with a careless shrug, lowering his hand. "Your choice."

To say Phoebe didn't like it was an understatement. Angry color rose to her pale cheeks, and she practically vibrated with fury. But she knew she'd been beat.

"You'll pay for this someday," she growled from between clenched teeth.

"Skip the whole saving-face thing, and just answer

my questions. Who the hell is this *Liberi* you've set us on?"

Phoebe's shoulders slumped in defeat. "His name is Justin Kerner. He's a descendant of Anubis, just like I told you."

Anderson gave a little snort. "That was the one part of your story I believed. What does this Justin Kerner have against our friend Konstantin?"

Phoebe hesitated, reluctant to part with the truth, but all Anderson had to do was wiggle the fingers of his right hand to get her talking again.

"There's a . . . bad seed. We believe it was handed down from the goddess Lyssa to one of her daughters."

Anderson glanced over his shoulder at me. "The goddess of madness," he explained, correctly guessing that the name was unfamiliar to me. "She's often associated with rabies." He turned back to Phoebe, who'd stalled out again.

"We think Lyssa infected the seed with her madness when she gave it to her daughter. Rumor has it that anyone who's possessed that seed has eventually gone mad."

"And what does any of this have to do with Konstantin?"

Phoebe swallowed hard and avoided all of our gazes. "We captured a *Liberi* who seemed to be insane. We didn't know if it had something to do with Lyssa's seed or if he was just a madman in his own right. We wanted to harvest the seed if it was any good, but we didn't want to risk one of our own people in case it turned out the rumors were true."

Anderson shook his head in disgust. "So you captured a non-Greek Descendant and forced him to kill your madman and take on the seed."

Phoebe nodded. "We figured we'd see how Kerner reacted to the seed. If he stayed sane, then we'd harvest the seed for one of our own. If he didn't . . ."

"Finish the story, Phoebe. What was your plan for if he went crazy, as he obviously did?"

"If Lyssa's seed showed evidence of being infected, then we needed it neutralized. We were afraid an insane *Liberi* would be an exposure risk. Obviously, we couldn't destroy the seed. So we figured the only way to neutralize it was to keep it contained."

"Oh, spit it out, already!" Blake snapped. "You buried him, didn't you?"

Blake's moment of impatience was almost enough to get us all in trouble, because Cyrus and the goon blinked and snapped out of the daze he'd had them in. The goon tried reaching behind him, where he probably had another weapon concealed, and Cyrus turned to glare at Blake, but that was all they had time to do before Blake put them under again. Blake gave Cyrus a shrug and a half smile that looked almost apologetic.

Anderson relieved the goon of a second gun, then speared Phoebe with a cold glare. "Is that what you did, Phoebe? You buried the man alive, knowing he'd be trapped in there, unable to die, forever?"

It's what Konstantin had said he'd done to Emma, although he'd actually chained her in the bottom of a pond instead. I shuddered and tried very, very hard not to think about what such a fate would be like.

"There was no other way to contain him!" Phoebe snapped.

"How did you manage to bury him without his jackals tearing you to shreds?" I asked.

"He hadn't figured out how to use his death magic yet. It takes time for a new *Liberi* to learn what he can do. Surely you know that yourself."

That I did. I suspected it might be years, even decades, before I fully understood my powers and was able to use them to the fullest extent.

"So if you buried him," Anderson interrupted before I could ask another question, "then how did he get out?"

Phoebe shifted her weight from foot to foot like a guilty child. "He figured out how to create the jackals while he was buried. We never thought he'd be . . . conscious enough to do anything."

I shuddered again as I put myself in poor Justin Kerner's shoes. He must have died of suffocation over and over and over, each time being brought back to life by his seed of immortality, only to die again within minutes. That would be horror enough to drive a sane person over the edge, but for someone who was already crazy . . .

"The jackals eventually dug him out," Phoebe continued. "If he'd just run, we might not have known he'd escaped for years, if ever. But he holds Konstantin personally responsible for everything, and he wants revenge more than he wants safety."

Anderson nodded. "Your vision warned you that

Kerner would get to Konstantin someday and that the jackals' bites would be fatal even to *Liberi*."

"Not just Konstantin," Phoebe said. "When he's finished taunting us with his mortal kills, he'll start coming after the rest of us. He'll come for Konstantin eventually, but not until he's decimated the Olympians first." Her brow furrowed suddenly. "How did you know the bites were fatal? Did you lose someone?"

"No," Anderson said. "We're all safe and accounted for, no thanks to you and the bounty of information you shared."

I hoped my poker face was working, because Anderson's failure to mention just what he'd had to do to cure me bugged the hell out of me. The only reason not to tell Phoebe what had happened to me was that he didn't want the Olympians to know how to save themselves if they got bitten. I wasn't a big fan of the Olympians, but I wasn't exactly into the "kill them all and let God sort them out" philosophy. Still, I managed to bite my tongue. I might argue Anderson's decision, but not in front of the enemy.

I got the distinct impression Phoebe wasn't satisfied with his answer, but she wasn't in any position to press him, and she knew it.

"What it all comes down to," Anderson continued, "is that you came here spewing lies simply because you wanted me and my people to protect Konstantin." The curl of his lip said just how appealing he found that prospect. "There is no higher purpose to be served, no risk that Kerner's actions might expose the *Liberi* to the government."

Phoebe swallowed hard. "Maybe not. But are you willing to let an untold number of innocent victims die horrible deaths just so you can get back at Konstantin? Because if you are, you'll have to give up any claim to the moral high ground."

"Oh, I intend to stop Justin Kerner, mark my words. But I'm *not* doing it for Konstantin's benefit, and I'm *not* handing Kerner over to you when I've got him. Obviously, the Olympians are incapable of keeping him contained."

Phoebe's jaw dropped open, like she couldn't believe anyone would say anything so outrageous about such pinnacles of perfection as herself and her comrades. "We—"

"Will stay out of my way. I will clean up your mess because it's for the greater good, but you have no say in the how of it. And if I find out you're withholding any more information, I will hold *you* personally responsible. Understand?"

Mingled fear and anger played across Phoebe's face. "You don't dare hurt me," she said. "The truce . . ."

Anderson's smile was fierce and chilling. "Right now, Konstantin needs me. Do you think he'd risk having me withdraw my help for *your* sake? He can always find another pretty trophy to warm his bed. He can't find another descendant of Artemis to do his hunting for him."

Phoebe's gaze flicked to me briefly, and I knew her general dislike of me because of my allegiance to Anderson had now become something much more personal. Konstantin would choose me over her—not for any sexual reason but for self-preservation—and she would never forgive me for it.

Great. I'd managed to make yet another enemy without even having to say anything. *Thanks a lot, Anderson,* I thought, grinding my teeth to keep from saying it out loud.

"Now that we've got that all straightened out," Anderson said, "is there anything else you'd like to tell us about Justin Kerner and what he can do?"

Phoebe hesitated, but in the end, she knew she was beat. "He draws power from the dead. No doubt, you've noticed that his kills take place near cemeteries. If you can get him far enough away from such large concentrations of dead, the jackals might not be so virulent, or he might not be able to create so many. It took him years to dig his way free, and we presume it's because he didn't have access to the dead where we were keeping him."

I could think of another reason that was perfectly plausible: that he needed concentration to control the jackals, and it was hard to concentrate when you were repeatedly suffocating to death.

"That's all I can tell you," Phoebe finished. "When he took on Lyssa's seed, he fell to the madness within weeks, so we didn't exactly have time to test him out and see what he could do before we had to subdue him."

Anderson stared at her intently for a few seconds, trying to intimidate her into talking more. When she didn't, he shrugged. He emptied out the guns he'd taken from the goon, then put them back into their concealed holsters.

"You promise your ape will be on his best behavior when Blake releases him?" he asked.

"Yes," she replied, though it looked like the promise physically hurt her.

"And I'm sure Cyrus won't do anything rash," Anderson added, but he looked to *Blake* for confirmation, not to Phoebe. Blake nodded, and his sexual magic evaporated. Phoebe's goon gasped in a deep breath and took several panicked steps backward, almost tripping over his feet in his haste to get away from Cyrus. He regained some of his composure almost immediately, stopping his retreat, but his face was pale and sweaty, and he couldn't seem to look anyone in the eye.

Cyrus's reaction was less dramatic. He blinked a couple of times, then fixed Blake with a heated look. "I'll pay you back for that someday," he said. His facial expression screamed of anger, but there was a completely different undercurrent in his voice. Unless I completely missed my guess, that threat had been as erotic as it had been angry, and I was almost certain that Blake and Cyrus had some kind of history with each other.

"I'm sure you will," was Blake's understated reply.

Phoebe gave Anderson one last withering look before turning on her heel and striding for the door. This time, I got out of her way.

"I'll show you out," Blake said. His offer had nothing to do with courtesy—he was just making sure the Olympians actually left. And didn't do any mischief on their way out.

I should have followed them, should have given

myself time to ponder and digest everything I'd learned from this conversation before saying word one to Anderson.

Even as I told myself that, I found myself closing the door and turning to face him. When I met his eyes, I found not Anderson the laid-back man who was friendly and easy to talk to but Anderson the god in disguise. He was still in his human form, showing no overt hint of the dangerous and powerful being within, but there was a weightiness to his gaze that told me he had no interest in hearing my opinion.

Getting the hell out of the room was probably a good idea when he had that look on his face. But I've never been all that good with authority—as most of my foster parents would be happy to tell you—and I refused to be intimidated.

All right, that's a lie. I *was* intimidated. But if Anderson wanted a good little toady who never argued his decisions, then he might as well kick me out, because that wasn't me.

"Tell me you're not seriously considering burying Kerner alive for all of eternity," I said.

I hadn't thought his expression could get any more forbidding, but I'd been wrong. "Burying him would be pointless," he said in a monotone that still managed to convey plenty of authority. "The jackals would just dig him out again." He frowned, the expression making him look almost human again for a moment. "Perhaps we'll need to encase him in concrete. Or steel. Then we can bury him somewhere far away from the dead so he'll have as little power as possible."

"Don't bullshit me. You're missing the point on purpose."

"He has to be contained." The humanity was gone again. I wondered if he was doing that to make himself more forbidding, or if he just had to cut himself off from his humanity in order to be such an ass.

"No, he has to be killed," I said. "And you can do it." As painful as death at Anderson's hands would be, it had to be the lesser evil compared with being buried alive for eternity.

"Perhaps I haven't made myself clear. My ability and my origins are top secret. A secret that only you and Konstantin have survived learning. When I find a way to get to Konstantin without witnesses, I will kill him. If you don't keep your mouth shut, I will have to kill you, too."

I was shocked by how much his words hurt. It wasn't anything I didn't know, wasn't anything he hadn't told me before. But in the past, it hadn't been so . . . blunt. Or so cold. Anderson was my friend, at least sort of, and though I'd been under no illusions that I was as dear to him as the rest of his people, who'd been with him for decades, I'd thought he would be at least a little reluctant to kill me.

Apparently, I'd been wrong, and to my shame, my eyes prickled with tears, and my chest felt heavy with loss. Loss I had no right to feel, because I was still an outsider, would *always* be an outsider, and I knew it. You can't lose something you don't have in the first place.

The ice in Anderson's expression thawed, and he

reached out to put his hands on my shoulders. I took an instinctive step back, but he followed and trapped me against the door. His hands squeezed the tight muscles in my shoulders, and I knew the gesture was meant to be comforting. But his last words were still echoing through my head, and it was an effort for me to hold still and not try to jerk out of his grasp.

"It's nothing personal, Nikki," he said gently. "I have good reasons for keeping this secret so . . . aggressively. I'm sorry to have to resort to threats, but I don't know how else to be sure you'll keep quiet."

My throat was tight, but I managed to get words out anyway. "You could try telling me the good reasons. Because from where I'm sitting, it all looks very selfish."

"I'm afraid you're going to have to trust me." His eyes met mine, and I found myself trapped by his gaze. Usually, those eyes were a perfectly ordinary shade of brown, but right now, there was a hint of white light coming from the centers of his pupils. "I've taken a huge risk in letting you live. Konstantin I know well and understand. I know he will not reveal my secret because he fears that if others know, it will diminish his power. You I can't predict as comfortably. I can't know that you won't someday get angry and blurt something out." He raised his hand to my cheek, stroking the backs of his fingers over my skin as he continued to meet my gaze with those unsettling, inhuman eyes.

"You're alive because I care about you," he continued. "I'm taking this massive risk because I like you

too much to hurt you." The light in his eyes grew a little brighter. "But I need you highly motivated to keep
my secret, and so my threat will always be there, and I
may at times feel it necessary to remind you. It doesn't
mean I don't care."

"Right," I responded in a hoarse whisper.

I knew he was telling the truth as he saw it. It even
made a sort of sense, in a coldly logical way. Anderson
was, after all, a god. He'd never been human, and to
expect him to have human values might not be very
fair of me. That didn't stop me from expecting it,
however.

Anderson gave a soft sigh, dropping his hands back
to his sides and giving me a little space. The light in
his eyes slowly faded until he was fully back in his
unprepossessing human guise. The look in those eyes
spoke of hurt and loneliness. It might have struck
me as funny that he found my inability to accept his
justification for threatening to kill me hurtful, except
nothing was going to strike me as funny under the circumstances.

I didn't know what to say to him. Maybe there just
wasn't anything else to say, at least not at the moment.
But if we managed to capture Kerner, I had a feeling
I wouldn't be able to stop myself from opening my big
mouth again.

I settled for shaking my head and making a grace-
ful retreat. Now that I had a name for our killer, I had
a lot of research to do. Work was always a powerful
balm for pain and fear, for keeping emotions at bay
while the mind was busy being productive and logi-

cal. The problem with using work as a balm was that it was like taking aspirin for a brain tumor. It might mask the symptoms for a while, but it didn't cure what was ailing you.

I had a nasty feeling I was going to be in a world of hurt when the emotional aspirin wore off.

THIRTEEN

I wasn't entirely shocked when my search on Justin Kerner didn't yield any exciting results. I found out he'd been an army brat, spent much of his childhood traveling from place to place, never setting down roots. He'd continued the trend as an adult, working as a consultant, going wherever the jobs took him. In fact, he traveled so often that it took almost two months for anyone to notice when he went missing from his home in Alexandria five years ago. He'd only moved in a few weeks before and hadn't even bothered to introduce himself to his neighbors.

He was still officially listed as missing, and the police had made zero progress in finding him. They weren't convinced that there was foul play involved.

What this all meant for me was that Kerner didn't have any ties I could exploit in my search for his whereabouts. No wife, no kids, no girlfriend, not even a real friend of any kind, as far as I could tell. No permanent home that might draw him back or sentimental locations he might want to revisit when he wasn't busy killing people. His parents were both dead—his father having met his end in a car accident very close to the time Kerner disappeared—and he had no other living family I could find. No doubt, the Olympians had been thorough in their attempt to wipe out this non-Greek line.

I slept on what little information I had, hoping I'd be able to make something of it in the morning, but no dice. When the Olympians had gotten their claws into him, Justin Kerner had left his old life in the dust, and it didn't look like he had much of anything to look back on. That meant his past wasn't going to help me catch him. Which left trying to anticipate his next move as my only option.

I unfolded my huge map of D.C. and its surrounding area, laying it on my desk. I'd already marked the murder sites on it, and I'd highlighted every cemetery I could find. Until the attack at Rock Creek, Kerner had been going on a generally northerly path, but to continue that pattern, he'd have to go outside the D.C. limits. Now that we knew for sure he was making a statement to Konstantin with the murders, I was fairly certain he wasn't going to keep going north.

There were two cemeteries within the D.C. limits to the south of Anacostia, the site of the first kill, and one that was southwest of Rock Creek, where he'd struck last. When I looked at my numbered dots on the map and if I eliminated any cemeteries not within the D.C. limits, it seemed like the Oak Hill Cemetery, in Georgetown, would be the next logical site in his path if he was planning to circle back to the beginning.

Had he realized what meeting a fellow *Liberi* at the cemetery had meant? Did he think it was just a strange coincidence, or did he know I'd been there waiting for him?

If he thought I was just a bystander who got in his way, then there would be no reason for him to change his pattern, and I could feel fairly certain he'd make an appearance at Oak Hill. If he realized my presence at Rock Creek was part of a bungled ambush attempt, then he might be too wary to stick to his pattern. Then again, he might think I was dead, and our "ambush" hadn't exactly been successful enough to strike fear in his heart.

And that's when the anomaly of his pattern finally struck me.

His first kill had been the southernmost of all of them, and yet there were two other cemeteries on my map within the D.C. limits and farther south. So why hadn't Kerner started with one of them if he was planning to do a grand tour of the cemeteries?

There was no record of Kerner owning any property in the area—the house he'd been living in when he disappeared had been a rental—and when I'd seen him, he'd immediately struck me as a homeless guy. He had to be living *somewhere* when he wasn't out hunting, and his pattern suggested to me that that somewhere was near one of those southern cemeteries, that he was avoiding them because he didn't want to crap in his own backyard. If he was avoiding them and if he was restricting himself to cemeteries within the D.C. limits, then Oak Hill had to be his next target. Unless he decided to go to one of his previous locations, of course.

I folded the map with a huff of exasperation. There were far too many ifs in this scenario. Even so, I had a hunch that Kerner would be at Oak Hill tonight. The big problem with my hunches was that it was really hard to tell the difference between a hunch that was fueled by my supernatural abilities and one that was fueled by wishful thinking. Was the fact that I could think of a logical reason for Kerner to be at Oak Hill and couldn't think of a logical reason for him to be at one of the others influencing my gut reaction?

A straightforward power, complete with step-by-step instructions on how to use it, would have been real nice.

Anderson held a strategy meeting in his office in the afternoon. I did my best to explain to everyone why I thought Kerner would show up at Oak Hill, although the argument sounded even flimsier spoken out loud than it had in my head. I saw more than one skeptical look directed my way, and there was what felt to me like an uncomfortable silence when I finished speaking.

"She was right about Emma," Jamaal said, breaking the silence. "I don't think the reasoning here is any more outlandish than that was."

"The guy is crazy, not stupid," Blake argued. "Why would he risk sticking to his pattern? Even if he doesn't think it's *likely* we're hunting him, he must have some idea it's a possibility. I mean, what were the chances that a *Liberi* just happened to be wandering around the cemetery at night and just happened to run into him?"

"I think the more important question is what good does it do us to assume Nikki is wrong?" Anderson put in. "If she's wrong, then we have no idea where he'll be, and we can't do anything to stop him. But if she's right, we might be able to get the drop on him before anyone else gets killed. I'd say that's a very good reason to act on the assumption that she's right."

No one could counter that argument, and though it wasn't exactly what I'd call a vote of confidence, it did make me feel better. We might be deluding ourselves, but at least now we felt like we had a chance of finding Kerner. Never mind what we would do with him if we actually did.

"Nikki," Anderson continued, "if you see Kerner, ignore the jackals and just shoot *him*. Got it?"

Of course, that was what I should have done last time, but I'd been too disoriented by the jackals' attack to think about looking for their master—until it was too late. I nodded.

"We'll divide into pairs like we did last time," Anderson said. Then he turned a regretful face to Jamaal. "I'm afraid you're going to have to sit this one out, though."

Jamaal clearly didn't like it, but he had to know it was coming after last week's performance. He nodded tightly, lips pressed together and hands clenched.

"So who gets to be my partner for the night instead?" I asked. I had a brief fantasy of going to the cemetery with Anderson at my side, capturing Kerner, and then persuading Anderson to kill him without anyone being the wiser, but of course, Anderson was partnering with Emma, and it was better for everyone that way.

"You're still the most likely of us to find Kerner," Anderson said. "And the most likely to be able to take him out if you do. I'd like Logan to go with you." His focus turned to Logan. Logan was probably tied with Leo in the category of people I lived in the same house with and knew least, but I *did* know he was the descendant of a war god and therefore pretty handy in a fight.

"You might want to bring a sword," Anderson instructed Logan. "If you do find Kerner, it'll be up to you to keep the jackals at bay."

"Sword's a little close-range for that," Logan said skeptically.

Anderson raised an eyebrow. "You were thinking maybe an automatic weapon? One gunshot might be dismissed as a backfiring car, but there will be more than one jackal. We got lucky last week in that Nikki ran into Kerner far enough away from houses that no one heard the shots, but we might not have that luxury this time. Unless you have a silencer somewhere in your arsenal?"

Logan looked chagrined. "Never thought I needed one. Guess I'll be polishing the rust off my sword. It's been a while since I've fought with one."

The statement made me wonder just how old Logan was. It had been a while since *anyone* had done any serious swordfighting, but I got the feeling he'd done a fair amount of it in his life.

"Let's hope it's like riding a bicycle, then," Anderson said.

There was a little more logistical discussion after that, and then we all went our separate ways to prepare. I was still a little less than my best after being dead for most of a week, so I took a nap. I was pleasantly surprised to discover that Jamaal was right, and the horror of closing my eyes had faded to almost nothing.

When the time came, we paired up for our hunt. I'd thought Logan, as a war god descendant, might be the kind of manly man who would insist on driving, but when I said I wanted to take the Mini, he didn't make a fuss. That won him a couple of brownie points in my book.

It was more than a little unnerving to see the long, sleek sword Logan stashed in the backseat as we got ready to go. He handled it with the careless ease of long familiarity, and he patted it almost affectionately when he put it down.

Among all of the other difficulties of tonight's venture would be avoiding the attention of the police. Logan was going to look a little conspicuous walking around with a sword, although he swore his trench coat would keep it hidden until it was needed. And I was once again carrying an illegal firearm within the D.C. city limits, which could turn out very bad for me if I got caught. Not as bad as things would turn out if I got caught unarmed, however, so I was more than willing to continue tempting fate.

The Oak Hill Cemetery was in Georgetown, and even at this time of night, we couldn't find enough parking for all of our cars together. I'd have preferred to have a central rallying point, but since we were going to split into four teams, I supposed it didn't matter.

I parked on Q Street at the southeast tip of the cemetery. Oak Hill was vaguely triangular in shape, with two sides of the triangle bordering residential areas. The longest side of the triangle ran parallel to the Rock Creek and Potomac Parkway and the scenic Rock Creek Trails. If Kerner was hitting this cemetery tonight, then it stood to reason he'd make an appearance in one of the residential areas, where there was more prey to choose from. I, however, was putting my money on the scenic route. There wouldn't exactly be a lot of joggers or bicyclists out at this hour, but Kerner liked his privacy, and the isolation of that trail might be a draw.

Logan climbed into the backseat and strapped on his sword as covertly as he could. When he emerged, I could still see the tip of the scabbard poking out from under the tail of his coat. We were just going to have to hope that wasn't enough to draw attention.

The other three teams were staking out the residential areas and the numerous side streets, while Logan and I got the trail all to ourselves.

We walked back and forth, eyes peeled, nerves buzzing, for a couple of hours, but we didn't see anything suspicious, nor did any of the others. Then, at a little after two, Anderson called.

At first, I hoped that meant he'd spotted our quarry, but that turned out to be wishful thinking.

"What's up?" I asked.

"Leo's been keeping an ear on the police scanner, just in case. There was just a report of someone seeing a pack of dogs in Fort Totten Park."

"That's near the Rock Creek Cemetery," I said with an internal groan, even as I started hurrying back toward the car, gesturing for Logan to follow. I'd *known* my reasoning was flimsy, but I'd definitely gotten my hopes up that it would turn out to be sound.

"Yes," Anderson agreed, and the jostling sounds I heard told me he was moving fast, no doubt heading for his own car. "I doubt we'll be able to get there fast enough to do any good . . ."

"But we have to try," I finished for him.

"Exactly."

I picked up my pace to a brisk jog as I told Logan about the police report. We dove into the car, and I pulled out with an embarrassing shriek of tires.

"If the jackals have been spotted," Logan said, holding on to the oh-shit bar, "we're already too late."

"I know," I answered, hoping I wasn't being unfairly snappish. I gave the car a little more gas, though I didn't dare go too fast, or I'd attract police attention. I could just see trying to explain to the nice officer why there was a sword in the backseat and why I was carrying an illegal concealed firearm.

Logan and I rode in silence for a few minutes as I worked to contain my impatience and not run any red lights or stop signs. And then a thought hit me.

"Weird that Kerner would let someone see his jackals and live to tell the tale," I said. "They're invisible unless they're in use, as far as I can tell."

"Maybe it really is just a pack of stray dogs," Logan suggested.

My foot eased on the gas pedal as something inside me shouted that this wasn't right. "Maybe. Or maybe it's some kind of trap. He knows we're out looking for him, and he's decided to lure us somewhere where he feels he has the advantage."

I slowed even more. The car behind me honked in indignation, then roared past me. The driver was probably giving me the finger, but I was too distracted to care. My gut was clenching with dread. I came to a stop as yet another theory popped into my head, one that resonated strangely.

"Or it's a diversion," I said. "He's luring us away from where he really means to strike."

I was halfway into the U-turn before I even realized I'd made a decision. I hit the gas, creating another scorched-rubber screech.

My heart was hammering with adrenaline now, and I was certain that we'd just been duped. Someone was going to die because I fell for the trick and ignored what my gut had been telling me from the very beginning.

"How could he lure us to Rock Creek with his jackals and still make an attack at Oak Hill?" Logan asked, bracing himself against the dashboard. I bet he'd think twice before getting into the Mini with me again. "I'm not sure how far there is between the two exactly, but it's a few miles at least."

He was right, and I had to admit I was puzzled. But something inside me was telling me Oak Hill was still the target, and as badly as I understood how my power worked, I felt certain my reluctance to leave the area was driven by more than a suspicion.

"I don't know how he created the diversion, but it doesn't matter. Like you said, if he's at Rock Creek, we'll get there too late to do any good. If he's at Oak Hill, we *might* get back in time to stop him."

Logan glanced at the dashboard clock doubtfully, and I wasn't that much more confident. We'd wasted a buttload of time rushing off after the red herring—if that's what it was—and instinct told me he would already have selected his victim by the time he created the diversion.

My former parking space was still available, so at least I didn't have to circle the block searching for a new one, but we'd been gone at least fifteen minutes, and I had a sinking feeling that we were too late.

I held on to the remnants of hope as I parked. I got out and hurried around the car to the sidewalk as Logan leaned in to retrieve his sword once more. When he stood up, his eyes suddenly widened at something he saw behind me. I started to turn but not in time.

A pair of furred bodies sailed through the air, impossibly high off the ground for such small creatures. They both slammed into Logan's chest.

His sword was still in its scabbard when he hit the ground. I fumbled for the gun in my shoulder holster, then froze when a voice spoke over the snarls of the jackals.

"Move, and they'll tear his throat out."

I looked around, trying to spot the source of the voice, but the only human form I saw was Logan. He lay on his back on the sidewalk, a jackal's jaws at his throat, teeth pricking his skin. There was no sign of blood yet, and we now knew how to cure the supernatural rabies, but I wouldn't put anyone through that if it wasn't absolutely necessary.

A second jackal stood on Logan's chest, its ears flattened to its skull, its teeth bared as it snarled directly into his face. I could almost feel its fierce desire to attack, but so far, at least, Kerner was holding it back.

I stood absolutely still, my heart pounding in my throat as I frantically searched for a way out of this mess. But I already knew the only way to stop the jackals was to stop Kerner, and it's hard to stop a guy you can't even see. Especially when you're standing stock still and hoping he won't order his jackal to tear out someone's throat.

"What do you want?" I asked. This was a calculated ambush, and I'd walked right into it, even parking in the same space I'd left from.

"Start by slowly putting your hands in the air," he said. For a psycho who was infected with rabid insanity, he sounded awfully calm.

I was finally able to pinpoint the sound of his voice, and I realized he was hiding behind a parked SUV. Even if I managed to pull my gun, I'd have no shot. My aim might be ridiculously good, but I wasn't carrying armor-piercing rounds.

Licking my lips and trying to stay calm, I did as he ordered, splaying my hands to show him I had no weapons. Out of the corner of my eye, I saw that three more jackals had joined the first two, menacing Logan. The three newcomers circled him restlessly, snarling and growling, every nuance of their body language showing how badly they wanted to attack. Even more disturbing, they had streaks of blood on their coats, and their muzzles were wet and red with it. I hoped Kerner's hands were steady on the reins.

Kerner stepped out from behind the SUV. He couldn't have seen me comply with his command, so I supposed the jackals were working as his eyes and ears in addition to being his attack dogs.

"What do you want?" I asked again as Kerner came closer and I could get a better look at him. And, unfortunately, a better smell. He was dressed in a filthy trench coat and too-long jeans. The cuffs of those jeans dragged on the ground and had collected a revolting crust of . . . whatever. And the smell wafting from him was rotting garbage, outhouse, and unwashed body.

I must have wrinkled my nose unintentionally,

because Kerner stopped and made a point of sniffing the air. Then he shrugged.

"My apologies," he said, smiling at me like we were having a pleasant conversation. "I'm so used to it I can't smell it anymore. I'll try to stay upwind."

This was not what I was expecting. His voice was calm and level, his words perfectly rational. There was no manic gleam in his eyes, no insane laughter or gleeful rubbing together of hands.

"You obviously want to talk to me," I said as my mind kept trying to figure out what the hell was going on. "So go ahead and talk."

"I would like you to stop interfering," Kerner said.

I blinked at him. "You ambushed me to tell me that? Hate to tell you this, but I could figure that out on my own." I braced myself, thinking maybe a show of attitude might bring out the screeching maniac I'd been expecting, but Kerner just smiled.

"I've pissed you and your friends off by killing civilians. I'll only get to kill the real Konstantin once, and that's a great pity. He deserves so much more after what he did to me. You have no idea . . ." Kerner shuddered, and I couldn't help a moment of pity as I thought about what he'd been through—and what he'd be going through for all eternity if we captured him and I couldn't persuade Anderson to do the right thing.

Kerner was a sadistic serial killer, but he hadn't been before the Olympians had screwed him up, and somewhere beneath the madness of Lyssa's seed was a scared, damaged human being. A scared, damaged human being I couldn't afford to feel sorry for, I reminded myself. A lot of serial killers have sob stories, but they're still monsters.

Kerner shook off the horror of his ordeal at Konstantin's hands. "But never mind my sad story. While I won't deny I enjoyed killing Konstantin in effigy, I have moved on to worthier prey. My quarrel is with Konstantin and his pack of gutless, soulless cronies, not civilians."

All right. This guy was crazy after all. "Let me get this straight. You want us to leave you alone so you can have your jackals rip various and sundry Olympians into shreds. Is that the gist of it?"

He furrowed his brow as if thinking, then nodded. "Yes, that's the gist of it. Once the world is rid of Olympians, it will be a much better place. And I love the irony of it all, that they used me as their lab rat to test Lyssa's seed and that in doing so, they created the one and only being who could destroy them."

Except for Anderson, of course, but Kerner didn't know about that.

"I wouldn't call it irony so much as poetic justice," I said. And if Kerner hadn't already killed four innocent victims, I might even have believed it.

Kerner looked delighted with what he must have taken as my agreement. "Exactly. And I think it only fair that Konstantin watch the ones he cares for die one by one, knowing he'll face the same fate himself, just as he made me watch as he slaughtered my family." He made a face. "Not that Konstantin truly cares about anyone but himself."

My research had turned up very little family for Kerner. His father had died in a supposed car accident near the time Kerner went missing, and I had no trouble believing Konstantin had killed him in front of Kerner's eyes. That didn't exactly sound like watching his loved ones die "one by one," but maybe Kerner thought it made him sound more sympathetic.

I nodded. "Like I said, poetic justice. But I'm still kind of getting stuck on the killing-innocent-bystanders thing."

Kerner stuck out his lower lip in a twisted pout. "I already told you I've moved on. I only meant to take out Olympians, but then I bumped into that first guy. He thought I was some panhandler harassing him for money." For the first time, there was a hint of a manic gleam in Kerner's eyes, one that said he wasn't as sane and rational as he pretended. "He was a condescending asshole, and he looked so much like Konstantin ... then he got spooked and started running away, just begging me to chase him." He shrugged. "I probably would have been able to contain myself if the stupid shit hadn't started running."

"So it's all his fault he's dead?"

Kerner's eyes flashed with anger, but his voice remained level. "When it was over, I felt more like my old self than I had since I was forced to take Lyssa's seed, and I realized I could get my revenge on Konstantin and stop being so . . ." He made a circular motion beside his head with his finger. ". . . at the same time. Two birds with one stone."

"And that makes it okay for you to kill people

just because they have the bad luck to resemble Konstantin?"

The jackals snarled their disapproval of my tone, and I reminded myself that antagonizing a crazy man who commands a pack of rabid jackals wasn't the brightest idea.

"I keep telling you, I'm finished with that," Kerner growled. His voice had deepened, and he sounded strangely like his jackals. "It was fun while it lasted, but I know now that it was stupid and unnecessary."

I glanced at the jackals and once again saw the blood on their coats. They had killed already tonight, and it sounded as if their victim had been an Olympian. Better than a civilian, but still . . . it was an awful way to die.

"Who?" I asked, not sure why I wanted to know.

Kerner smirked. "Someone whose loss Konstantin might actually regret a little. A pretty little blonde, descendant of Apollo. The Olympians call—*called*— her the Oracle."

I fought to suppress my reaction. Phoebe had no redeeming qualities that I could tell. And yet it freaked me out enough to learn that complete strangers had been torn to shreds, partially eaten. Learning that something like that had happened to someone I *knew* . . . My stomach gave an unhappy lurch.

"There is one less Olympian to blight the earth tonight," Kerner concluded with obvious pride.

I swallowed hard to keep my gorge down. "But she'll come back," I said. The body would somehow mend itself, regenerate the missing organs, and come back to life in the throes of the supernatural rabies.

"No, she won't," Kerner said with a smug smile. "Konstantin made the biggest mistake of his life when he chose me to host Lyssa's seed. The madness *infected* the seed—which means it operates on a metaphysical level as well as a physical one. Pair it with death magic, and you have something that can destroy a *Liberi,* body and soul." His voice was replete with satisfaction, then he frowned at me. "But *you* didn't die," he said speculatively. "I thought at first it was because my jackals didn't eat your heart—did you know the heart was the seat of the soul?—but the Oracle expired before they'd managed to do more than nick her heart. I felt her seed snuff out, right here." He patted the center of his chest. "Even without having directly contacted your heart, the infection should have worked its way there eventually. I wonder why it didn't."

I tried really hard not to picture a jackal tearing my heart from my chest and devouring it, but my stomach heaved anyway. I had no intention of letting Kerner in on the secret of how I'd survived. "No idea," I mumbled.

The physical effects of his death magic were somehow mirrored on a metaphysical level. So much so that when the infection reached the heart, the body and the seed of immortality were both destroyed. If Anderson hadn't broken my neck, if he'd let the super-rabies run its course, I would have died. And *stayed* dead.

Anderson had saved my life by killing me.

But that was a paradox to ponder at another time. I still had to get Logan and myself out of this mess, preferably without either of us being bitten.

I could tell Kerner was still curious about my continued existence, but he didn't press me on it. "All I'm asking is that you stay out of it until Konstantin is dead," he said. "I'm through with the civilians, and I have no quarrel with you or your friends."

"No? Then why did your damn dogs bite me?" Once again, I was failing to humor the crazy person, and the jackals growled their displeasure. I checked on Logan out of the corner of my eye. He was lying very still, eyes closed, and he looked very Zen about having a rabid jackal's fangs pricking the skin of his throat.

"That was unintentional," Kerner said with an edge in his voice that said he was getting tired of my attitude. "For future reference, you might want to avoid shooting my jackals. They're a manifestation of my death magic, and if you take one out, the magic comes back to me. The rebound effect makes me a little cranky." He gave me a teeth-baring smile that was closer to a snarl.

"I'm not a fool, and my mind is still reasonably intact, at least when I have a recent kill under my belt. I understand why you feel the need to stop me. I'm just asking you to put it off for a while."

He averted his eyes and ran a hand through his lank, greasy hair. "I know I'll end up in the ground again eventually. I'm just one guy, and you're all out to get me. But I can't ever die." He met my gaze again, and I saw a shimmer of tears in his eyes. "I can't ever be released from the horrors of the prison you will put me in. And if I have to go to that prison knowing that Konstantin still walks the earth, then I will be spending eternity in hell."

His Adam's apple bobbed as he swallowed hard. "I'm begging you to let me have my revenge before you condemn me. Give me the one thing that will make my eternity bearable."

Bleeding-heart alert—I was standing there facing a psycho who'd killed innocent people just because they vaguely resembled Konstantin, and I was feeling sorry for him. Not to mention the vengeful side of me that was overcome with glee at the idea of Konstantin getting killed by a man who was one of his victims.

Of course, it wasn't like I was in any position to stop Kerner at the moment. Not unless I didn't mind letting Logan get savaged. Sure, he'd probably live through it if they didn't tear out his heart, but it would seriously suck. And while I'm a good shot, I'm not a quick-draw expert. With the gun still in my pocket, in all likelihood, the jackals could make short work of both Logan and me before I got a shot on Kerner.

"I'm attempting to show you a sign of good faith," Kerner said with a little edge in his voice. I guess he was getting tired of my hemming and hawing. "I could have killed both of you before you even knew I was here."

"Yeah, thanks for not doing that. But you're asking me to stand by and let you kill people. I have a hard time saying yes to that." And I had a hard time believing that Kerner would *believe* me if I said yes. So what was he really after?

"All right," Kerner said, and there was now an angry glitter in his eyes. "Let me be more blunt: I'm hunting the Olympians now. Keep out of my business until I've finished with Konstantin, and the Olympians will be the only ones who get hurt. But if I see you or any of your friends near me again, civilians are going back on the menu. I've been controlling the death magic, only letting it loose for one kill a week, but the death toll if you don't keep your nose out of my business will be considerably higher. Are we clear?"

Funny how I felt a lot less sorry for him all of a sudden. "Crystal," I grated out.

He smiled, looking very pleased with himself all of a sudden. "I knew we could work this out. And if you or your friend make any attempt to follow me, I'll take that as a sign that you're rejecting our agreement. If that's the case, check out the local news tomorrow to see how many people I chose to punish for your mistake."

He winked out of sight before I could answer, as did all the jackals. I could tell he was still nearby, because I could smell his rancid stink. Logan lay still on the sidewalk, his breaths shallow, as if the jackal's jaws were still around his throat.

"Is the jackal still there?" I asked, because it was

abundantly clear that just because I couldn't see it didn't mean it was gone.

Logan just blinked at me, which I figured was answer enough. I wouldn't want to talk if I had a jackal's teeth at my throat, either.

Kerner's stink was fading, which told me he was leaving, though he was still completely invisible. I had no idea which way he was going, and I wasn't about to move until I was positive he was gone.

As positive as it was possible to be with an invisible man, anyway.

After maybe three minutes, Logan finally sucked in a deep breath and slowly sat up. We both tensed for an attack, but none came.

Kerner and his jackals were gone. Maybe.

Fourteen

Later that night—or, more accurately, later that morning—we regrouped in the kitchen at the mansion. We were all tired and dejected from the failed hunt. I started a pot of coffee brewing, then did my best to recount everything Kerner had said, word for word, with Logan filling in a few details I had missed.

The coffee maker's death rattle announced it was finished brewing, and those of us who were so inclined filled our mugs. Logan got a bottle of Jack Daniel's from the cabinet over the sink, and Maggie boiled water for tea. When everyone had their beverage of choice, we gathered around the table in the breakfast nook. There weren't enough chairs for everyone, so Jack hopped up onto the counter, and Jamaal, who had waited up for us, stood leaning against the wall. Emma stood practically in the doorway and looked like she was bored and wanted to slip away while we weren't looking.

Jamaal's knee was bouncing, which worried me. He'd seemed relatively calm in the week since he'd unleashed his death magic, but I didn't think the fidgets were a good sign. Kerner said the killings had calmed his death magic, and his one-per-week schedule seemed to suggest the calming effects lasted for about seven days. Which might mean Jamaal was creeping back toward his usual dangerous edge. Then again, he *was* drinking coffee, so maybe he just had a caffeine buzz going.

"If Kerner was in Georgetown killing Phoebe," Jamaal said, "then how did he create the diversion at Fort Totten Park?"

No one had an answer to that.

"If it was a diversion engineered by Kerner," I said, thinking out loud, "then either he has an accomplice with a bunch of dogs, or his jackals can cover a hell of a lot of territory without him being nearby." That was not a thought that put me in my happy place.

"Or he can travel between cemeteries a lot faster than human beings can," Anderson suggested. We all turned to him with varying expressions of inquiry.

"I've known some death god descendants who've been able to use cemeteries as gateways to the Underworld," he continued. "When they leave the Underworld, they can reenter our world anywhere there's a cemetery or burial ground. They need to draw power from the dead to open the gateway. It's a rare power, but it does exist. And I suspect our man has it."

"You're telling me he can teleport from cemetery to cemetery whenever he wants?" I asked. I wondered if this was something Anderson could do himself. After all, he was Death's son.

"Something like that. It would explain how he's getting around."

"So what do we do now?" Logan asked. "How do we stop Kerner without getting a bunch of innocent people killed?"

"We don't."

Everyone turned to look at Emma, who rarely participated in these little staff meetings of ours. I didn't get the feeling she cared about much of anything, and she certainly wasn't eager to talk to anyone except Anderson. Though she yelled at him more than she talked to him.

"Emma . . ." Anderson said in a warning tone, which she completely ignored.

"If he wants to take out the Olympians, I say more power to him."

Anderson looked pained. "I'll admit, they're not good people, but—"

"But nothing!" she snapped, eyes flashing. "Anything Kerner does to them, they deserve. And I quite like the idea of Konstantin watching as his people get savaged one by one, knowing what's coming and unable to stop it."

She was dead serious and had a fanatical gleam in her eyes that reminded me a little of Kerner. She'd moved away from the doorway, finally interested enough in the subject matter to join in. As far as I could tell, the only thing she truly cared about was getting her revenge.

"We'll talk about this later," Anderson said with quiet authority, but Emma wasn't finished.

"No, we'll talk about it now! It's past time you get off your ass and avenge me! You don't want to go to war with the Olympians because you like your status quo so much? Fine. But if there's another *Liberi* out there willing and able to go get that pound of flesh, then you're damn well not going to stop him!"

Everyone in the room must have overheard snippets of this argument before. It wasn't like Anderson and Emma were quiet when they fought. But they'd usually at least made a show of keeping it private.

Emma stalked through the assembled chairs toward Anderson. The anger that radiated from her was palpable, and I don't know about the rest of Anderson's people, but *I* wanted to get the hell out of the room before things went any further. But I don't think any of us wanted to draw Anderson's attention or Emma's ire, so we sat still and silent, unwilling witnesses to what could soon become something truly ugly.

Anderson rose slowly as Emma approached, his full attention on her. "Konstantin deserves to suffer for what he did to you," he said. "But not like this. Not when innocent lives are at stake."

Emma snorted and tossed her hair. "Innocent lives! There's no such thing as an innocent Olympian. The only way more innocents get hurt is if you insist on playing the fucking hero and Kerner decides to make you pay."

"You don't know that."

Considering Emma was in complete battle-ax mode, Anderson was remaining impressively calm. In fact, he looked more sad than angry.

"He may mean what he said," Anderson continued, "or he may not. Either way, I don't trust him, and if you were thinking straight, you wouldn't, either."

I thought for a moment Emma was going to hit him. She looked that pissed.

"I'm thinking perfectly straight," she said in a low growl that reminded me of an angry cat. "Even if there turns out to be some collateral damage, it would be worth it if Konstantin dies."

Anderson gaped at her like he couldn't believe she'd just said that. Maybe whatever she'd been through at Konstantin's hands had warped her beyond recognition, because I had a hard time believing Anderson had married someone this cold and vindictive. I hated Konstantin for what had been done to my sister on his orders, but it would never have occurred to me to let innocent people suffer in order to hurt him.

"You can't mean that," Anderson said weakly.

"Yes, I can." She lowered her voice, attempting to sound calm and reasonable. It would have worked better if there weren't so much insanity and hatred in her eyes. "I don't understand why you're so dead set against it. If you don't care enough about what he did to me, then surely you care about all the hundreds of others he's hurt and killed in his lifetime. If he dies, it will save untold innocent lives. You know that."

She was probably right. Konstantin and his Olympians were a scourge, wiping out whole families of

Descendants and taking whatever they wanted without a thought. But there was no great conviction to her argument, no sign that the saving of innocent lives meant anything to her whatsoever. She was merely looking for the angle that would convince Anderson to do what she wanted.

"Everyone out," Anderson said without taking his eyes off Emma. "I need to have a private conversation with my wife."

The haste with which the rest of us jumped to our feet and stampeded toward the door might have been funny in other circumstances.

Despite the coffee, I was dead tired. I could hear Emma's and Anderson's shouting voices behind me, and I suddenly realized I had had all I could take of them, of this house, and of my new and not improved life. For the last two weeks, I'd lived and breathed the *Liberi* and their troubles. I had not once stopped by my condo, nor had I even thought about spending the night there. I was letting myself get drawn in more and more deeply, letting the life I had once known slip through my fingers.

While the rest of the *Liberi* trooped upstairs to get some sleep, I found myself heading out the front door. I might have thought someone would try to stop me or at least ask me where the hell I was going at oh-dark-thirty, but either they were in too much of a hurry to get out of earshot of the argument, or they didn't give a damn. I assumed the latter and felt sour about it.

I let out a breath of relief as I drove through the front gates and pointed my car toward Chevy Chase. I wasn't free of the *Liberi,* not by a long shot, and I still had a lot to do in the fight to stop Kerner. In a few hours, I would be back at the mansion, hard at work. But maybe for a precious few hours, I could take a mental vacation from the turmoil.

The air in my condo felt stale when I let myself in, but I was pretty sure that was just my imagination. I walked from room to room, reacquainting myself with my things, waiting for the tightness in my shoulders to ease, waiting for my body to acknowledge that I was home.

Maybe I was just too tired and stressed to relax, but being surrounded by my own things in my own home didn't have the soothing effect I'd hoped for. The apartment felt cold and empty, oppressively quiet, and although it wasn't unwelcoming, it didn't feel like *mine* anymore. It reminded me of spending the night in my old bedroom at my adoptive parents' house: I still felt emotional ties to the place, the bond formed from years of memories, but that was all in the past. I was just a visitor now.

More disturbed than I'd have liked to admit by the direction of my thoughts, I slipped between the sheets of my no-longer-familiar bed and tried to sleep. It took me far longer than it should have.

I hadn't kept the kitchen stocked, so when I woke up in the morning, I had to go out for breakfast if I wanted anything to eat. I wanted to stay longer, to give myself an extended time-out, but staying in my apartment wasn't giving me the kind of boost I'd been hoping for. Just the opposite, in fact. There was a hollow feeling in the pit of my stomach, and I feared the life I was trying to cling to had passed me by forever.

I left the apartment as soon as I was showered and dressed. I drove through McDonald's for an elegant breakfast, then headed back to the mansion. I parked in the garage and walked to the front porch, where I found Jamaal lighting one cigarette from the butt of another.

It was none of my business if Jamaal was chain-smoking, but I found my footsteps slowing as I climbed the front steps and ventured onto the porch. He stared at me with neutral eyes while he took a deep drag on the fresh cigarette, holding the smoke in his lungs before letting it slowly out. It was then that I realized he wasn't smoking one of his usual clove cigarettes.

"You're smoking pot?" I asked, surprised. It was something I'd never seen him do before.

He shrugged and took another drag, then held the joint out to me.

For all my rebellious ways, I'd never been into drugs. Of course, if the Glasses hadn't taken me in when they had, I'm sure I'd have headed down that road as a teenager. Luckily for me, the Glasses had cured me of the need to act out in self-destructive ways.

"Um, no, thanks." I boosted myself up onto the rail that surrounded the porch, trying to read Jamaal's face without being too obvious about it. "Everything okay?"

He laughed a cloud of smoke. "You're kidding, right?"

"You know what I mean. You seem to be getting edgy again." And there was a reason he'd graduated from cigarettes to joints.

He took another drag, then stubbed out the joint, putting the remains in a little tin, which he then slipped into his jeans pocket.

"This is normal for me," he said, but he didn't look happy about it. "Releasing the death magic made it better for a little while, but I can feel it building up again. Just like always."

"But it wasn't like this when Emmitt was around," I said tentatively, always afraid to bring up his friend's death. The death *I'd* caused. Emmitt had possessed some death magic of his own, and he'd been teaching Jamaal how to control it, apparently with some success.

Jamaal moved over to the porch swing, dropping into it like he was bone-tired. Maybe he was.

"It was better then," Jamaal admitted. "We'd kind of . . . vent the death magic together. Send it at each other to ease the pressure inside."

I shivered. "You sent death magic at each other? Wasn't that kind of dangerous?"

He shrugged. "It wasn't like we could do each other any permanent harm. And our magics tended to cancel each other out." His eyes had a faraway look to them, and there was a faint smile on his lips.

Guilt niggled at me for the umpteenth time. If only I'd listened to my common sense that night, or if only

I hadn't gone so fast on that icy road, Emmitt would still be alive today. I'd still be mortal, with no idea that the *Liberi* even existed.

"Why can't you just do the same thing with someone else?" I asked. "It's not like you can kill another *Liberi*."

"Yes, I can. Emmitt's magic canceled mine out, but it would kill any other *Liberi*. They wouldn't stay dead for long, but people seem strangely reluctant to try it. Would you like to volunteer?"

"You know, that sounded almost like a joke. If you're not careful, I may start suspecting you have a sense of humor buried somewhere deep down inside."

"Who says I was joking?"

His voice was completely deadpan, and his face revealed nothing, so I don't know what it was about him that told me he was kidding. It was something, though, because no shiver of fear passed through me, despite the very real reasons I had to be afraid of Jamaal.

I didn't respond, instead thinking about the mysteries of death magic. Was it something specific to being a descendant of Anubis that allowed Kerner to channel his death magic into phantom jackals the way he did? Obviously, the *jackals* were specific to Anubis, but . . .

"Isn't there any other way you can vent the death magic? Kerner thinks creating the jackals is helping him keep in control. At least, as in control as a psycho can be."

"I can't make it manifest itself physically, if that's what you're asking."

"Have you ever tried?"

He blinked at me like the thought had never occurred to him. "No, but—"

"Then how do you know you can't? My powers didn't come with an instruction manual, so I see no reason to assume yours did."

He dismissed my question with a shake of his head. "If we believe anything Phoebe told us, Kerner hasn't been *Liberi* a tenth as long as I have. If I had a power like that, I would have figured it out by now."

I swung my feet between the balusters like a little girl, hoping the small movement would both help me stay warm and help me follow my own train of thought.

"But you haven't *needed* to figure it out. Kerner had been buried alive. He had a desperate need to do something to get him out. You know what they say about necessity being the mother of invention."

Jamaal arched an eyebrow. "Are you suggesting you'd like to bury me somewhere and see if I can make my magic dig me out?"

"Why are you being willfully obtuse about this? If you're so unhappy about the effects of your magic, maybe you should try *doing* something about it instead of just whining."

Jamaal rose slowly to his feet, eyes locked on me with simmering fury. I'd been treating him like a regular guy, allowing myself to forget just how terrifying he could be when he was angry. And how easy it was to set him off.

I held my hands up in a gesture of surrender.

"Sorry. I didn't mean to be so abrasive. I'm just trying to help."

The apology did nothing to appease him. "I don't need your help. I don't *want* your help."

So much for any sense of calm the joint might have given him. A smart woman would have retreated in the face of Jamaal's Mr. Hyde, but no one's ever accused me of being smart where men are concerned.

"You need to smoke like five packs a day to keep from completely wigging out, and you gave in to the death magic last week at the cemetery. I'd say that means you need help."

I slid off the railing and straightened to my full, but decidedly inadequate, height as Jamaal stalked closer. There was too much white showing around his eyes, and his pupils were little black pinpricks in a sea of chocolate brown. His nostrils flared like those of a predator who'd scented his prey. All very bad signs. Signs I chose to ignore as I held my ground.

"Are you really going to give in to it this easily?" I asked as my heart drummed frantically and my sense of self-preservation begged me to shut the hell up. "You've fought it for so long. And you've gone through so much to keep from being turned out of the house. Don't fuck it all up just because someone tries to help you."

Jamaal blinked in surprise, and I almost smiled. Amazing how much more effect an F-bomb has if you don't make a habit of using them. He stared at me a little more, and I watched the anger fade from his eyes until he took a deep breath and lowered his head.

"Why would you want to help me?" he asked so softly I could barely hear him. "You have every reason in the world to hate me."

There was a wealth of pain and loneliness in his words. He was not someone who was used to forgiveness. I'd explained to him numerous times by now that I'd forgiven him for his actions when I'd first become *Liberi,* but there was no sign he'd believed me.

I stepped a little closer to him. My feminine instinct was to reach out and touch him, give him a little human contact to anchor him in the now. But I knew he didn't like to be touched, especially by me, so I resisted the urge.

"You know I don't hate you," I said, picking my words carefully. "You and I are too much alike."

Amusement lit his eyes, and his lips twitched with a smile. "Yeah, we have a lot in common."

He meant that sarcastically, but he was right.

"You saw my file, saw how many foster families I went through. I didn't get bounced around like that because I was Miss Sweetness and Light. I spent years lashing out at people. I remember what that need felt like, remember what it was like to try to keep it buried and have it explode out of me at the least provocation. If the Glasses hadn't seen past all that crap and adopted me, I don't know where I'd be today. In jail is as good a guess as any.

"I got lucky, Jamaal. That's the only reason I don't have serious anger-management issues anymore. Maybe it's my turn to see past someone else's crap now."

Chocolate-brown eyes met mine, warmer than I'd ever seen them, and I thought maybe I was getting through to him. Then, before I had a chance to get my hopes up, his expression clouded.

"You were just a kid when that shit happened," he said. "And you didn't have death magic beating down your barriers. I'm glad you were able to get help, but it's too late for me."

He started to turn from me, and I knew he was planning to retreat to the house without another word. I couldn't let him do that, couldn't let our conversation end on such a hopeless note. So I reached out and grabbed his arm.

He whirled on me, braids lashing through the air like whips. I stood my ground, refusing to let go as he glared down at me for daring to touch him. His biceps were as hard as marble, well defined, and almost completely devoid of fat. He could have broken my grip easily, and the fact that he didn't gave me the courage to hold on.

"It's not too late unless you want it to be," I said.

"You don't know what the fuck you're talking about, so shut the fuck up."

F-bombs from Jamaal were a dime a dozen, so I wasn't particularly surprised by his response. I also couldn't help noticing he still hadn't tried to pull his arm from my grip. There was a battle going on inside him, a battle between the part of him that wanted to avoid all human contact to prevent being hurt and the part that was desperate not to be alone anymore. It was a battle with which I was intimately familiar.

"I know exactly what I'm talking about, and you know it," I countered. "I know exactly what it's like to be abandoned by someone I love, and I know exactly what it's like to build up that suit of emotional armor so—"

Jamaal jerked his arm, the motion making me stumble forward, right into his chest. I expected him to shove me away, so what he did next shocked me.

His free hand plunged into my hair, grabbing a handful and pulling my head back. I started to gasp out a protest, but before a sound escaped me, his mouth crashed down on mine.

He smelled of cloves and smoke, with a sweet over-tone of pot. His braids tickled my face and throat, and his lips . . .

This was not a soft kiss, not a kiss inspired by ten-der emotions and affection. This was rage and pain, loneliness and frustration, and, most of all, fear. His lips pressed against mine so hard I half expected them to fuse. My mouth was open from my interrupted pro-test, and he thrust his tongue inside.

I won't lie and claim I wasn't a bit turned on. There was no question I was attracted to Jamaal, had been even when he'd hated me and wanted to kill me. He was beautiful and exotic and dangerous, all of which made him sexy as sin. Desire stirred in my belly as his tongue brushed against mine. I wanted to shut off my brain and return the kiss, press my body up against his. I wanted to take him upstairs and get him out of his clothes, see if his body was as beautiful as his face.

But this was wrong on so many levels. Jamaal and

I didn't even like each other, and I'd never seen any sign before now that he shared my attraction. He was violent and dangerously unstable, and he was kissing me because he wanted to shut me up—although I had to wonder why he hadn't just pulled free and slammed into the house.

I tried to pull away from the kiss, but Jamaal wouldn't let me. His hand was still buried in my hair, strands wrapped around his fingers as he tasted the inside of my mouth. I put my hands on his chest and pushed, but I might as well have tried to move a tank. He pressed me closer to his chest, close enough that I could feel the impressive bulge in his pants. He might be doing this just to make a point, but he wasn't completely unmoved by it.

His scent filled my head, blurred my mind. His taste threatened to overwhelm me, and his touch threatened to make me forget why I should be stopping him. But I'm nothing if not stubborn, and I held on to my reason with desperate strength. This was not a battle I could allow him to win.

I pressed my teeth gently against his tongue in warning. Of course, he ignored the warning. I pressed a little harder, silently begging him not to make me hurt him, but he was well beyond being warned off.

Wincing in anticipation, I bit down hard enough to draw blood.

Jamaal's mouth jerked away from mine, his hand in my hair tightening to painful levels before he suddenly let go. His chest was heaving with his breath, and his eyes were dilated with lust. If he weren't using this to cover up a whole lot of other, less savory emotions, I might have found the expression on his face smoking hot.

I opened my mouth to force out an apology for biting him but swallowed it before any words escaped. He'd deserved it and was lucky I hadn't done anything worse.

"Leave me alone," he said hoarsely, shoving on my shoulders so hard I almost fell on my butt. "I don't need your interference."

Instead of seeking refuge in the house, Jamaal ran past me, jumped down the porch steps, and sprinted toward the garage. I guess he was afraid that if he ran into the house, I'd follow him.

FIFTEEN

Even though Jamaal had shut me down in no uncertain terms, I decided to do a little research on Kali, to see if there was an animal associated with her that perhaps Jamaal could try to use to make his death magic take physical form. I'd already seen evidence that animals associated with the gods had real significance when it came to *Liberi*. I couldn't be sure the doe that had led me to find Emma had been supernatural in nature, but it seemed a bit of a stretch for it to be a coincidence that Artemis is often pictured with a deer by her side. It all seemed a little whimsical and perhaps not at all useful, especially if Jamaal refused to try anything, but arming myself with knowledge couldn't hurt.

Let me tell you, Kali is one hell of a scary goddess, and I wouldn't want to meet her in a dark alley. She isn't evil—despite some of the really nasty cults that had sprung up in her name—and most of the stories about her involve her killing demons, not people. Still, when you've got a goddess who's often depicted standing on a dead body and wearing amputated body parts for jewelry, it's hard to feel much in the way of warm fuzzies. I did notice that she was often associated with tigers. Perhaps Jamaal already knew that, but I decided that the next time I saw him, I'd try to work the fact into the conversation. Assuming the embarrassment of what had happened this morning didn't make conversation impossible.

I was trying to figure out what to do next when the lights suddenly went out.

It was broad daylight, and while the windows in my sitting room were a little small for my taste, they let in plenty of light. However, when the lights went out, my room was suddenly pitch dark, like someone had switched off the sun.

My adrenaline spiked as I reached up to rub my eyes, not believing what I was seeing. Or, more accurately, what I *wasn't* seeing. But rubbing my eyes didn't suddenly make everything better. No matter how much I blinked, the room remained dark.

The hairs on the back of my neck rose, and my breathing shallowed. I'm not afraid of the dark, but this was something else entirely, and it reminded me far too much of being dead. I forced myself to take a deep breath, forced myself to acknowledge that I had a body and that it was following my orders. I wasn't dead, no matter how much the empty blackness made me feel like it.

Slowly, I rose from my chair as I mentally mapped out the room and tried to keep myself oriented. If I was careful, I should be able to make it to the door and out without falling over anything.

As I stood there hesitating, wondering if the whole house was draped in this unnatural darkness, I heard the faint sound of my door swinging open. No light poured in from outside, and I wondered if I'd suddenly gone blind. Maybe it was some lingering effect of the super-rabies. I grabbed the back of my chair, needing an anchor as panic skittered around the edges of my mind.

The door clicked shut. I was no longer alone in the room.

I closed my eyes and tried to pretend that was the only reason I couldn't see. I could still try a run for the door, but I had no idea who'd just come in, and whoever they were, they could well be in my way. Besides, the fact that I hadn't seen any light from outside when the door opened made the prospect less appealing.

"Who's there?" I asked, but I wasn't surprised when there was no answer.

I was seriously creeped out, my skin crawling, but I was also getting just a tad pissed off. Especially as a suspicion crept into my mind about just who might be behind the unnatural darkness.

Who in this household didn't like me *and* was a descendant of Nyx, the Greek goddess of night?

My fingers began exploring the surface of my desk, looking for something that would make a useful thrown weapon. Something other than my laptop, which I'd never dream of risking.

The most weighty thing I found was my empty coffee mug, and I hefted it experimentally. It wasn't exactly a lethal weapon, but it was all I had. Plus, I'd once taken out Jamaal's eye with a thrown shoe, so ordinary objects could be more dangerous than they looked when I wielded them.

My blood rushed in my ears, the only thing I could hear in the hushed silence of the room. I closed my eyes again, straining my ears for the slightest hint of movement, anything that would help me target the intruder.

There! Something that sounded like the brush of a shoe over carpet.

With a grin that was probably a less-than-attractive expression, I heaved the coffee mug in the direction of the sound, letting my body make the toss on autopilot. I might not understand how my supernatural tracking abilities worked as well as I'd like, but I *did* understand my miraculous aim.

There was a distinctive thump as the coffee mug hit its target, followed by a cry of pain and surprise. Another thump, sounding like a body hitting the floor. And then the lights came back.

I had to blink in the sudden brightness, but it hadn't been dark long enough for my eyes to adjust fully, so I wasn't blinded for long.

Emma was sprawled inelegantly on my floor, and I could practically see the stars and chirping birds circling as she blinked and shook her head. A thin trail of blood snaked down her face from her temple, and I might have felt bad about it if she hadn't been sneaking into my room to terrorize me. My coffee mug lay in pieces on the carpet around her.

I took a couple of steps to my right and grabbed the hardback book that was sitting on a nearby chair, in case Emma decided to object to my treatment and go ballistic. I hadn't hit her hard enough with the coffee mug to knock her out, but the book felt heavy enough to cave in the side of her head.

"How nice of you to come pay me a visit," I said, hefting the book dramatically in case she didn't get the hint.

She shook off the lingering effects of the blow to the head and glared up at me. She pushed herself into a sitting position.

"If you're going to stand up," I said, "do it real, real slow." I held up the book for emphasis.

The look she leveled on me then was pure malevolence. "I'll make you pay for this."

"For *what*?" I cried in exasperation. "You're the one who attacked *me*." Though I supposed, strictly speaking, making the room go dark wasn't exactly an attack. I was sure she'd had more on her mind than just a little optical illusion.

Moving at a normal pace, as if the book in my hand didn't worry her for a moment, she stood up, touching the blood on her face. "I did *nothing* to you," she snarled, staring at the blood on her fingers. "And you drew my blood."

"Oh, cut the crap, Emma. I don't know exactly what you were planning on doing, but I know it wasn't anything good."

She wiped her bloody hand on her shirt, leaving a crimson smear. Scalp wounds bleed like a son of a bitch, even when they aren't deep.

"I came here to apologize, and this is how you treat me?"

My mouth dropped open in shock as for half a second, I thought she meant what she said—no matter how loudly her actions contradicted her. Then I saw the sly smile on her lips and realized she was already crafting her own version of this story. A version that would make *me* look like the aggressor. Once again, she wiped blood from her face and then smeared it on her shirt, making her look like she'd just left a war zone. The small wound on her forehead might fade before she tattled on me, but the blood on her shirt would not.

The bitch had played me.

I shook my head, hating that I'd stepped right into her trap. Anderson should know me well enough to know I wouldn't just pitch something at Emma's head for no reason; however, he had an obvious blind spot where Emma was concerned. If she told him I'd attacked her, there was a chance he'd believe her, no matter how outlandish the claim. If he believed her, things could go very badly for me.

"What the hell, Emma?" I asked as my stomach dropped to my toes. "If it hadn't been for me, you'd still be down at the bottom of that pond." I'd long ago given up on the romantic idea that she might be grateful to me for her rescue, but for her to hate me so much . . .

"Oh, thank you sooo much," she said, oozing sarcasm. "I'm so glad I get to be around and watch you throw yourself at my husband while talking him out of avenging me. I will owe you for all eternity, and you can treat me like your bitch whenever you want."

Throwing myself at Anderson? I couldn't think of a single thing I'd done that any halfway reasonable person would even think of labeling "throwing myself" at him. And did she honestly think *I* could talk Anderson out of *anything*? As for treating Emma like my bitch, I'd done my best to keep my distance from her from the very beginning. I barely spoke to her at all, if I could help it.

Obviously, the woman was delusional. But knowing that didn't help me.

"You need professional help," I told her. "You're being completely paranoid and irrational. And whatever problems you and Anderson are having, you should be working it out yourselves, not dragging me into the middle of it."

The cut on Emma's forehead had stopped bleeding and was probably well on its way to healing completely. But the streaks of blood on her shirt would look very damning if Anderson was prepared to take her story at face value.

If she heard a word I said, she didn't acknowledge it. Instead, her eyes filled with cunning, suggesting that as crazy as she was, she still had enough wits about her to be dangerous.

"I won't tell Anderson what you did to me," she said. "On one condition."

I did *not* like the sound of that. Nor did I like her self-satisfied tone and gloating expression. It told me she was sure she'd won.

I wished I could be sure Anderson would be rational, would realize I wasn't the type of person who would just attack his wife out of nowhere. Maybe he would, but *maybe* wasn't good enough, not with a man who had threatened to kill me on more than one occasion. And even if he did believe me, he might decide this was evidence that Emma and I couldn't live in the same house together, and I was damn sure *she* wasn't the one who would be asked to leave.

"What condition?" I asked through gritted teeth.

"Make no effort to catch Justin Kerner until after Konstantin is dead. Lead everyone on a merry chase, pretend you're trying your hardest. But stay away from him. Do we have a deal? Or should I go speak to Anderson right now?"

I seriously considered throwing the book at her in hopes that another blow to the head would jar some sense loose. I didn't do it, but I'm sure my face conveyed the message of how much I wanted to.

"All I'm asking for is *justice*," Emma said earnestly. "Konstantin deserves to die. And Kerner has sworn he'll stop killing civilians. It's like the gods themselves dropped a solution to the Olympian problem straight into our laps!" Her voice was steadily rising with her excitement, but she seemed to notice and pull back. She was nuts, but not so nuts as to not realize how nuts she was making herself sound.

"Anderson refuses to declare war on the Olympians because he's afraid some of his people might get hurt if he does," she continued more calmly. "But if we just let Kerner take care of things himself, there won't have to be a war. I don't know why Anderson refuses to see that."

There was a certain amount of logic to what Emma was saying. If I could be certain Kerner would only kill Konstantin, I might even have agreed with her. I'm not the bloodthirsty sort as a rule, but I did want Konstantin dead. Maybe the rest of the Olympians deserved it as much as he did. But no matter what, my conscience couldn't swallow the idea of standing idly by while who knows how many people got torn apart by phantom jackals. I just didn't have it in me to let that happen when I could possibly stop it.

Emma didn't like my hesitation. She plucked at her bloody shirt. "I'm asking you to do the right thing," she said while fixing me with a cold glare. "But if you refuse, I'll tell Anderson you attacked me. Believe me, I'll make it very convincing. After all, I'm his wife . . . and you're just some stray he picked up from the street."

I tried not to let her see that she'd scored, but I must have flinched or something, because she smirked. "Oh, yes. Anderson *will* toss you back out on the street without a single regret, and you and your sister will both lose his protection. How long do you think the two of you will last before Konstantin finds you?"

Dammit, she'd just scored again. I felt the blood draining from my cheeks and could do nothing to stop it. Emma's eyes practically glowed with satisfaction.

"Do you want me to describe in graphic detail what Konstantin likes to do with pretty female captives?" Her lip curled. "*You* he wouldn't touch, but I bet he'd make you watch while he—"

"Shut up!" I shouted, trembling with rage. Steph had already suffered terribly because of me. My conscience would hate me for letting a crazed serial killer continue his reign of terror, but I refused to put Steph at risk again.

"Okay, fine, you win," I growled. "I'll lay off Kerner until Konstantin is dead. But someday, this is all going to come back and bite you in the ass. And I'll be there to see it."

Emma smiled at me, so smug in her triumph that I wanted to slap her.

"I'm glad we could come to an understanding," she said, then frowned down at the bloody shirt. "I guess I'll have to go change my shirt. But don't worry; I'll keep it nice and safe somewhere, in case I should ever need it."

She waited for my response, but when there was none forthcoming, she sighed in satisfaction and sauntered out of my room.

I'm not a big drinker, but after what had just happened, I felt that a little alcohol was in order. I found an open bottle of Chardonnay in the fridge downstairs and brought the whole bottle and a wineglass back up to my suite. I hadn't even eaten lunch yet, but that didn't stop me from pouring a glass immediately.

What was I going to do about Emma? Sure, I was

caving to her demands, and that would appease her for the moment. However, I had just established my willingness to be bullied, and that was a terrible precedent to set. Not to mention that my reaction to the threat to Steph had amply demonstrated where my weak spot was.

I finished my glass of wine and immediately poured another.

Emma's threat was a declaration of war.

For now, she was content to bully me, but as long as she misguidedly saw me as a rival for Anderson's affections, she was going to hate me. And I had no illusions that her hatred wouldn't turn into an all-out campaign to get me kicked out of the house. And hell, if that didn't work for her, I had no doubt the threats would escalate. Steph was an obvious, easy target, and I was under no illusion that Emma would hesitate to hurt an innocent bystander. And that meant it was time to start planning for the worst.

From the beginning, I'd told myself that my stay at Anderson's mansion was temporary. When he'd first offered me shelter, I'd figured my choices were to move in—thereby obtaining protection not only for myself but also for my adoptive family—or to leave everything I knew and loved behind and go into hiding in hopes the Olympians would leave my family alone as long as I wasn't around. I hadn't wanted to lose my job, my home, my family, or my way of life, so I'd chosen to accept Anderson's protection.

Finding Emma was supposed to have cemented

my position within Anderson's *Liberi*. It was supposed to be the proof of my sincerity, the proof that I was not a secret Olympian spy.

And it might ultimately turn out to be my downfall instead.

Grim reality was staring me right in the face. I was never meant to be part of Anderson's team, not for the long haul. Believing he and the rest of his *Liberi* could give me the home and the sense of belonging I'd lacked all my life had been a nice fantasy, but it was time to wake up. I would stand on the sidelines and let Kerner continue his reign of terror against the Olympians, and that would keep Emma out of my hair for a while. When Konstantin was dead, I would resume my hunt in earnest, and I would stop Kerner from ever killing again.

But the only way to protect Steph in the long run was for me to get out of her life.

I doubted the Olympians would pick on her if I was gone, but even if they did . . . I felt sure Anderson and his people would look out for her. Especially Blake, who I thought really did care about her.

To make her safe, I had to give up everything that was important in my life, including her, including my parents . . . and including the *Liberi,* the only people in the world I would not outlive. I would be alone, in the most fundamental of ways, always keeping secrets, always on the run. At least, when I'd been bouncing around between foster homes, I'd been able to hope for the future, for the day when I would be an adult with the power to control my own destiny and create my own home. If I fled from the *Liberi,* there would be no hope to cling to.

But Emma was a threat I couldn't protect Steph from. Not when Anderson refused to see her for what she really was. A threat from the outside I might have had a chance against, but not this. I owed Steph and her parents way too much to reward them by subjecting them to this kind of risk. So no matter how much it hurt, no matter how terrifying my future might be, I had to leave.

Sixteen

My resolve to let Kerner have his way with the Olympians lasted almost forty-eight hours. Right up to the time I found out he'd abandoned his once-a-week schedule and made another kill already.

I'd spent most of my time since Emma had confronted me sitting at my computer in my room, avoiding all human contact. I didn't want to get any more attached to Anderson's *Liberi* than I already was, not when I was planning my escape. Instead of trying to make any progress on finding Kerner, I'd been working on picking a new home and planning the new identity I was going to have to adopt. My work as a P.I. had given me plenty of experience finding people who didn't want to be found, so I knew what traps to avoid, but it was still going to be damned hard. I was going to have to swallow my scruples and dip into my trust fund, because I was going to need the cash. I would have to find a new job—there was only so long the cash would hold me unless I wanted to carry suitcases of it—and it would have to be one where I could get paid under the table. And I'd have to find somewhere to live, with a landlord who wouldn't start asking questions when I paid my rent in cash. All in all, it was a daunting, depressing prospect.

It wasn't until after dinner that I decided to check up on the day's news to give myself a break from all of the questions and anxieties that pinged back and forth in my brain. The first screaming headline I read rocked me back in my chair: CAPITAL MAULER STRIKES AGAIN.

I wondered when the press had started referring to Kerner as the Capital Mauler. Perhaps as soon as the police had admitted that the killings were not the result of wild dogs.

A prominent lobbyist had been mauled in his home sometime after midnight, along with his wife and their live-in maid. Police were called to the scene after neighbors were awakened by the screams, but no one saw anything. They wouldn't, of course, since Kerner could make himself and his jackals invisible.

I was willing to bet that both the lobbyist and his wife had been Olympians. However, the maid couldn't have been, because there was no way in hell an Olympian would be willing to do menial labor. The poor woman must have gotten in the way.

Goddammit. I wanted to punch my computer screen. So much for Kerner's vow that he wouldn't target civilians anymore. Though perhaps from his point of view, he *was* keeping his promise. It was possible the maid would have lived if she hadn't some-how gotten in Kerner's way, that he hadn't actively targeted her.

Not that the distinction meant squat to the maid, or her family, or me. Yet another innocent bystander was dead. Maybe I couldn't have prevented last night's attack—after all, I'd had no reason to think the next attack would come so soon—but if I spent any more time wringing my hands and worrying about Emma, then the next death definitely *would* be on me. And I couldn't have that.

Trying to contain my rage, I stomped out of my room and headed for Anderson's office. The door was open when I arrived, but he wasn't inside. Which was probably just as well, because I didn't know what to say.

No matter what, I had to stay on Anderson's good side, or I'd never be able to stop Kerner. I might be able to *find* the crazy son of a bitch on my own, but I didn't think I could single-handedly defeat him. Which meant I needed Anderson to keep trusting me, something he likely wouldn't do if I starting slinging accusations at his wife. Especially not after she started slinging her own back.

Crap. I couldn't bring Anderson in on this. The moment I started flapping my gums, Emma would bring out her accusations. And if I got lucky and Anderson didn't believe her, then I would have to worry that she'd retaliate against me by hurting Steph.

No, whatever I ended up doing, I was going to have to keep Anderson out of it. I might have hoped that

Emma would take pity on the maid who'd died and change her mind about stopping Kerner, but I didn't bother trying to fool myself. As long as Kerner was a deadly weapon aimed at Konstantin, she wouldn't care who else got hurt along the way.

I took a few deep breaths to calm myself, then left Anderson's office. I'd felt fairly muddled until the moment I learned of the maid's death, but now everything was coming clear in my mind.

I couldn't let Kerner run free, no matter what horrendous threats both he and Emma had made. And I couldn't take Kerner down alone, no matter how much simpler it would have been if I could. Which meant I needed an ally. Someone who would understand my dilemma and be willing to go behind Anderson's back to help me.

My first thought was Maggie. She was my best friend among Anderson's *Liberi,* and her super-strength might come in handy. Asking Maggie would have felt safe and comfortable, but it took only a moment's thought for me to realize it would be anything but.

I hadn't known her—or anyone in this house—for all that long, but I knew she was not a rule breaker. She regarded Anderson's word as law, and if I brought this to her, she would insist we tell Anderson everything. Maybe there was an off chance I could persuade her not to spill the beans once I shot my mouth off, but there was no way she'd risk Anderson's wrath by helping me.

In the end, there was only one person I believed

might see things my way and might be willing and able to help me. If I was wrong about this, I was massively screwed. So I crossed my fingers and prayed that I wasn't wrong.

Jamaal wasn't in his suite. Or if he was in, he wasn't answering the door. The next most logical place to look for him was on the front porch, but he wasn't there, either.

Somehow the whole day had slipped away from me, and the sun had gone down. The temperature had dropped, and I went back inside to grab a jacket. It wasn't until I was slipping the jacket on that I wondered why I was going back outside when Jamaal clearly wasn't there. I hadn't seen him since he'd stormed off after kissing me. For all I knew, he'd never come back to the house.

I decided to treat my impulse to put on a coat as if it were one of my hunches and headed out to the garage to see if Jamaal's car was there. Sure enough, the black Saab was inside.

If he were anyone else, I would have checked inside the house first, maybe looked in the kitchen or the den, but my instincts were telling me he wasn't there. I let those instincts guide me and wandered around to the back of the house.

There was a nicely manicured lawn in the back, but Jamaal wasn't there. From the lawn, I could look through the kitchen windows and confirm my hunch that he wasn't inside.

Shivering and wishing I'd gone with a heavier

jacket, I crossed the lawn and headed into the woods. The last time I'd been out this way at night, I'd been carrying a lantern to light the path, but tonight I had to rely on the moonlight. Luckily, the night was clear, the moon just past full, and I could see well enough to pick my way through the trees toward the clearing about a hundred yards from the woods' edge.

It was in that clearing that Jamaal had twice been executed, once by beheading and once by hanging. It was also in that clearing that he'd voluntarily allowed himself to be tied to a stake with kindling at his feet, willing to suffer the torment of burning if that was what it took to convince Anderson of his commitment to controlling himself.

Anderson had never ordered the fire lit, had been satisfied that Jamaal was willing to do whatever it took to avoid being kicked out. Logically, the clearing should be the last place I expected to find Jamaal. If I'd been in his shoes, I would have forever associated the clearing with pain and death. But Jamaal was not me.

I kept going until I finally broke through the trees and into the clearing.

The silver-blue moonlight revealed Jamaal's tall, imposing form as he stood in the center of the clearing. He was facing me, but his eyes were closed, his face a picture of concentration. His muscles were taut with tension, and despite the cold, there was a faint sheen of perspiration on his brow.

I stopped at the edge of the clearing and just watched him stand there, fighting whatever personal demons were troubling him. If he was in the process of trying to curb his death magic, I had a feeling it would be a very bad idea to interrupt him.

On the other hand, I felt like a voyeur for standing there and watching him like that. Especially when I couldn't resist drinking in his masculine beauty. As long as his eyes were closed, I could finally drink my fill without worrying about the consequences.

Moonlight and shadows accentuated his high cheekbones and sensuous mouth, and his stark white T-shirt fit tightly across his muscled chest. If I'd been wearing a top that light, I'd have been freezing, but he showed no sign of being cold. His breath frosted the night, but the sweat on his brow shone in defiance.

As I watched, Jamaal began trembling with strain, and I bit my lip in worry.

I didn't know exactly what he was doing, but I suspected the trembling and sweating was not a good sign. I took a careful step backward, thinking that now might be a good time to make myself scarce. I'd seen Jamaal out of control before, and I never wanted to see it again.

I should have retreated, but something inside me held me rooted in place. Jamaal's trembling increased, his chest heaving with heavy pants. Then his legs seemed to give out under him, and he dropped to his knees.

"Jamaal!" I cried in alarm, and I found myself running toward him instead of away.

Even on his knees, he was swaying, and he propped himself up with his hands, his head bowed to his chest. I scrambled to a stop beside him, my body working on autopilot as I knelt and put a hand on his shoulder.

Heat seemed to radiate from his body, and I almost snatched my hand away in surprise. He was burning up.

"Jamaal, are you okay?" I asked, wondering if I should be running back to the house to get help. "What's happening?"

He made no effort to jerk away from my touch, and I took that as a bad sign. Or maybe I should have considered it a good sign, in that he wasn't going berserk and attacking me, which was what I might have expected him to do if he'd just lost a battle against his death magic. I moved even closer to him, sliding my arm around his shoulders in hopes that I could help keep him upright. If he collapsed, I wouldn't be able to get him back up again.

Sweat soaked his thin cotton T, but even in the few moments I'd been by his side, the intense heat of his body had begun to recede. He was still breathing hard, and his muscles quivered beneath my touch, but I hoped his cooling off meant that whatever it was had passed.

"Do you need me to get help?" I asked, and he shook his head. It was the first sign he'd given that he even knew I was there. His teeth started chattering. I hastily unzipped my jacket and threw it over his shoulders. It was probably too small to be much help.

Jamaal had recovered enough to give me a withering look at the gesture, but I ignored it. As long as I didn't know what was wrong with him, I thought the chances were good he needed the warmth more than I did.

"What happened?" I asked again.

He took a shaky breath and raised his head. The sweat had cooled on his brow, but his eyes seemed to have sunk deeper into his head, and he looked exhausted. He glanced at me quickly, then looked away. I thought that meant he wasn't going to talk, but he surprised me. In more ways than one.

"You were right," he said, with a grimace that said it physically pained him to admit it. "What you said the other day about channeling the death magic."

My feet were falling asleep, so I shifted so that I was sitting on the ground instead of kneeling on it. I gave Jamaal a slight smile. "I know I was right. But which point are you conceding? I think I made a bunch of them."

Jamaal didn't smile back. But then, his sense of humor never had been exactly well honed.

"Take it easy," I said, still smiling despite the chill of his stare. "I'm just trying to lighten the mood." He seemed to be inching his way back toward normal, and I couldn't see that as anything but a positive sign. "Tell me what happened." Third time was the charm, right?

"I just tried to channel the death magic. Tried to make it manifest like Kerner does. Only I have no idea how to do it."

Considering how violently he'd rejected the idea when I'd suggested it, I was pretty surprised he'd even tried it.

"Well, *something* happened," I said. "Aside from the fact that you collapsed, you were burning up when I first touched you. Is that normal for you when you use death magic?" I remembered how he'd collapsed after killing Kerner's last human victim. Obviously, the death magic had some serious side effects.

Jamaal slipped my jacket off his shoulders and dumped it in my lap.

"I'm not cold anymore," he said when I opened my mouth to protest. "And to answer your question, no, that isn't normal. It exhausts me when I unleash it, but that feels different." He touched his chest, then made a face and pulled the damp cotton away from his skin. "It doesn't make me sweat like this."

And it probably didn't make him into a human radiator, either.

"So maybe that's a sign that you're on the right track," I suggested. "If it were an exercise in futility, it probably wouldn't have had any effect on you at all, right?"

Jamaal might not be cold anymore—though I suspected that was a bit of alpha-male posturing—but *I* sure was, so I slipped my jacket back on. It was still warm from his body, and I hugged it around me to chase off the lingering chill.

Jamaal shrugged. "That's one way of looking at it." He reached into his jeans pocket and pulled out his tin of cigarettes and a book of matches. His hands shook slightly as he flipped the tin open and selected a half-smoked joint.

"But I'm guessing from the fact that you're skipping the cloves and going straight to the pot that it didn't relieve the pressure at all."

Jamaal lit up and drew in a deep drag, closing his eyes as he allowed the smoke to linger in his lungs. He blew it out slowly, and some of the tension in his shoulders eased.

"Nope," he said, offering the joint to me.

I declined with a shake of my head, and he took another drag.

"I'm sorry," I said, wishing I had something more productive to say.

"I'll try it again later, when I don't feel like I've been run over by a truck. You're right that *something* happened." He met my eyes, and for the first time since he'd snapped out of it, his gaze held. "I've never *tried* to use the death magic before. It's always been something to fight against, something to suppress. Even when Emmitt and I were venting, it was more like I was letting the magic go than I was actually trying to *use* it."

He was scared of it, I realized, though I was smart enough not to say it. No one else I knew, except for Anderson, had so destructive a power. If I could kill someone without even touching them, and I didn't know exactly how my power worked, you can bet I wouldn't go around experimenting with it, either. It would be like going into a nuclear submarine and pressing a random button just to see what it did.

Jamaal cocked his head at me. "What are you doing out here, anyway?"

"Looking for you."

The wariness in his expression was almost insulting. "Why?"

I took a moment to rethink my decision to confide in Jamaal. Spending more time with him than absolutely necessary was dangerous to both my physical and my mental health. Not to mention that he still looked kind of out of it.

I couldn't tell whether that was the voice of wisdom talking or just cowardice. Either way, I couldn't stop Kerner by myself, and though I couldn't say I trusted Jamaal unreservedly, I thought he was the most likely of Anderson's *Liberi* to help me without telling Anderson. Besides, I'd already determined that once I'd stopped Kerner, I was going to have to bite the bullet and leave to protect myself and Steph from Emma's malice. So even if I found myself getting more attached to Jamaal, it wouldn't matter, because I'd be gone.

Crossing my fingers, hoping I wasn't making a big mistake, I told Jamaal about Emma's ambush.

"You should tell Anderson," was Jamaal's prompt response. "If you tell him what happened, she won't have anything to blackmail you with."

I hadn't been expecting that response from Jamaal, so I hesitated a moment before I responded. "But even if I tell him what happened, Emma will just give him her side of the story afterward. Which one of us do you think he'll believe?"

Scorn lit Jamaal's eyes. "Any fool can see that Emma is out of her fucking mind. She was always a drama queen, but she's gone completely around the bend."

"Yeah, any fool can see that. But can Anderson?

He's in love with her, and love does funny things to people's perceptions."

"He's too smart to fall for such blatant manipulation," Jamaal retorted, but there was doubt in his voice.

"I don't think smart has anything to do with it. He blames himself for what she went through, and he's going to put up with a hell of a lot of shit from her he wouldn't take from the rest of us."

Jamaal chewed that one over for a bit. I figured the fact that he hadn't dismissed my argument out of hand was a good sign, though he wasn't jumping up and down with enthusiasm at the idea of keeping secrets from Anderson.

A wisp of chilly air made me shiver, even in my jacket, and I couldn't imagine how Jamaal could be sitting there in his short-sleeved T-shirt without seeming to notice that it was freezing out. My teeth were starting to chatter.

"Do you think we could continue this conversation inside somewhere?" I asked as I hugged myself for warmth. "You may not have noticed, but it's the middle of winter."

I thought I saw a hint of amusement in his eyes. "You're the one who came out here looking for me, remember? You could have just waited until I came back to the house."

I gave an indelicate snort. "Yeah, because I was really in the mood to sit around twiddling my thumbs waiting for you. Can we go back to the house now, or would you rather sit out here and freeze your tail feathers off some more?"

I rose to my feet and brushed off the seat of my pants, then offered Jamaal my hand to help him up. I wasn't at all surprised when he didn't take it. Nor was I surprised when he got to his feet and swayed dizzily. Even knowing that he wouldn't appreciate my help, I couldn't stop myself from reaching out to steady him. His biceps twitched under my hand, and I couldn't tell if that was from tension or from the aftereffects of death magic.

He pulled away from me, but for once, there was no rancor in the gesture.

"All right, you win," he said. "Let's go back to the house."

I bit my tongue to keep from offering him any more help, even though he still looked unsteady on his feet. I already knew the answer would be an abrupt refusal. Instead, I settled for walking intimately close to him, ready to help prop him up if gravity started winning the battle of wills. Based on the way the corners of his mouth tugged downward, I guessed he knew exactly what I was doing. The fact that he didn't snap at me for hovering told me that somewhere behind the testosterone, he knew he might end up having to lean on me whether he wanted to or not.

Jamaal's footsteps steadied as we neared the house. We entered through the back door near the kitchen, and I was severely tempted to take a detour for some coffee or hot chocolate. But Jamaal was being relatively accommodating at the moment, and I didn't want to risk any interruptions.

Even though he seemed to be doing much better

by the time we were inside, I kept hovering, sure the stairs were going to get the better of him. We hadn't discussed exactly where in the house we were going to continue our conversation, but I'd assumed we would go to my suite, which was, unfortunately, on the third floor.

Jamaal seemed to handle the stairs just fine, but when we got to the second-floor landing, he veered off toward his own suite instead of tackling the next flight. He didn't gesture for me to follow, but I did so anyway.

I'd never seen his suite before, and I have to admit to a great deal of feminine curiosity about it. I imagined his rooms being cold and austere, with a bare minimum of furniture and decoration. He just didn't seem the type to live in luxury or to care about appearances. But when he pushed open his door and I got a glimpse of his sitting room, I was immediately slapped upside the head with the realization of how little I knew Jamaal.

Most of the mansion's walls were painted a generic shade of ivory meant to be ignored. Jamaal's walls were painted a rich, golden tan that immediately lent warmth to the room. Burgundy drapes and a burgundy futon sofa added to the warmth. A small but elegant cherry-wood dining set was tucked into one corner, and the wall beside the door was covered in floor-to-ceiling bookcases. Those bookcases held mostly large, coffee-table-type books, some of them displayed face out so that their covers served as further decor. If those books were any indication, Jamaal had a connoisseur's taste in art, particularly Eastern art. Several of the proudly displayed books were catalogs from museum exhibits, though it was hard for me to imagine someone like Jamaal strolling through a museum.

I took all of this in with one quick glance before my eyes found the true focal point of the room.

It was a small, square painting set in a plain gold frame, showcased by a discreet museum-style light set into the wall above it. A figure I recognized from my research as the goddess Kali stood on the body of a naked man against a background of metallic gold. She was painted in a blue so dark it was almost black. Unlike many of the other depictions I'd seen of her, she was adorned not in severed body parts but in lotus blossoms and pearls, although, rather disturbingly, she also had a couple of hooded cobras twining around her torso.

I stepped closer to the painting and saw that there was a little wear and tear around the edges, proving that this was the real thing, not a print or a reproduction. It was beautiful, in a creepy kind of way.

"How old is it?" I asked Jamaal without looking away from the painting. On closer inspection, I noticed that there were little bits of iridescent blue-green paint decorating Kali's jewelry, and I figured the painting couldn't be that old after all if the artist had access to iridescent paint.

"Late sixteen hundreds or thereabouts."

I blinked in surprise, then looked over my shoulder at Jamaal, who had come up close behind me while I was focused on the painting. "Really?" He nodded. "Then what's the iridescent stuff?"

"It's actually little pieces of beetle wings."

"Oh."

Strange how one little painting could throw me for so much of a loop. I'd have thought it was some kind of family heirloom, except considering what Jamaal had told me of his background, I knew he didn't have any family heirlooms. Had he bought a work of fine art, or had it been a gift? And if it was a gift, who was it from?

I dragged my attention away from the painting and faced Jamaal. If I hadn't known better, I would have sworn he was embarrassed at having revealed this unexpected aspect of his personality. He averted his eyes and plucked at his T-shirt.

"I'm going to put on a fresh shirt. Be right back."

He disappeared into the bedroom without awaiting a response, leaving me with inappropriate images in my head. I couldn't help picturing him dragging that T-shirt off over his head. From the fit of his clothes and the cut of his biceps, I knew he would look spectacular without a shirt on. My hormones were more than happy to provide me with a mental image.

Jamaal hadn't closed the bedroom door, and despite my best intentions and a stern lecture from my common sense, I found myself drifting across the sitting room. I angled toward the bookcase, but the moment my vantage point allowed me to, I glanced through the bedroom door.

Like the sitting room, Jamaal's bedroom was decorated with a distinctly Eastern flavor in warm, inviting colors. A platform bed covered with a plush mahogany-colored bedspread dominated the room, which was so painfully neat it was hard to believe a single guy resided in it.

Jamaal was bending over to open the bottom drawer of his cherry-wood dresser when my eyes found him, and the sight was enough to steal my breath away. His jeans clung lovingly to his butt and thighs, and I decided the rear view was just as mouth-watering as the front view.

And then he stood up straight, a black and red football jersey in his hand, and I got a look at his naked back.

It shouldn't have come as such a shock to me, not after what he'd told me about his childhood. He'd been a *slave,* and though his father had apparently treated him "well," he'd admitted he'd had a hard life after Daddy Dearest kicked him out to appease the little missus. I just somehow hadn't allowed myself to think about what that kind of hard life might entail.

Ridged scar tissue riddled his back from his shoulders all the way to the waistband of his jeans, and I suspected it continued on below. I couldn't even imagine what kind of pain Jamaal had endured when those wounds were inflicted. Obviously, he hadn't been *Liberi* yet, or there wouldn't be scars, and I realized that although he'd told me about his childhood, I had no idea when and how he'd become *Liberi.*

The scars marred what would otherwise have been a perfect back. With his broad shoulders and narrow waist, Jamaal was a work of art in his clothes, but shirtless, he was even more stunning. I'd never seen someone who wasn't bulked up like a weightlifter and yet had had such perfect definition in his back muscles. Even with the scar tissue, I could see the ripple and play of those muscles as Jamaal stuck his arms into his shirt and pulled the neck opening over his head.

I stood there like an idiot, entranced by what I was seeing, as the shirt slid down his back and hid both his scars and his beauty. In fact, I was so entranced that I think somehow he sensed me staring, because he suddenly whirled around.

I was busted.

SEVENTEEN

I could have turned and pretended to be looking at the books on his shelf. He probably wouldn't have been fooled, but I didn't even bother to try. As long as he knew—or at least strongly suspected—that I'd been looking, I didn't want to do anything that might suggest I was repulsed by what I'd seen. Jamaal wasn't what I'd call the shy, sensitive type, but instinct told me those scars represented a serious chink in his armor.

Something dark and dangerous lurked in Jamaal's eyes as they locked with mine and he stalked toward me. His expression spoke of rage, of pain, and of something else, something I couldn't identify. I wanted to back away from what I saw in his eyes, but again, my instincts insisted doing so would be a mistake, would hurt him even more than he'd been hurt already. For all of the angry words he'd flung at me, for all of the times I'd seen him practically out of his mind with fury, I knew that at his core, he was a fragile and damaged human being. And I didn't want to be the one to make that damage irreparable.

Jamaal's lips curled away from his teeth in a feral snarl. "Get a good look?" He was still coming closer, and my pulse drummed in my throat. "Want a close-up?"

He lifted the front of his shirt, and I practically swallowed my tongue in my effort to keep from gasping. The scars weren't restricted to his back; their pale ridged lines sliced through his sculpted pecs and six-pack abs. It looked like he'd been through a paper shredder, and the sight of that devastation made my throat ache.

Without conscious thought, my hand reached for him, fingers wanting to trace his savaged skin as if I could somehow erase the marks. Jamaal's eyes widened in what looked like fear, and he dropped his shirt down and took a hasty step back before I could touch him.

I kept staring at his chest, even though the travesty of those scars was now covered. In my peripheral vision, I was aware of the way he was looking at me, a combination of hostility, scorn, and challenge on his face, but my vision was starting to blur with tears.

"Sometimes I really hate people," I murmured hoarsely, then cleared my throat as if that could dislodge the lump that had formed there.

Jamaal let out his breath with a loud whoosh, like the air rushing from a punctured tire. I seemed to have passed some kind of test, a test I hadn't realized I was taking, and Jamaal backed away from the edge, his intense glare replaced by an ironic half smile.

"You and me both," he said. He crossed his arms over his chest as if trying to build a thicker shield to keep those scars hidden.

"Did you kill whoever did that to you?" I blurted without thinking.

He laughed bitterly. "I was a slave, remember? If I'd killed anyone, I wouldn't be around today, believe me."

"But you killed someone eventually, or you wouldn't have become *Liberi*." He had to have taken his immortality from *someone,* and it would have been poetic justice if that someone was the sadistic bastard who'd tortured him.

Jamaal moved away from me, but he didn't go far, instead dropping down onto the futon sofa. I wanted to press him for information but managed to control my curiosity. His body language suggested he might continue talking, and I didn't want to say anything that might discourage him.

"It happened during the Civil War," he said. "My master at the time was neither particularly kind nor particularly cruel, but I hated him anyway. I pretty much hated everybody, black or white."

Considering what had been done to him, I could hardly blame him.

"Our plantation was attacked by a bunch of Union soldiers. And believe me, just because they were fighting on the side of the angels didn't make the men themselves angels. These guys were more like a rioting mob than an organized troop of soldiers. My master surrendered without a fight, and they shot him down in cold blood anyway.

"When the soldiers first came, I was thrilled to see them. I figured my life as a slave was over, and I could join the Union army and get my revenge on the people who'd oppressed me. I was angry enough that I probably could have looked the other way even after they'd killed an unarmed man, but then they started going after his family. They raped his wife, and they made his daughter run so they could chase her down. She was only twelve."

"I hate people," I muttered again.

Jamaal ignored me. "I didn't have much of a conscience left at the time. It had mostly been beaten out of me. But I couldn't just stand by while they raped a little girl, so I got my master's gun and started shooting the men who were chasing her.

"It was suicidal. I was just one man, and there were at least a dozen soldiers. I couldn't save the poor kid, but I figured at least I could go out trying to do a good deed." He shook his head. "Maybe at that point, I just wanted to die. I'd seen these soldiers as my salvation, and then to find out they weren't really any better than the people who'd tormented me most of my life . . ." He fell silent, his eyes clouded with memories of his haunted past.

"Did you save her?" I prompted, although everything about his body language told me the answer was no.

He shook his head. "I shot three of the soldiers before they got me, but like I said, I was badly outnumbered. I must have taken twenty or thirty bullets by the time it was all over. I should have been dead, but apparently, one of those three men I'd shot was *Liberi*. I woke up hours later, covered in blood, to see the plantation burned to the ground, still smoldering. There were bodies everywhere. The soldiers had slaughtered everyone, even the slaves they were supposedly there to free. That was probably because of me."

I made a sound of indignation on his behalf, but he shushed me before I could voice the objection.

"They were war-maddened thugs who got a kick out of raping and murdering civilians. By killing some of them, I gave the rest of them the excuse to view the slaves as the enemy. All because I was disillusioned and decided it was time to die." He gave a bitter laugh. "Kind of funny that I tried to commit suicide by soldier and wound up becoming immortal because of it."

"Hilarious."

My heart ached for everything he had been through. He'd been broken—or at least severely damaged—even before he became *Liberi* and had to deal with death magic that had a mind of its own.

"Did you have any idea what was going on?" I asked. "Had you ever heard of the *Liberi*?" As confusing as my own transition had been, at least I'd been surrounded by *Liberi* who could explain to me what was happening. I'd thought they were completely delusional, of course, but at least they'd provided me with some explanation.

What would it be like to awaken after being shot twenty or more times and have no idea why you weren't dead? I shuddered. I thought about the time when he had actually been dead, when he must have thought the airless dark was his own personal Hell. To go through that, having no reason to believe it would ever end, was unimaginable.

"Nope," Jamaal said. "I had no clue what was going on. Thought I'd gone crazy, actually. I thought I'd make it better by blowing my own brains out, but I woke up again after that. It wasn't until after the war was over that I ended up meeting another *Liberi*. He was a descendant of Odin, and he kind of taught me the ropes—including telling me about the Olympians and emphasizing how important it was to avoid them.

"Problem was, the bastard was bat-shit crazy and hated the world even more than I did. I lost myself under his influence for a very long time, and I did some very bad shit, let the death magic have its way with me. Until Anderson found me and convinced me it didn't have to be that way."

And then I came along, killed his best friend, who'd been helping him keep the death magic tamed, and put everything that was good in his life at risk.

My mind took me back to that fateful night, replaying a picture of that dark, sleet-slicked driveway, of my struggles to keep the car in control. A figure appeared out of nowhere, only a couple of feet in front of my car, no time to stop or swerve. My headlights illuminated his face as he raised his head and smiled at me in the instant before I slammed into him.

I shook my head violently to stop the playback in my head. I wished there were some way I could expunge those images from my brain for good. I'd relived them more than enough already.

"It wasn't your fault," Jamaal said gruffly, and I guessed my face had told him exactly what I was thinking about.

I swallowed hard, trying to keep my emotions under control. Jamaal was making a huge concession by admitting that, though I supposed he'd stopped blaming me long before. Now, if only *I* could stop blaming me.

"I know that," I forced out through my tight throat. "He set me up, and he basically did it to himself. But I had to make a couple of bad decisions for his plan to work, and I can't help wishing I'd made different ones."

When Emmitt had called and asked me for help, I'd agreed because I'd wanted an excuse to cut my bad date short. My gut had told me from the very beginning that there was something hinky going on, but I'd ignored it. That was Bad Decision Number One. Bad Decision Number Two—also known as Worst Decision Ever—was to go looking for Emmitt when he failed to show up at the rendezvous. Driving through those gates and onto private property was against the law, even if Emmitt had left them enticingly open, and I'd known that. I should have—

"But you know that if you'd made different decisions, Emmitt would have found some other way. The goddamned bastard had made up his mind and didn't care what anyone else wanted."

It was the first time I'd heard Jamaal express any anger toward Emmitt for what he'd done. Personally, I'd thought a number of times that I'd like to go back in time and kill Emmitt all over again for being so selfish. He had to have known how devastated Jamaal would be, and he had to have known, or at least have had an inkling of, what I would be put through thanks to his decision. But he hadn't cared enough about anyone to trouble himself about the consequences.

"Why didn't he talk to anyone?" Jamaal asked, the pain in his voice so deep I wanted to draw him into my arms. "If he felt so fucking bad he wanted to die, why didn't he say something, let us try to help him?" His voice was turning hoarse like he was crying, although his eyes were dry. "Hell, why didn't we just *know,* without him having to tell us anything? Why didn't *I* just know? We vented the death magic practically every day, and the days we didn't vent, he was teaching me to meditate to help calm my temper. How could I spend that much time with him and not realize he was fucking suicidal?"

Jamaal was on his feet and pacing before I could answer. There was so much fury in him he could barely contain himself, and I half expected him to start smashing up the room. But at the heart of that fury was pain. And, apparently, guilt. He was furious at

Emmitt for killing himself, but he was equally furious with himself for not seeing how depressed his friend and mentor had been.

"*No one* realized," I said gently. "He was obviously very careful to hide it." I stood up, moving slowly because I knew Jamaal was on a hair trigger. "You can't blame yourself."

He was in my face between one blink and the next, hands gripping my biceps as he leaned down and snarled at me. "The fuck I can't!"

I should have been scared of him at that moment. He was so furious I half expected to see sparks flying off him, and I'd had firsthand experience with how savage he could be when his temper snapped. I should have said something noncommittally soothing, appeasing the dangerous madman. Instead, I found my own temper rising to meet his head-on.

"Oh, get over yourself!" I snapped, making no attempt to escape his bruising grip. "First, you decide I'm the one and only person to blame for Emmitt's death, and now you've decided it's all your fault and you're using it as an excuse to act like an asshole. Why don't you just grow up and deal with it like everyone else has to?"

As soon as the words left my mouth, I wondered if I was doing the equivalent of lighting a match while wading in a pool of gasoline. I held my breath and waited for the explosion.

Jamaal stood frozen in speechless shock. His hands still gripped my arms, but they weren't squeezing as hard, and his eyes went comically wide, like he couldn't believe I'd just said that. To tell you the truth, *I* couldn't believe it.

When he didn't immediately go ballistic, I forced myself to let go of the breath I'd been holding. Yelling at him had been cruel when I knew how wounded he was, and I felt like a mean-spirited bitch for doing it.

"I'm sorry," I said, shaking my head in amazement at myself. "I didn't mean that."

Jamaal's shoulders relaxed, and the rage drained from his eyes. I didn't think the bleakness that replaced it was much better. "Yes, you did. And you were right. I just . . . I can't seem to keep a lid on it. All this shit keeps bubbling out, no matter how hard I try to keep it together."

He finally seemed to realize he was touching me, and his hands quickly opened and dropped to his sides. He sank back onto the sofa, his head in his hands.

"I don't know what to do," he said, and I could barely hear him because he was talking to the floor.

I joined him on the sofa and put my arm around his shoulders. Maybe he didn't like to be touched— especially by me—but I just couldn't help myself.

"You'll figure it out," I told him as I ran my hand up and down his back. "Either you'll figure out how to make it manifest and vent it that way, or you'll figure out how to keep it leashed. I have confidence in you."

Don't ask me where all these words of encouragement were coming from. I'd lost my rose-colored glasses long ago. Jamaal had all the signs of being a ticking time bomb, and logic said that that bomb would eventually go off. I did not want to be around when that happened, and I had no reason to believe Jamaal could control himself indefinitely.

So why was I telling him I had confidence in him? And, even more mystifying, why was that actually the truth?

Jamaal raised his head and met my eyes. He started to say something—something scathing, judging by the look on his face—but he stopped himself.

"Why?" he asked, still holding my gaze. "Why would you have confidence in someone like me? I'm a total fuck-up."

"Beats me," I responded, coaxing a hint of a smile out of him. My heart did a little flip at the sight of that smile. I swear, if that man actually let the smile take over his face, he'd stop traffic.

And just like that, all of the angry energy that had been zipping around the room changed into something entirely different.

EIGHTEEN

I'd been attracted to Jamaal practically from the first moment I'd laid eyes on him. It was an attraction that was purely physical, but that didn't make it any less real. Until recently, I hadn't had any evidence that he'd shared even one iota of that attraction.

Okay, yeah, he'd kissed me that one time, but that hadn't been a *real* kiss, so it didn't count.

The way he was looking at me right now *did* count. His luscious dark-chocolate eyes practically smoldered—with something other than rage, for once—and he seemed to be holding his breath, like he was stunned into immobility by a sudden bolt of desire. No, wait, that was me.

I leaned in to him just slightly, unable to stop myself. His scent of cloves and smoke, which had once made my nose wrinkle, now evoked an erotic cologne, making my pulse soar. His lips were so lush and sensual, made even more so by the elegant lines of his face, with its high cheekbones and artistic curves.

I told myself to back off, to get off the couch and run if that was what it took to snap myself out of the fog that was overtaking me. I reminded myself of all the reasons even trying to be friends with Jamaal was a bad idea, never mind trying to be anything more. I even tried reminding myself of the awful night when Jamaal had ambushed me, preventing me from getting to Steph and saving her from Alexis's clutches.

That memory was almost enough to kill the arousal, because, let's face it, it had been one of the worst nights of my life. Not because of the beating Jamaal had delivered—that hadn't been any fun, but I'd been too hopped up on adrenaline and fear to be much affected by it—but because of what had happened to my sister because of it.

I should hate Jamaal for getting in my way, even though he'd had legitimate reasons at the time to think I was a traitor. A guy beating me up was not something I should be able to forgive and forget, even granted my history of being attracted to inappropriate men.

None of that mattered as our eyes remained locked and he slowly lowered his head.

I breathed in his scent as his braids clickity-clacked with his movements, my eyes half-closed and my lips parted. A little voice in the back of my head was still trying to talk me out of it, but it was no more than background noise, easily ignored.

When his lips touched mine, my nice, sane inner

voice, the much-vaunted voice of reason, abandoned me completely.

Who'd have thought a broody, angry man, a death goddess descendant with a badly damaged soul, could kiss like an erotic dream come true?

His kiss of the other day had been all aggression and dominance, with neither tenderness nor subtlety behind it. This, however, was something different altogether.

Those full, sensual lips of his brushed over mine lightly, teasingly, drawing a little sound of need from somewhere deep inside me. My hands found their way around his neck and locked on, prepared to fight for what my body wanted if he came to his senses and backed off.

That, however, was not a valid concern.

Jamaal put his arms around me and drew me closer as his lips continued their delicate exploration. I had no objection whatsoever to getting closer, having yearned to get to know his body better for quite some time. My hands slid down from his neck to his back, exploring the muscles that rippled beneath his shirt as I returned his kiss and tried to be patient.

I didn't have to try for very long, because Jamaal was apparently as impatient as I. He deepened the kiss, his tongue sliding into my mouth for a delicate taste.

Seeing as he was a smoker, his tongue should have tasted like an ashtray to me, a flavor I would tolerate as the inevitable price for the pleasure of his kiss. Apparently, my brain never got that memo, and a hungry, raw sound rose from my throat.

I wanted to get closer still, so I squirmed until Jamaal's grip loosened enough to let me move; then I straddled him on the sofa. His hands slid down my back until they cupped my ass, and I groaned at the touch. Then, as I settled myself on his lap, I felt the significant bulge in his pants, growing bigger and harder by the moment.

Oh. My. God. I'd thought I was hot before. But that oh-so-tangible evidence of Jamaal's desire seemed to set my very nerves on fire.

I buried my hands in his hair as I opened myself completely to his kiss, my rational mind consumed by my desire. I played with the coarse braids, explored the intricate beading, all the while pressing myself more firmly against him. Without my even noticing, my hips started to rock, and he rose to meet me.

My hands couldn't get enough of him, eager to touch bare skin. I started to pluck at the bottom of his shirt, but he distracted me by shifting in his seat so he could lay me on my back on the sofa. His body came to rest between my legs, sending a flush of heat and hunger through me.

My hands slid down Jamaal's back. The football jersey was thin enough that I could feel the ridges of the worst of his scars. His weight shifted on top of me, the movement dislodging my hands. I made a little sound of protest, until I realized he was just making room for his own hands to explore.

His fingers trailed from my throat down my collarbone to the little V of skin revealed by my button-down shirt.

Our eyes met as he began opening the buttons one by one. The heat in his eyes made me wish we were already naked in his bed.

He only made it through two buttons before he impatiently thrust his hand inside, cupping my breast. I gave a soft cry of pleasure, raising my head and demanding his kiss. He obliged me as he worked his hand under my bra. The brush of his fingers over my nipple fanned my hunger even higher. I hadn't thought that was possible.

I reveled in the sensation of skin on skin, but I wanted more, *much* more. One of my arms was trapped between my body and the back of the sofa, but my other hand was free. I smoothed that hand down Jamaal's back once more. I couldn't reach the hem of his shirt, so I just grabbed a handful of fabric and pulled up until the small of his back was revealed. Finally, bare skin.

I let go of the jersey and touched my hand to his back.

And the moment my fingers made contact with bare skin, Jamaal went stiff, and not in a good way.

He broke the kiss and jerked away from me, jumping to his feet so fast it would have been comical in another situation. One where I wasn't lying there on the sofa so desperate for the touch of his hands that I practically wailed. My nipples ached, and there was that low, insistent buzz of hunger in my belly, a hunger that could only be satisfied in one way.

But though I was still all achy and desperate, Jamaal had clearly lost the mood. His back was turned to me, and I forced myself up into a sitting position in hopes I could at least get a glimpse of his face.

What I saw there dampened the fire inside me.

Jamaal's eyes were too wide, white showing all around the irises, and there was a glazed look to them. This wasn't the way he looked when he was about to go Incredible Hulk, but I still got the impression that the Jamaal I knew had left the building. I wouldn't have believed it if I hadn't seen it with my own two eyes, but it sure as hell looked to me like he was afraid.

But of what?

"Jamaal?" I asked tentatively. "Are you all right?"

Stupid question; I could see that he wasn't, though I had no idea what was wrong.

Stupid question it might have been, but at least it seemed to draw him back from wherever he'd disappeared to. He blinked a couple of times, and his eyes cleared. He glanced quickly in my direction, then averted his eyes and slid his hands into his pockets. His shoulders hunched a bit, and he turned away from me.

I took a deep breath to compose myself, then stood up and went to him, putting a hand on his shoulder but not making any more intimate gesture. His muscles quivered under my touch, like he was fighting the urge to pull away. I'd have been hurt, except I didn't think whatever was going on had much to do with me.

"Tell me what's wrong," I urged him, though I honestly didn't know if a man like him was capable of sharing anything that might resemble intimate details. Even the things he'd told me about his past had been lacking real depth, like he was giving me the Cliffs Notes version.

"It's not you," he said hoarsely, and if it had been someone other than him, I might not have been able to resist making some wisecrack about the famous cliché. "I just . . ." But he couldn't seem to finish his own sentence, falling instead into a brooding silence.

I might not be a genius where relationships are concerned, but I could put two and two together with the best of them.

Jamaal's back was riddled with scars. He'd pulled away abruptly the moment I had touched those scars skin-to-skin. Ergo whatever was wrong had something to do with the scars.

Was he self-conscious about them? He certainly had seemed to get prickly about me having seen them, but I didn't think it was self-consciousness that had made him run away from me as abruptly as he had. This was something more visceral than self-consciousness.

Should I press him about it? Or should I just figure he'd tell me in his own good time?

I honestly don't think of myself as a particularly pushy person. Sometimes I'm almost embarrassingly ready to ignore the elephant in the room and skip out on potential conflict. But with Jamaal, I was having a damn hard time finding my emotional balance, and I found myself incapable of letting it go.

"You don't like when someone touches your scars," I said.

Jamaal moved away from me, his body language screaming of tension. "Just leave it alone," he said tightly. "We have more important things to talk about, like—"

"Not right this second we don't." Yes, I did still have a sense of perspective. I knew figuring out a plan to stop Kerner was more important than having a Dr. Phil moment. I also knew neither of our minds would be fully in the game if we were both distracted by what had been left unsaid between us.

"Tell me what that was all about," I insisted.

Jamaal's eyes flashed, telling me he didn't appreciate how I'd made that into an order. Not that I was in any position to give orders.

"It's none of your business," he grated.

"You can't honestly believe that. Not under these circumstances."

His glower became even fiercer. "I believe you need to back the hell off. We shouldn't have let things get that far, anyway."

He was sealing the cracks in his emotional armor with alarming speed, and there was nothing I could do to stop him. Maybe what had caused him to back off had nothing to do with me touching the scars; maybe he'd just been scared he was letting me get too close.

Curiosity, desire, and common sense battled within me, but common sense won out. I could see that Jamaal had fortified his defenses against me, and any further attempts I made to breach them would only make him dig in his heels more firmly.

It wasn't easy to let it go, but I managed somehow.

"Fine. We won't talk about it. Yet. But someday, when this whole mess with Kerner is over, you and

I are going to have a long talk." My stomach knotted up as I remembered that when this mess was over, I would be hitting the road and wouldn't be having any long talks with anyone.

Secure in his victory, Jamaal visibly eased back from the edge. He arched an eyebrow at me. "You think so?"

I nodded briskly and hoped my face hadn't given away my sudden burst of gloom. "Yep."

The arousal of our little make-out session hadn't fully faded yet, but I did the best I could to shove it to the background of my mind. Later, I'd probably regret letting things go as far as they had, and I'd be grateful that Jamaal had put on the brakes, but for now, I had to battle my own frustration.

Rebuttoning my shirt, I plopped back down onto the futon. I really wanted to go back to my own suite to pull myself together and lick my wounds—possibly even to do a little sulking—but I'd sought Jamaal out for a reason, and sex wasn't it.

"All right, then," I said with a sigh of resignation. "Let's talk strategy."

Nineteen

Not surprisingly, it was a little hard to change gears back into problem-solving mode. Especially when Jamaal was brooding and I was suffering from an acute case of sexual frustration. I knew Jamaal still wanted to tell Anderson about Emma's threat, but, at least for the time being, he was willing to respect my desire to keep Anderson out of the loop.

From hours of staring at my map, I had determined approximately where Kerner spent his days—or at least, I had a theory about where he spent his days. That didn't necessarily mean I was right, and even if I was, I didn't know which of the likely cemeteries Kerner actually hung out in. The fact that Kerner was most likely hiding in a cemetery made Jamaal into a less-than-optimal ally, but I had no other choice but to use him as my co-conspirator.

"I won't go apeshit the moment I set foot in a cemetery," he assured me. "It took a couple of hours for me to lose control that first time. We'll just have to make sure we don't need that much time to track Kerner down."

I bit my tongue to avoid pointing out that my power wasn't as predictable as that. He already knew.

"So what do we do if we find him?" I asked. "I'd really rather not be a jackal's chew toy again. That wasn't fun."

"If the jackals are a manifestation of Kerner's death magic, then it's possible they wouldn't be able to hurt me; Emmitt's magic couldn't." He frowned. "At least, it couldn't when I countered it with my own. I'm not sure if I'd have to target Kerner or the jackals."

Whichever one he didn't direct his death magic at would be all over me. Assuming his death magic had any effect at all. Which sounded like a pretty big, scary if.

"I could act as a diversion," Jamaal continued. "Draw off Kerner's jackals while you take him out with a shot to the head. It wouldn't kill him permanently, of course, but if you can knock him out of commission, that'll take care of the jackals, and we can . . . do what we need to do."

I found it interesting that Jamaal was unwilling to put into words exactly what it was we needed to do to keep Kerner contained. I couldn't blame him, and I still hoped that somehow I'd be able to persuade Anderson to do the right thing. Which was almost certainly wishful thinking on my part, because Anderson was not an easy man to persuade, and he obviously felt very, very strongly about keeping his damn secret.

"But if you're wrong about the death magic . . ." I said.

Jamaal shrugged. "If I'm wrong, then I get mauled. I'll still be a distraction, and we know how to 'cure' the rabies. I'd rather not go through that, but I'm willing to if that's what it takes."

I have to admit, I was impressed at the nonchalance with which he offered himself up. No, he didn't act like he was all eager or anything, but he was willing to put himself through hell—a hell he'd personally experienced before, so he knew exactly what he was getting into—to stop a bad guy. I like to think that I'd have been able to do the same thing, take one for the team if it were necessary, but I wasn't so sure. I'm not a total wimp or anything, but I've never thought of myself as particularly brave, either.

"All of this assumes we can even find him," I said, not at all secure in my ability to do so. All I had was a hunch that he was in one of two places. The cemeteries were relatively small, compared with, say Rock Creek, but if Kerner realized I was there, he could lead us on a merry chase, and we might never catch up to him. At least, not until the proximity to the dead pushed Jamaal over the edge.

"Maybe we need him to find us instead," Jamaal suggested.

That might be the way it happened, whether we wanted it to or not. After having warned me off, Kerner would probably turn out to be a little grumpy if he saw me poking around. Maybe he would come out of hiding to show his displeasure. But I didn't know if we could count on it. He was crazy but not stupid. If he saw us looking for him, he'd know we were rejecting his deal, and he might play hide-and-seek with us, then go find some innocent victim on whom to take out his frustrations.

"Maybe isn't good enough," I said. "We need to draw him out for sure, or we'll get people killed."

What would draw Kerner out of hiding?

The first thing that came to my mind was Konstantin. Kerner's plan was to torment and terrify Konstantin by taking out his Olympians one by one, but it was Konstantin himself he hated most, and he might not be able to resist the temptation if he thought Konstantin was within his reach. Of course, there was the small problem that in order to use Konstantin to draw Kerner out, we'd have to get hold of him. Somehow I didn't think that would be so easy.

"Do you think there's some way we can trick Konstantin into meeting us at one of the cemeteries?" I asked, thinking out loud. "If we could jump him, we could use him as bait." And wouldn't it be a shame if we used him as bait and then didn't manage to stop Kerner until Konstantin was dead?

I felt a brief twinge of shame for thinking like Emma, but all I had to do was remind myself what had happened to Steph on Konstantin's orders, and I didn't feel bad about it anymore. If we could kill Konstantin *and* capture Kerner, it would be an entirely satisfying mission.

Jamaal gave me an incredulous look that told me just how impressed he was with my idea.

"That was a joke, right?" he asked. "Konstantin would smell this rat from a mile away. And even if we could trick him out into the open, he's a descendant of Ares. He could take the two of us in a fight with his hands tied behind his back. There's a reason he's been the leader of the Olympians for so long, and it's not because he's an easy target."

I gave him a dirty look. "Come up with a better idea. Then you can criticize all you like."

We mulled things over for a few minutes, both lost in thought. I could see the moment an idea struck Jamaal by the way his eyes suddenly sharpened with interest.

"You've got something?" I asked.

Jamaal frowned thoughtfully. "Yeah. I think. But you'd have to be willing to let someone else in on the plan. You willing to do that?"

I didn't like that idea one bit. The more people who knew, the more likely someone was going to blab to Anderson, and that could be a disaster.

"Depends how good your idea is," I answered cautiously. "And who the someone is."

"Getting hold of Konstantin would be the next best thing to impossible. But getting hold of someone who could *impersonate* Konstantin would be doable."

I had to think about it a second before I got it. "Jack," I finally said. I still hadn't taken the time to look up Loki on the Internet, but clearly Jack possessed strong illusion magic. And he could change into a dog. It wasn't much of a stretch to imagine he could disguise himself as Konstantin.

Jamaal made a face—he couldn't seem to help expressing distaste when Jack's name came up—but he nodded. "He can create an illusion that no one would be able to see through."

The idea had merit, I had to admit. "So we have Jack disguise himself as Konstantin, then we drag him out to the cemeteries and parade him around until Kerner makes an appearance." A few more things clicked into place in my mind, and I found myself liking the idea more and more.

"We can pretend we grabbed Konstantin to hand him over so that Kerner won't kill any more innocents on his way to his main goal. Maybe we can have Jack make his illusion look like Konstantin is in rough shape, extra vulnerable."

Jamaal shrugged. "I suspect if Kerner gets a look at Konstantin, his brain will short-circuit, and he won't bother worrying that it's too good to be true. Some temptations are strong enough to make people forget to be cautious."

He had a point, but I suspected we were getting just a bit ahead of ourselves. It sounded like Jack might be an extremely useful ally if we were going to take Kerner down, but . . .

"Are we really willing to make a plan that relies on Jack?"

I didn't feel like I had much of a read on Jack. Being part of Anderson's crew made him automatically one of the good guys—I trusted Anderson's judgment where anyone but Emma was concerned. But his trickster heritage made him unpredictable. Would he think it was more "fun" to rat Jamaal and me out to Anderson, thereby getting us into trouble he might find entertaining to watch? Not to mention the fact that he and Jamaal weren't exactly the best of friends.

Jamaal made a dismissive sound. "The little shit will get a kick out of going behind Anderson's back."

Was I crazy, or was there a hint of gruff affection beneath Jamaal's expressed disdain? He made such a habit of snarling it was hard to take it very seriously or personally, but I'd always assumed his animosity toward Jack was real and heartfelt.

"That isn't exactly what I'd call a rousing endorsement," I pointed out.

"Come up with a plan that doesn't require illusion magic, then."

"You're not being very helpful," I grumbled.

Jamaal didn't bother with a response, which was just as well. He was right, and for the plan we'd come up with, we'd need Jack's help. I still didn't like it. I was used to working alone, and it had taken some adjustment to get used to thinking of myself as part of a team. I didn't like having to trust other people, especially someone as mercurial as Jack.

There was that, and there was also the fact that even if our plan worked out perfectly, Anderson would be furious with us. Then, if Emma threw a little more gasoline on the fire by trotting out her accusations against me, I could find myself in big trouble. There were makeshift prison cells in the basement of the mansion—Anderson's version of the preschooler's "time-out"—and I didn't want to think about what would happen to Steph if I found myself locked up in one. Emma would have a field day. And that was the best-case scenario! If our plans failed, it would be much, much worse.

If I'd been able to think of another plan, even if I'd just had an inkling of one, I'd have seized it. But I had nothing, and I wanted to stop Kerner before he killed again.

"All right," I said reluctantly. "Jack's in. Assuming he agrees to join us, that is."

"Oh, he'll join us, all right," Jamaal said with complete confidence.

I gave him an inquiring raise of the eyebrows.

"Sneaking around? Doing something recklessly dangerous? That is so his cup of tea. He'll be all for it."

"Great," I answered while trying to silence my internal alarm bells. Either my gut was trying to tell me that this plan sucked, or I was suffering an acute bout of paranoia. I wished like hell I knew which one.

TWENTY

After reaching our decision, Jamaal and I sought out Jack—who was surprised to see us, to say the least—and laid it all out for him.

Jamaal was right, and Jack was more than eager to participate. I would have liked to have gone running out to the cemetery right that moment and get the whole mess over with, but I managed to put a lid on my eagerness.

The phases of the moon seemed to have an effect on my hunting abilities, and though the moon was near full tonight, it was cloudy out. If I had more moonlight, I'd have a better chance of tracking Kerner down, and the clouds were supposed to clear during the day.

I discussed timing with Jack and Jamaal, and we all agreed it would be best to wait until the next night to implement our plan. We needed to stack the odds in our favor as much as possible.

Not surprisingly, I couldn't sleep that night. Let's face it, I was scared. There were so many things that could go wrong with our plan. And even if everything went perfectly, I knew I had to make myself disappear before Emma realized I was reneging on our "deal." The only reason I was still hanging around was that I needed to stop Kerner first.

In the wee hours of the night, I packed my bag, taking only the essentials, and snuck through the darkened house out to the garage while no one was around to see me. I stashed the bag in the trunk of my car. Tomorrow night, regardless of what happened with Kerner, I would make my escape.

I didn't think I could bear to say good-bye, but I couldn't just disappear without a word. I spent the rest of the night composing letters of farewell to those who mattered most to me: Steph, my adoptive parents, Anderson—who needed to hear the truth, even if he refused to believe it—and, yes, Jamaal. I even wrote a short note for Blake, asking him to take good care of Steph.

It was a good thing I composed those letters on my laptop, because if I had been writing by hand, I'd have smudged the ink with my tears. You never appreciate what you have as much as you do when you've lost it. I wished I could hug the Glasses one more time before I disappeared from their lives completely— thanks to their cruise, it had been weeks since I'd seen them. More than anything, I wished I could hold on to the fantasy of being part of Anderson's team, of living with fellow immortals who knew my secrets and would remain constant as the years, decades, and centuries passed. I had tried to keep myself aloof from them, and I had failed miserably.

As the long, slow hours of the night crept by, I couldn't help wondering if the best-case scenario wasn't for the jackals to get me. But I wasn't Emmitt, to think only of myself and my own needs. If I went on the run tomorrow, it would hurt Steph and our parents—and maybe some of the *Liberi*—pretty badly, but at least they'd know I was alive. And maybe in their own minds, they could imagine a better and brighter future for me than the one I knew was coming.

As consolations go, it wasn't much.

We met on the front porch at a little after nine the next night, going out one at a time so that no one would see the three of us leaving together and wonder what we were up to. I was the last to arrive, because I'd waited until the last possible moment to print out my farewell letters, seal them, and leave them on my desk. Seeing those envelopes neatly lined up on my desk had made everything seem much more real. My heart was already aching with loss, and I hoped like hell Steph would one day forgive me for leaving her like this. I was pretty sure she would understand, but understanding isn't the same as forgiving.

I wondered if this was how my mother had felt when she'd walked out of that church without me. Had she had a good reason? Had she hoped I'd forgive her someday?

I shook the thought off. This wasn't the same thing. Steph wasn't a child, and I wasn't disappearing without a word. *Yeah, like leaving a typewritten note is going to make it all better.*

Jeez, I was a maudlin bundle of nerves tonight, but who could blame me under the circumstances? When I stepped out onto the porch and found Jamaal smoking a joint, I was almost tempted to ask him to give me a puff. But somehow I didn't think adding drugs to my anxiety and sleep deprivation was going to be an improvement.

While my stomach was tight with dread and Jamaal was smoking the joint because he needed it to help him stay calm, Jack seemed more excited than nervous. He watched Jamaal smoking with a hint of amusement in his eyes.

"You gonna share that?" he asked hopefully. Jamaal gave him a withering look, and Jack pouted.

"You're bad enough sober," I said, to save Jamaal the trouble of responding. "I don't want to be around you if you're stoned."

Jack grinned at me. Sometimes I swear I thought his face had frozen that way. "But it doesn't bother you to be around a stoned death goddess descendant?"

"I'm not getting stoned," Jamaal snapped, playing right into Jack's game as usual. Amazing how easily Jack was able to provoke him. And that he'd lived to tell about it. "I'm just trying to keep the death magic quiet."

"Riiiight," Jack drawled. "And you read *Playboy* for the articles."

"Guys," I interrupted before Jamaal could react, "let's not start this, okay?" I glared at Jack, though I'd never seen any evidence that glares affected him. "If you set Jamaal off before we even get in the car, you'll have screwed up our plan at step one, because it'll be noisy, and someone will wonder what the hell we're up to."

Jack's eyes twinkled with mischief, and Jamaal grumbled something under his breath that I was perfectly glad not to have heard. I ignored them both and headed out to the garage, glancing over my shoulder at the lighted windows behind me, hoping no one would see us. But who sits around looking out windows at night?

We made it to the garage without incident and without anyone from the house seeming to notice us. The moment we were inside the garage, Jack started in on the troublemaking again, reminding me of all the reasons why I'd hesitated to include him in the plan.

"I'm driving," he announced, pulling a rabbit's-foot key fob out of his jeans pocket.

"No," Jamaal and I replied in concert.

I'd ridden in a car Jack was driving once, and I had no desire to repeat the experience. Besides, my bag was in the trunk of *my* car, and I intended to drive myself. I knew Jamaal wouldn't want to get into the Mini, so that meant we'd have to take two cars— which was perfect, because I didn't want to leave Jamaal and Jack stranded when I made my getaway from the cemetery.

"I'm never getting in a car you're driving again," I said. "At least, not without a blindfold and Valium."

"That can be arranged," Jack answered, undaunted. "Jamaal's stoned, and you're going to need all your concentration for the hunt."

"I am *not* stoned," Jamaal gritted out. "Stop being such an asshole."

"I'm driving," I declared. I unlocked the Mini and reached for the door. "If you have a problem with that," I said over my shoulder to Jamaal, "then you can drive your own car, and we can do rock, paper, scissors to figure out who gets stuck with Jack."

To my surprise, Jamaal opened the passenger door like he was fine with the idea of riding with me. It meant I was going to have to strand them at the cemetery after all, but I wasn't going to renege now that I'd already offered.

Jamaal started folding the seat forward to let Jack into the backseat, then paused with a thoughtful look on his face.

"We shouldn't take the chance that Kerner might see Jack riding around in the backseat while we're looking for a place to park. We should have our cover all ready to go by the time we get there." He turned and looked at Jack, his expression almost gleeful. "You should ride in the trunk and be in your Konstantin disguise by the time we open it to get you out."

Crap. This was not a contingency I'd planned for. I didn't want the guys to know I was planning to bolt. Maybe they wouldn't try to stop me—I doubted Jack cared one way or another, and with the dangerous undercurrents that ran between us, Jamaal might be just as happy to see me go. But even if they didn't try to stop me, I knew they wouldn't let me go quietly and without fuss.

"You won't give me a hit, *and* you're going to make me ride in the trunk?" Jack said. "Man, you two are cold."

Jamaal surprised me by holding the joint out to Jack, which made Jack laugh.

"No, thanks," he said. "Never touch the stuff."

Jamaal took one last drag, then stubbed out the half-smoked joint and put it away. He blew his smoke directly into Jack's face. Jack laughed again but not until after he stopped coughing.

"My trunk is too small for Jack to ride in," I said, trying to sound casual. "Maybe you guys should take the Saab, and I can meet you there."

Jack's form shimmered, and seconds later, there was a fluffy white miniature poodle, complete with a pink bow and painted toenails, sitting where he had been. The poodle made an impossibly long leap and landed on the passenger seat, then put its paws on the dashboard and panted eagerly, tail wagging furiously, looking for all the world like a real dog excited for a car ride.

Jamaal rolled his eyes. "Size isn't an issue," he informed me unnecessarily as he grabbed the poodle by the scruff of its neck and lifted it off the seat. He held the poodle up to his face and glared at it. "This is not a laughing matter, so quit with the hilarity."

The poodle nodded solemnly, then flicked out its

long, almost froglike pink tongue and licked Jamaal's face. Jamaal made a choking sound and tossed the poodle away from him hard enough to make me wince in sympathy. Jack resumed his human form before he slammed into the wall of the garage. He let out a soft "oof" and slid to the floor on his butt, but it didn't seem to put a damper on his sense of humor.

"You should have seen your face!" he said, laughing at Jamaal as he picked himself up off the floor. "Priceless! If only I'd had a camera."

"Whose idea was it to bring Jack?" Jamaal asked me with a look of chagrin. He wiped at his face where Jack had licked him but showed no sign that he might be losing control of his temper. Which was pretty impressive, considering *I* might have lost my temper in his shoes.

"Yours," I reminded him, then smiled, realizing he'd just made something approximating a joke.

He scowled but with less ferocity than usual. "Pop the trunk."

And here I'd been hoping Jack's prank might miraculously make Jamaal forget about his brilliant idea for deception. I tried to think of a good excuse not to put Jack in the trunk, but I came up empty. Either I had to let the guys see that I was ready to bolt, or I would have to change my mind about taking my own car. The latter meant I'd have to come back to the mansion later, and I didn't think that was a good idea.

While I was still hemming and hawing, looking for a third option, my trunk popped open of its own volition. I leapt out of the car with a startled gasp and saw Jack peering curiously into the trunk.

"How did you . . . ?" I let the words trail off as I realized my car keys were no longer in my hand. I tried to remember what I'd done with them after I'd opened the locks, but I couldn't recall. Not that it mattered—one way or another, Jack had relieved me of them and opened the trunk.

"What's all this?" Jack inquired, blinking at me innocently.

Jamaal peeked over Jack's shoulder and made a low growling sound. So much for my clandestine getaway. I fought the urge to hang my head. I hadn't done anything wrong.

"Emma's going to take this as a formal declaration of war when she finds out," I explained. "I can't be around when that happens. If she were just going to come after me, that would be one thing, but she's threatened Steph."

Jamaal's face was hard and cold. "And you think the rest of us are just going to sit idly by and let Emma hurt your sister?"

"What are you going to do to stop her?" I asked, shaking my head in exasperation. "Are you going to put her under twenty-four-hour surveillance? Lock her in the basement? Besides, I'm getting you two into enough trouble with Anderson as it is. I've got enough crap eating away at my conscience already. It's better for everyone if I just get out of here as soon as this is all over."

Jack shrugged like it didn't matter to him one way

or another—which it probably didn't. "Suit yourself," he said, then reached into the trunk and pulled out my suitcase, lugging it to the backseat and shoving it in. "We'll call Anderson to come pick us up—and help us get Kerner permanently contained—after you've blown his brains out and taken off."

Jamaal just stood there looking at me reproachfully. The needy little girl in me wanted him to argue with me, wanted him to show some evidence that he wanted me to stay. Even if that evidence was him yelling at me for being a coward. But all I was getting from him, apparently, was the evil eye. And that wasn't anywhere near enough to persuade me.

Since no one seemed inclined to say anything more, I got back into the car and fussed with the rearview mirror, though its angle was just fine. The trunk slammed shut, presumably with Jack inside, and Jamaal slid the passenger seat as far back as he could get it before climbing inside. He didn't look at me, and I couldn't read the expression on his face. Which was probably just as well.

Blowing out a breath and telling myself I'd worry about my future later, after I'd survived the night's mission, I started the car and headed out.

The Hebrew Cemetery was the closest of the likely candidates for Kerner's home base, so I drove there first. Neither Jamaal nor I spoke for the entire ride. It wasn't a companionable silence. I'd have broken it if I could have thought of something to say.

The moon was conveniently high in the sky,

and there was nothing more than the occasional wispy cloud to block its light. The perfect night for a hunt. As I neared the cemetery, I tried to listen to my instincts and get a feel for whether Kerner was there or not, but I felt nothing. No surge of excitement, no quickening of my heartbeat, no conviction that this was the place. I drove around the block, circling the cemetery, just to be sure, but there was nothing. Either Kerner wasn't here, or my powers weren't going to lead me to him.

Jamaal still hadn't spoken to me, and he made no comment when I veered away from the Hebrew Cemetery and started wending my way toward our next destination, a pair of cemeteries to the northwest. I suppose he figured out that my radar hadn't picked up anything without having to ask me about it.

The silence had taken on a life of its own, and I squirmed with discomfort. I wished I knew what Jamaal was thinking.

Did he think I was a coward for running? Was he pissed off at me for trying to sneak away without telling him good-bye? Was he regretting the fact that we could no longer explore whatever it was that was going on between us? Or was he glad I would finally be out of his life because of all the ways I'd screwed him up?

I mentally growled at myself to keep my head in the game. What Jamaal was feeling, what *I* was feeling, was irrelevant at the moment. All that mattered was finding and catching Kerner. When that was over, I could wallow to my heart's content.

Jamaal cleared his throat, and I jumped, realizing I'd spaced out a bit while getting a head start on the wallowing. I looked around, disoriented and not sure where I was.

"Is there a reason you turned onto Suitland?" Jamaal asked.

I glanced at the street sign as I came to a stop at an intersection. Sure enough, I had somehow ended up on Suitland Road when I was supposed to be on Alabama Avenue. There was no traffic, so I could easily make a U-turn, but I felt a strange reluctance to do it.

I started the car rolling forward into the intersection and was about halfway into the U-turn when it occurred to me I might have made that wrong turn for a reason. I mentally pictured my map of D.C. and its environs, with all of the cemeteries marked with little stickers.

Just across the D.C. limits into Maryland, there was a cluster of three cemeteries, and Suitland Road led directly to those cemeteries. I didn't think it was a coincidence that I'd turned down Suitland while I was spaced out.

I made my U-turn into a clumsy circle and kept going down Suitland. It felt right.

"I think Kerner is in one of the cemeteries on the other side of the D.C. border," I told Jamaal when he gave me a strange look. He nodded but didn't say anything, still giving me the silent treatment.

I drove until the cemeteries came into view, then found a conveniently dark parking space off one of the side streets. We might not want Kerner to see Jack riding around in the backseat, but we also didn't want civilians seeing us dragging our Konstantin lookalike from the trunk of the car. The pool of shadow formed by a burned-out streetlight was perfect for our purposes.

I looked at Jamaal and swallowed hard as my palms began to sweat with nerves.

"I guess this is it," I said, and I hoped I didn't sound as scared as I was. It was one thing to plan a confrontation with Kerner and his jackals from the safety of the mansion, quite another to actually walk out into a darkened cemetery as bait for a crazed serial killer.

Jamaal nodded sharply at me without making eye contact. "Let's do it," he said, and stepped out of the car.

I took a deep breath for courage, then popped the trunk and stepped out onto the sidewalk.

Despite knowing what to expect, I still did a double take when I looked in the trunk and saw Konstantin's body wedged in there. Jack had apparently decided Konstantin would have needed a lot of subduing, because his disguise included an impressive array of swollen, angry-looking bruises, as well as handcuffs, rope, and even some duct tape. Not only that, but he lay still in the trunk with his eyes closed, as if unconscious. Or dead.

I looked at Jack's disguise more closely and saw what looked like a bullet wound in the middle of his chest.

"Jeez," I muttered, "isn't this a bit of overkill?"

"Konstantin is a war god descendant," Jamaal

reminded me, his voice just as low as mine. "It would take a lot to subdue him."

Jamaal checked up and down the street, looking for potential witnesses, but there was no one around. Then he leaned down and hefted Jack out of the trunk, throwing the supposedly unconscious/dead man over his shoulder. I noticed Jack had left a large bloodstain on the trunk's upholstery from his phony bullet wound.

"That blood better not be there when we come back," I said, and though he didn't move, I could swear I heard a little snort of amusement from Jack.

I slammed the trunk closed, then checked to make sure my gun was easily accessible. I'd stashed it in my coat pocket, not having a holster for it. A situation I should probably remedy if I was going to be trotting around D.C. carrying a concealed firearm on a regular basis.

Of course, I *wouldn't* be doing that, I reminded myself, because I was leaving as soon as we'd accomplished our mission.

The fence around the cemetery was purely ornamental, so low we could step right over it. I managed to trip anyway and almost went sprawling on the grass. My cheeks heated with embarrassment—not the most auspicious start ever—and I stared straight ahead so I didn't have to see Jack laughing at me.

"Which way?" Jamaal asked.

I didn't feel sure of anything, but I felt slightly more inclined to go to my right than my left, so I went with it. Jamaal, with Jack still draped limply over his shoulder, followed me as we wove our way through the headstones. The light of the moon was just enough to keep us from tripping and stumbling over the various obstacles.

We made it all the way to the fence on the opposite side of the cemetery without any sign of Kerner, and my senses were blurred and confused from thinking too hard. Probably the only reason I'd managed to bring us to this cemetery in the first place was that I'd distracted myself enough with my brooding that my body was able to follow subconscious signals.

Spacing out involuntarily is pretty easy, especially when you're stressed and sleep-deprived. Doing it on purpose, however, proved to be impossible. I tried to let my conscious mind drift, but I was too aware of the creepiness of walking through a cemetery at night and of the fear of facing Kerner and his jackals again.

I picked a direction at random and started walking again, reminding myself that our plan was for Kerner to find us, not the other way around. For all I knew, he was watching us right now, trying to figure out what we were up to.

"Kerner?" I called into the night. My voice was too soft to carry—it's hard to get yourself to shout in a cemetery—so I tried again. "Justin Kerner. We've brought you a present."

I waved my hand at Jamaal and his fake Konstantin. If Kerner could hear me, he wasn't answering.

"I guess we keep walking," I decided, and Jamaal fell into step beside me.

Our haphazard path took us all the way to the

fence once again, and I had a sinking feeling that Kerner wasn't going to bite. Either he knew this was a trick, or he had more self-control than we'd thought and wasn't willing to give up his slow revenge for the quick kill.

Jamaal and I turned around, preparing to plunge back into the heart of the cemetery, but we both came to an abrupt halt when we saw that we were not alone. A figure stood in the shadow of a tree, his features hidden by darkness.

I started to draw my gun, but when the figure stepped forward out of the shadow, the moonlight revealed that it wasn't Justin Kerner.

It was Anderson.

And boy, did he ever look pissed.

TWENTY-ONE

What the hell was Anderson doing here? I was certain no one had seen us leave the house, and even if I'd been wrong about that, surely I would have noticed if someone had been following us the whole way. I wondered for a moment if Kerner was a shape-shifter of some sort—like Jack—and could make himself look like Anderson, but I quickly dismissed the idea. He wouldn't know Anderson well enough to match that uniquely pissed-off body language.

Jamaal slung Jack's body off his shoulder. He probably expected Jack to shift back into his real form and join us to face the music, but Jack just allowed himself to fall limply to the grass, still in his Konstantin disguise.

Anderson stalked to within a few feet of us, his eyes fixed on me the whole time like he knew this was all my idea. I had to fight the urge to hang my head in shame. I was only doing what I had to do to catch Kerner—without putting myself or my sister in Emma's sights. There was nothing to be ashamed of in that.

"How did you find us?" I asked when the pressure of silence became too much.

"I got a phone call from your accomplice," Anderson grated, "saying you were going to kidnap Konstantin and try to hand him over to Kerner. Without having discussed your Lone Ranger plan with me or the rest of the team."

Confusion struck me speechless, and I shared a puzzled look with Jamaal. If someone had told Anderson what we were up to, then he'd know we hadn't really kidnapped Konstantin.

Anderson glared down at our faux Konstantin, and I suddenly understood. He might be so angry he was thinking of whipping out his Hand of Doom, but Anderson wasn't going to blow our cover story just in case it was working and Kerner was nearby.

"Jack called you," I said in a flat voice, careful not to look at Jack as I spoke and give anything away. Obviously, putting him in the trunk where we couldn't see him had been a bad idea. "Why would he do a thing like that?"

"Perhaps because he thought you two are acting like idiots," Anderson snapped. He turned his glare to Jamaal. "I can understand why Nikki would do this under the circumstances, but what's your excuse?"

If I didn't know what I knew about Anderson, I would have found it almost comical to see a big, intimidating guy like Jamaal shrink from the rage of a much smaller, unprepossessing man. I don't think Jamaal was *afraid* of Anderson, per se, but he definitely held him in considerable respect.

"Maybe this isn't the right time or place to talk about it," Jamaal suggested.

I couldn't have agreed with him more. As angry as Anderson was right now, he was at least keeping his cool enough to maintain our cover. I didn't know exactly what Jack had told him, but I suspected hearing the details would send his temper into overdrive.

Anderson, apparently, didn't give a damn about any of these concerns, and I felt a shiver of unease when I saw just a momentary hint of white light in the center of his eyes, gone before I could be sure it was there. Jamaal might be able to dismiss that as some kind of optical illusion, but I knew I'd just seen a hint of the being who resided beneath Anderson's mild-mannered human facade. A being—a *god*—I wanted to stay as far away from as possible.

"I want to know what the two of you thought I would do if you'd brought this to me instead of going behind my back," Anderson said, flexing his right hand.

Surely he wasn't going to use his Hand of Doom on us. Not here, at least. Not if he thought Kerner might actually fall for our trick, which he must, or he wouldn't be keeping our cover.

"I wasn't worried about what *you* would do," I told

him, fighting a cowardly urge to step backward and out of range of his hand. "It was Emma I was worried about."

The little growling sound Anderson made in the back of his throat told me just how much that distinction meant to him. He started reaching for me, and I couldn't fight my instinctive retreat.

Anderson opened his mouth to say something, but his words were drowned out by a sudden chorus of feral growls.

Kerner's jackals appeared out of nowhere, surrounding us. There were eight of them that I could see, although there could have been others that were still invisible or hidden by tombstones or trees. I swiveled my head around but saw no sign of Kerner. I slipped my hand into my coat pocket, grabbing the gun, although I didn't draw it. As long as Kerner was out of sight, I had to pretend I was here in good faith.

The jackals circled us, growling and snarling, the circle growing tighter and tighter, but at least they weren't attacking. Not yet.

Beside me, Jamaal was standing with his eyes squeezed shut, and there was a thin sheen of sweat on his face. I couldn't understand why—even if Jamaal was afraid, he was the kind of alpha male who'd never dream of showing it. I reached out to him, but before my hand made contact, I felt the heat that radiated from his body and realized what he was doing.

"You're trying to do that *now*?" I asked incredulously. I was all for using every weapon at our disposal, but unless Jamaal had been practicing when I wasn't looking, a physical manifestation of his death magic was not on the menu. And if he failed, he'd be so weak and exhausted he'd be useless in a fight, which this was bound to come down to.

Jamaal, naturally, ignored me.

Anderson had, at least momentarily, forgotten his anger and was scanning the cemetery past the jackals, no doubt trying, like I was, to spot Kerner. I didn't think it was a coincidence that Kerner's jackals had pinned us in an area with lots of trees for cover.

One of the circling jackals broke from the pack and began stiff-leggedly approaching our faux Konstantin. I wasn't sure Jack's disguise would hold up to close examination. Did the jackals have a sense of smell? And if so, would they be able to tell the blood wasn't real?

I withdrew my gun from my coat pocket and pointed it at the jackal.

"Tell your dog to keep its distance!" I yelled.

The jackals growled more loudly, and I took a slow, deep breath to try to calm myself, but it was hard. The jackals weren't that big, but there were a lot of them, and I already had more than enough firsthand knowledge of their ferocity. Never mind the extremely unpleasant consequences of being bitten.

"If you're here to deliver Konstantin into my hands, then why do you want my jackal to stay away?"

Kerner's voice called, and sure enough, it was coming from behind a tree. He might be crazy, but he wasn't an idiot.

He had a good point, but right now, he had all of the advantages on his side. I couldn't see him, we were surrounded by his jackals, and we were on his home turf. I needed to keep him talking until we could somehow tip the scales to our advantage.

"Because I want some assurances before we hand him over," I said, improvising. Anderson looked at me with a raised eyebrow, then frowned at Jamaal, who was starting to breathe hard in his efforts to manifest his death magic.

Kerner laughed, and it sounded like he'd lost a few more inches of his sanity since we'd last spoken. Either that, or he was just embracing his cackling-villain role.

"You think you have any option *other* than handing him over?" Kerner asked, then laughed again.

I still couldn't see him, dammit! I wondered if I could make a trick shot and get my bullet to ricochet off one of the tombstones. I'd never tried anything like that before, so I didn't know just what the limitations of my supernatural aim were. Of course, if I tried that stunt and it didn't work, the jig was up. Kerner would bolt, and we'd be hard-pressed ever to track him down again. Somehow, I had to get him out from behind that tree.

I was trying to think of something to say that might tempt him to be incautious, but before I came up with anything, Kerner's jackal took a flying leap at Jack. My finger squeezed reflexively on the trigger, and the jackal went down with a very realistic yelp. I reminded myself that it was a phantom, not a real animal.

Kerner roared in rage but stayed behind the tree.

"I warned you not to do that!" he yelled, and then all of the jackals charged us at once.

Jack jumped to his feet, his form changing in mid-air until he was himself again, only this time clad in chain mail. In his hands, he held a baseball bat, which he swung at one of the oncoming jackals, making solid contact.

Hoping the sound of gunfire wouldn't bring any civilians running, I started shooting jackals right and left. Anderson disappeared from sight, but I knew he was still there because one of the jackals suddenly went flying backward with a yelp for no apparent reason.

Realizing I had a bit of an opening, I tried to scramble sideways so that I'd have a clear shot at Kerner—or at least at the spot where I thought Kerner was standing. It was only when I'd moved away a bit that I noticed Jamaal had fallen to his knees, his eyes still closed despite the chaos around him.

"Jamaal!" I screamed as I saw two jackals leaping at him. Jamaal didn't react.

I shot one of the jackals, but I wasn't fast enough to get both of them, at least not before one of them latched on.

I winced in anticipation even as I moved my hand to try to belatedly target the second jackal, but before I could steady my aim, Jack slammed into Jamaal from the side, knocking the bigger man to the ground. And leaving himself completely vulnerable.

The leaping jackal landed on Jack's back, its jaws snapping at the hand that held the baseball bat. Jack screamed and dropped the bat. I pulled the trigger and hit the jackal square in the head, but the damage had already been done. Jack was bitten, and that meant he had some serious hell to go through. Assuming he survived this, that is.

It was damned hard to turn away when my friends were in danger, but I knew my best chance of defending them lay in finding a clear shot at Kerner. Gun held out in front of me in hands that shook despite my best efforts, I continued moving away from the battle so I could get a look at the shadowed area behind the tree.

I got to where I had an angle, but there was no sign of Kerner. Either he had moved, or he was invisible. I suspected the former, because if he was invisible, he wouldn't have needed to hide in the first place. I shot at the empty space behind the tree, just in case, but there was no telltale cry of pain.

As soon as I fired off that shot, I cursed myself for stupidity. I'd been shooting at the jackals as if I had unlimited ammo, but my gun only held six bullets at a time. My shot into empty air was number six.

With my supernatural aim, six shots would usually be more than enough, but with Kerner's ability to re-create the jackals after I "killed" them, ammo was definitely an issue. I should have ignored the jackals from the beginning, just as Jamaal and I had planned, and gone straight for Kerner.

I had stuffed a handful of extra cartridges into my pocket, but it's kind of hard to reload a revolver during a fight, especially when ninety-nine percent of your experience with guns came from the firing range. My hands shook with adrenaline, and the various growls, snarls, and screams from the battle kept ratcheting the sense of urgency up and up and up. I was so rattled that I dropped the first cartridge when I fumbled it from my pocket.

With a curse, I bent to grab the cartridge, trying to move as fast as possible without rushing. Rushing was what made me drop the cartridge in the first place.

A deep-throated roar split the night, and I was so startled I almost dropped the cartridge again. Unable to resist the temptation, I spared a glance for the battle between my friends and the jackals.

Anderson was still nowhere to be seen, but that was only because he was using his death-god stealth. Jack was on his knees, cradling his bloody right hand to his body while he swung out seemingly at random with his baseball bat. And Jamaal sat on the ground with his eyes closed, not moving despite numerous bleeding wounds. But none of that was what stunned me into near immobility.

An enormous tiger ripped a jackal open from shoulder to hip with a casual-looking swat of its skillet-sized paw. The tiger roared again, and if the jackals had been real animals, they would have fled the scene with their tails tucked between their legs. But these were a crazy man's phantom constructions, and they didn't have the good sense to flee.

I forced my eyes away from the battle as I finally got a firm grip on the cartridge, and that was when I caught sight of Kerner, slipping through the trees away from the battle at a pace just short of a full-out run. I didn't dare lose sight of him, so I leapt to my feet in pursuit, even though it would be even harder to get the gun reloaded in the dark while running. A semiautomatic with an easy-to-change clip would have come in real handy.

Kerner glanced over his shoulder and saw me, and I thought for sure he was going to manifest another jackal just for me. Instead, he picked up speed, running toward a deeper patch of darkness amid another small stand of trees.

Just looking at that deeper darkness made the hairs on the back of my neck stand up. It was *too* dark. I remembered Anderson telling us that some death god descendants could open up entrances to the Underworld in cemeteries and that Kerner was one of them. If he made it into that darkness, he could reemerge anywhere, at any cemetery he wished, and who knew how many people he would kill in retaliation for my attempted trickery?

I wasn't skillful enough to reload while running, and if I stopped running, Kerner would make it through that portal before I could finish and shoot. So

I forgot about trying to reload and instead pumped my arms to give myself more speed, putting everything I had into an all-out sprint.

I was closing the distance between us at a good pace, but even so, I knew I wouldn't make it. He had too much of a head start. If only I hadn't fired that last bullet!

Hopeless though it was, I kept running. Kerner glanced over his shoulder in the moment before he hit the patch of blackness, and even in the dark, I saw his snarling smile of victory. As a last resort, I tried heaving my gun at him. I'd crushed a *Liberi*'s skull with a thrown rock once, but the gun wasn't as heavy as the rock, and though my aim was perfect, I'd waited too long. The gun struck Kerner in the temple, knocking him back—right into the portal.

My rational mind insisted it was time to wave the white flag. I was running headlong, and Kerner was even now disappearing into the darkness. If I didn't stop, either I'd find myself following him into the damned Underworld—assuming that was possible— or, more likely, I'd end up crashing headlong into a tree or a monument or something that was hidden behind the portal.

But this whole thing had been my idea, and even though I had accomplices, I held myself fully responsible for the result. If the result ended up being both Jack and Jamaal getting the super-rabies and having to go through the terrifying cure while Kerner escaped and killed a bunch of innocent people to punish me, I would never, ever forgive myself.

So I didn't listen to my rational mind. I kept sprinting even as Kerner disappeared into the blackness and the portal started shrinking in on itself. And when it became clear the portal would be gone in a fraction of a second, I threw myself forward, diving for the darkness like it was home plate.

TWENTY-TWO

My stomach crawled up into my chest as my arms and legs flailed through empty, black air.

I let out a breathless scream as I fell into what could very well turn out to be a bottomless pit. There was not a hint of light anywhere, nothing but complete blackness. I would have been completely disoriented if it weren't for the sickening falling sensation that let me know in no uncertain terms which way was down.

I couldn't help flashing back to the empty darkness of death, momentarily terrified that I had just plunged headlong into it, but there had been no falling sensation in death. And I hadn't been able to breathe or move my limbs, both of which I was doing just fine.

I wasn't dead. Not yet, at least. But assuming I wasn't going to fall forever, I might well be when I hit the ground, especially if I hit headfirst.

I'm not an acrobat, and the only time I ever went skydiving, I did it in tandem, where I didn't have to try to control anything. Still, I tried my best to orient myself and twist in the air until my feet were pointing vaguely downward, just in time to burst through the blackness into a lighter darkness. One that allowed me to see the rock floor rushing up to meet me.

My feet hit the floor with teeth-rattling force, and I rolled with the impact. My ankle twisted painfully, and I banged my hip so hard I was surprised I didn't break it. When I came to a breathless stop, I was pleasantly surprised to find I *still* wasn't dead. In fact, although I ached from head to toe and no doubt had a host of bruises to go with my twisted ankle, I was pretty sure I hadn't even broken any bones.

For a moment, I could do nothing but lie there on my back where I'd come to rest, staring at the black nothingness from which I'd emerged. Then I reminded myself that Kerner had come through before me, and I groaningly forced myself into a sitting position.

I was in what looked like a tunnel of some sort, although the walls disappeared within about seven feet into the blackness above. If I hadn't just fallen through that blackness, I would have said the tunnel was dark, but there was just enough ambient light for me to see the roughly hewn walls and the uneven floor. Don't ask me where that ambient light was coming from, though, because though I looked in all directions, I could see no source.

I'd obviously clocked Kerner pretty good with my gun, because even in the dark, I could see the smear of blood on the floor where he'd landed. There was another, hand-shaped smear on one wall, and a few drops on the floor marked which way he had gone.

I didn't have time to explore or absorb my surroundings. I had to catch up to Kerner before he disappeared back into the mortal world at some unknown location.

What I was going to do with him when I caught up to him was anyone's guess, as I was now officially unarmed. I glanced around on the off chance the gun had come through the portal with Kerner, but I didn't see it.

I started following the trail of blood, moving cautiously despite the sense of urgency that hammered at me. It was dark enough that I could only see a few yards ahead of me, and I had no idea what might be lurking in these tunnels.

The air was uncomfortably warm and smelled stale. I hoped there was enough oxygen. Then I wondered how the hell I was going to get out of here, but I shoved the thought aside. I would worry about that after I'd taken care of Kerner. And no, I still didn't have a plan for how I was going to do that.

I patted down my pockets in search of a weapon, anything heavy enough to take Kerner down with a really good throw, but the best I could come up with was my keys. Even throwing them as hard as I could and with perfect aim, I doubted I could kill Kerner with them or even knock him out. But it was all I had, and I wasn't going to accomplish anything by sitting around in the dark twiddling my thumbs.

The tunnel broadened as I followed it, but there were no branches. I could have stayed on Kerner's tail even without the helpful blood trail. But with every step I took, I became more and more convinced I'd done something unutterably stupid by diving into that portal.

I was unarmed and in unfamiliar territory. If Kerner caught sight of me, all he had to do was conjure a single jackal, and I had no way to defend myself. Who did I think I was to pit myself single-handedly against a supernatural serial killer? In the Underworld, no less, a place I wasn't sure I could escape from if I didn't have Kerner around to create one of his portals.

My mouth was dry, my skin clammy despite the heat, which seemed to be growing more oppressive by the second. Was I imagining things, or was there a hint of sulfur in the stale air? What *was* the Underworld, anyway? Was it Hell?

I blew out a steadying breath and continued forward until a soft growl emanated from the darkness in front of me. I came to an abrupt stop, hardly daring to breathe, as I strained my eyes, trying to see farther down the tunnel. Was there a patch of deeper darkness up ahead, darkness that might be the shadowed form of a jackal?

The beat of my heart seemed unnaturally loud

in the echoing silence of the tunnel. A bead of sweat rolled down the center of my back.

There was a scraping sound from up ahead, like claws scratching across stone, and the deeper pool of shadow moved. Enough that I could tell it was approximately jackal-shaped.

"You tried to trick me," Kerner's voice rasped from far enough down the tunnel that I couldn't even see him as a shadow. "I thought we had an agreement."

There was another growl, and I realized there was more than one jackal hiding just beyond the edge of the weak light. I was going to be torn apart, just like Phoebe had been. Unless I could find some way to talk Kerner out of it. But how do you reason with a madman?

"I thought so, too," I said, and I was proud of myself for not letting my voice quaver. "Then you killed that poor maid just because she was in the wrong place at the wrong time."

"She worked for an Olympian," Kerner argued with no hint of remorse. "She lived in his house. That makes her not a civilian."

"I don't see it that way."

"That's too bad."

I didn't get the feeling our conversation was increasing my chances of survival. The problem was, I didn't know what would. I could try throwing my keys, using Kerner's voice to target him, but I didn't know if that would work, and if it didn't, I could be sure the jackals would come for me immediately.

Anything that bought me just a little more time was worth it.

I took a couple of cautious steps forward. There was no point in retreating—I couldn't outrun jackals. Maybe if I could get closer to Kerner, I could figure out a way to stop him.

"Let's talk about this," I said in my best therapist voice. The jackals voiced their displeasure, and I stopped immediately.

"There's nothing to talk about!" Kerner snapped. And yet the jackals still hadn't attacked me. There had to be a reason for that.

"Maybe we can make another deal." My mind raced as I tried to think of what Kerner might want from me. And almost immediately, I came up with the answer.

Kerner wanted from me what *everyone* wanted from me.

"I could make it a lot easier for you to find all of the Olympians. And Konstantin, when the time comes." He didn't say anything, and I took that as a sign of encouragement. "I'm a descendant of Artemis." I was pretty sure he already knew that, but it didn't hurt to make certain. "I'm really good at hunting. It's why I've been able to find you as many times as I have."

There was more movement beyond the reach of the light, and I caught a hint of Kerner's foul reek blending with the sulfur smell of the air. He was moving closer, though he was still careful to stay out of sight.

"Why should I believe you'd help me?" Kerner asked. "You came with your friends to kill me. Not even kill me—to bury me alive for all eternity."

The jackals snarled and snapped, a couple of them stepping to the edge of the light so I could see the long, sharp fangs they bared. I swallowed hard.

"I'm descended from Artemis, not a death god," I said, hoping my voice sounded level and reasonable. "I wasn't really thinking about what I was doing when I followed you here, but I'm pretty sure I can't get out without your help. That's a pretty powerful incentive for me to help you, if you'll let me."

He thought about that for a long moment. "It's incentive for you to help me until you get out. Then you'll just turn on me. Like you did this time." The edge in his voice grew sharper, and I knew that I had to redirect him before his rage took over.

"I came after you this time because I considered that you'd already broken our agreement. I understand now that we were working off of different definitions of the word 'civilian.' It was a misunderstanding, not a breech of faith."

I found my own argument a bit of a stretch, but Kerner's silence suggested he was thinking about it. I decided my best strategy was to shut up and let him think.

"Follow me," he finally said, "but don't get any closer."

The jackals retreated into the darkness, and I heard the echoing sound of Kerner's footsteps. He hadn't indicated one way or another what he thought of my proposal, and I was not at all happy with the prospect of following him into more unknown territory. But what choice did I have?

I followed Kerner through the tunnel for what I'd guess was a couple hundred yards, timing my footsteps to his, getting growled at by jackals if he thought I was getting too close.

"Where are you taking me?" I asked once, but he didn't answer.

I kept my eyes peeled the whole way, looking for something, *anything,* I could use for a weapon. But there was nothing any more lethal that the keys I held clenched in my fist. If I could get Kerner into good enough light, I could try aiming for his eye. The keys weren't the most efficient throwing weapon in the world, but they could do an impressive amount of damage to something as vulnerable as an eyeball.

There was light coming from the tunnel up ahead. Dim gray light that wasn't particularly inviting, but who was I to be picky? As we approached the light, Kerner's form—and those of his jackals— was silhouetted. I could toss the keys and hit him in the back of the head—except I was too far away to get much oomph on the throw. I needed a more vulnerable target than the back of his head, and I needed to be closer so the keys would hit hard enough to do damage.

The jackals were quite determined that I wasn't to get closer.

The tunnel eventually opened out into an enormous cavern. And when I say enormous, I'm talking big enough to hold a small city. Which apparently it did. I came to a stop at the tunnel's opening and stared at what I saw laid out in front of me.

For as far as I could see, white marble buildings rose from the gray stone floor of the cavern, some of them so tall they flirted with the blackness of the ceiling—a ceiling that was considerably higher in the cavern than it had been in the tunnels.

The city was laid out in an orderly grid pattern, with one main road about three times as broad as any other leading up to something that reminded me very much of the Acropolis—only not in ruins. I shivered, even though the air was still uncomfortably warm. Some of the buildings were small and simple, little more than rectangular boxes with windows, but the larger, more elaborate buildings were adorned with columns and carved with bas-relief. In the dimness of the light, the carvings were nothing more than formless collections of shadow.

Nothing moved in the silent white marble city. Nothing except Kerner and his jackals, that is. The buildings looked like homes and temples and courthouses, but in the silence and stillness, they seemed more like elaborate mausoleums.

Uncommonly courteous for a crazed serial killer, Kerner gave me a moment to stand there and look around in awe before he started forward again. He didn't say anything to me, but I knew I was supposed to follow. The city gave me a serious case of the creeps, but I forced myself onward anyway.

Kerner led the way to the main street, turning down it and continuing on toward the big temple-like structure at its end. He was keeping me about thirty yards behind him, but the oppressive silence made his every footfall sound like a drumbeat in my ears. Or maybe that was just the beating of my heart. Empty windows stared down at me like malevolent eyes, and though the city felt dead, I kept expecting something to jump out at me from the shadows. It didn't help when I got close enough to one of the more elaborate buildings to make out the details of the bas-relief. It looked like the kind of thing you would see carved into the top of your average Greek or Roman ruin, with rows of figures in action. Except the figures were all skeletons.

Maybe it was just my imagination, maybe it was the dim gray light that gave everything an ominous look, or maybe it was just because I knew this was the Underworld, but I had a powerful sense that I didn't belong here, that the city wanted me gone. How an empty city could *want* anything is anybody's guess.

Every step I took involved a battle with my fight-or-flight instinct, which was all in favor of flight. Licking my dry lips with my dry tongue, I took a deep breath of sulfurous air and kept alert for any hint of something that I could use as a weapon. The city looked so ancient that it should be in ruins, but there were no convenient hunks of rock sitting by the side of the road.

At the base of the temple was a pair of circular

stone pits in the floor, looking for all the world like empty swimming pools, though I doubted that's what they were. They were about eight feet deep, their walls polished so smooth that the stone gleamed. As I neared those pits, Kerner had to go partway up the stairs leading to the temple's entrance to keep his distance.

"Stop there!" he commanded when I was a couple of yards from the pits. His jackals stood at the base of the stairs and growled at me in case I didn't get the hint.

Kerner turned around, and for the first time, I got a good look at him. Blood coated the left side of his face and neck and stained his already filthy coat. My gun had hit him right above the left eyebrow, and the damage it had done was more than a bloody scalp wound. I was surprised Kerner wasn't staggering around with a concussion. Then again, with the insanity he'd inherited from Lyssa's seed, his brain didn't exactly function like normal in the first place.

"I will accept your deal," Kerner announced from his perch on the stairs.

"Um, great," I said, though I knew it wasn't going to be as simple as all that. Kerner had led me here for a reason, and it wasn't just because he'd look impressive pontificating from the temple stairs.

"But I need a guarantee," Kerner continued.

I already didn't like it. "What kind of guarantee?"

Kerner smiled at me, an expression that couldn't help but look sinister on his bloody face. "I want you to hop into one of those cisterns. Either one, it doesn't matter. Then I'm going to go fetch a hostage or two. I'll put the hostages in the other cistern, and then I'll get you out, and we can go hunting together. Unless you want the hostages to die a slow and miserable death here in the Underworld, you'll need to keep me alive so I can free them for you."

No, I definitely didn't like this plan. I jumped when a jackal growled from behind me.

"Choose a cistern," Kerner commanded as I backed away from the jackal that menaced me.

The good news was that the cisterns would make the perfect place for me to contain Kerner once I'd subdued him—assuming he couldn't just create a portal back to the world above anywhere he pleased, but if he could do that, I was screwed no matter what I did. Now all I had to do was figure out how to get him into one of them. Maybe if I did as he asked, he would come closer to gloat at me.

I kept backing away from the jackal, looking back and forth between the two cisterns while keeping an eye on Kerner out of my peripheral vision. He was still too far away for me to hurt him with my keys, but he wasn't trying to maintain his distance anymore, and every step I took closer to the cisterns was a step closer to Kerner.

No matter what, I couldn't follow his instructions and jump into the cistern. If I did that, even if he came close enough for me to hit him afterward, he would just heal, and I wouldn't be able to get him into the cistern because I'd be stuck in it myself.

"I'm losing patience," Kerner said, and I realized what I had to do.

I was too far away to get a good shot at Kerner's head, and the jackals would attack me the moment I made a hostile move. They could run a hell of a lot faster than I could, but if I caught Kerner by surprise . . .

I took a deep breath, my hand spasming on the keys I still held, hard enough that I was sure I'd have key-shaped marks on my palms. This might be the craziest, most suicidal plan in the history of the universe. Even in the best-case scenario, I would be stuck in the Underworld forever. A frightened little corner of my mind suggested I go along with Kerner's plan and figure out how to rescue the hostages after I'd gotten out of there and taken care of Kerner.

But I couldn't do that. If I let Kerner get away, a lot of people would die for my cowardice. Maybe I'd find a way to rescue whatever hostages he brought, but I couldn't forget that in Kerner's mind, I'd violated our first agreement. When we'd made the agreement, he'd warned me he would kill innocents if I broke it, and I had no doubt he was still planning to do so. If I let him go now, he would return to the Underworld later with his hostages and with proof of how many innocents he'd killed to punish me.

It was now or never.

I hung my head as if in defeat, but I was really just trying to hide my face, making sure Kerner could read nothing in my expression that might give me away. I took a couple of hesitant steps forward, turning my body like I was going to head for one of the cisterns.

Then I charged Kerner.

TWENTY-THREE

Kerner and his jackals were so taken aback that for a moment, they didn't react. I let out a battle cry as I picked up as much speed as I could within a few steps.

Kerner recovered from his moment of shock, and suddenly, his jackals all leapt into action at once.

Hard though it was, I ignored the jackals, pulling back my right arm for a throw. I was still a bit farther away than I'd have liked, but at least I had the momentum of my brief sprint behind me as I hurled my keys at Kerner with every drop of strength I could muster, aiming not at his eye but at his wounded temple.

I put so much into the throw that I lost my balance, landing on the stone floor on my hands and knees. It turned out to be a lucky break, as a jackal sailed right through where I would have been if I'd kept my feet. I lashed out at one of the onrushing jackals with one foot, knowing it was a lost cause. A single bite was all they would need to kill me—assuming I never found my way out of the Underworld, which was a frighteningly good assumption.

A choked scream from above told me my keys had hit their mark, and the jackal I'd been trying to kick suddenly disappeared, my foot going through empty air. I looked up in time to see Kerner put both hands to his wounded head as fresh blood welled between his fingers. He staggered woozily and lost his footing on the stairs, tumbling down them and hitting his head numerous times on the way. When he reached the bottom of the stairs, he lay still.

I stayed on my hands and knees for a moment, hardly daring to believe I wasn't buried under a blanket of jackals. A vicious, fang-filled blanket. But I saw no sign of them, and Kerner wasn't moving.

Slowly, I rose to my feet and approached his body. A pool of blood was forming on the stone beneath his head. I wasn't sure whether he was unconscious or dead, but even if he was dead, it would only be temporary.

I didn't understand how Kerner's power worked. Could he create a portal anywhere in the Underworld he wanted to? Or were there certain places—like the tunnel we'd fallen into from the cemetery—that led back to the world above? I had to hope for the latter, or even trapping Kerner in one of the cisterns wouldn't keep him from escaping once he came back to life. Unless I were willing to stay by his side and pound his head into hamburger every time it came close to healing. I had the disturbing thought that if

I really was trapped down here till the end of time, I wouldn't have anything better to do. Though I supposed I would starve to death or die of dehydration periodically, which might give Kerner the time he needed to heal and escape.

Kerner reeked, and I didn't want to touch him, but I did it anyway, bending down and feeling for a pulse. There was none. Even if the blow from my keys hadn't been enough to kill him, the fall down the marble stairs had done the trick. Now all I had to do was drag him to the cistern and hope he couldn't just form a portal and escape.

Along with being disgustingly filthy, Kerner was also malnourished and as thin as a rail, but he still weighed more than I did. Dragging his dead weight— pardon the pun—toward the cistern was harder than I thought it would be, and I had to stop every couple of feet to suck air into my lungs. I was physically and emotionally exhausted, and fear hovered around the edges of my mind as I tried not to contemplate my bleak future. I wanted to sit down, hug my knees to my chest, and let loose with a fit of hysteria. Then maybe fall asleep and wake up later to find this was all a bad dream.

All of which I promised myself I'd do once I'd gotten Kerner into the blasted cistern. Gritting my teeth in determination, I bent down and grabbed Kerner's ankles to pull him another few feet closer to the cistern, which I could have sworn was moving farther away every time I turned my back.

"Need some help with that?"

The unexpected voice made me screech with alarm, and my clumsy attempt to whirl around was made even clumsier by my unfortunate mistake of putting my foot down on the edge of Kerner's leg. I fell awkwardly, getting blood and filth on me as I landed partway on Kerner's body.

I scrambled away, adrenaline still whipping me into a frenzy even as my rational mind realized it recognized that voice.

When I stopped my panicky retreat, I looked up to find Anderson standing a few yards away, his arms crossed over his chest as he regarded me with amusement. I closed my eyes and tried to calm my racing heart.

I'd allowed myself to forget that Anderson was a death god. I'd wondered once before whether he had the ability to travel into the Underworld. Now I had my answer.

I took a deep breath and let it out slowly. When I opened my eyes, Anderson was bending over me, offering me a hand up. I accepted his help, but he didn't let go once I was on my feet. He'd been smiling at me when I first caught sight of him, but he wasn't smiling now. I guess he was still mad that I'd gone behind his back.

"You could have gotten yourself, Jamaal, and Jack all killed tonight," he said, his hand tightening on mine enough to make my bones ache.

I swallowed hard, hoping he wasn't going to do the Hand of Doom thing. I'd have tried to pull away, but I knew it was pointless.

"I couldn't just let him keep killing people," I said. "And I couldn't let Emma know what I was doing. I couldn't risk Steph."

Anderson closed his eyes, but not before I saw the flash of pain in them. He let go of my hand, and I rubbed at my sore knuckles.

"She wouldn't have hurt Steph," Anderson said, but his voice held a trace of doubt. "Emma's not like that."

"Maybe she wasn't like that before the Olympians got to her. But she is now."

"Why didn't you come to me?"

"Is that a trick question?" Anderson scowled at me, and I held up my hands in surrender. "Because I didn't think you'd believe me. You want the old Emma back so much you refuse to see what she's become."

Anderson shook his head, either in denial or in disgust, I wasn't sure which. My heart ached way more than any of my physical injuries.

"I have a bag packed in my car," I said, forcing words through my tight throat. "I'll be out of your hair as soon as you get me out of here. Maybe if I'm not around, Emma will start to stabilize."

I didn't believe my own words, but it felt right to say them. "You *are* planning to get me out of here, right?"

Anderson sighed. "Of course."

I couldn't help hoping that he would ask me to stay, that he would somehow keep a leash on Emma and make sure that both Steph and I were safe from her malice. But I wasn't shocked when he merely squatted by Kerner's side and touched the dead man's throat. I thought he was checking for a pulse. Until his hand started to glow.

I took a couple of hasty steps back, primal fear urging me to run. I'd seen what Anderson could do with that glowing hand, and I didn't want to see it again.

I turned my back and squeezed my eyes closed as the light in the cavern brightened. I remembered the screams of agony from the men I'd seen Anderson kill before, and my entire body was taut with horrified anticipation. Only Kerner was already dead, so there were no screams. No sounds at all, except for the pounding of my pulse.

When the light dimmed, I turned around. Anderson was still squatting, but instead of a dead body at his feet, there was only Kerner's empty clothes. His body had been entirely consumed by Anderson's magic, leaving not even a trace of him behind.

Anderson dusted off his hands and rose to his feet, eyes averted. "Come on," he said, still without looking at me. "Let's get out of here."

I nodded my agreement, then gingerly picked up my bloodied keys from where they had landed on the steps. There were already bloodstains on my coat, so I used it to wipe off as much of the blood as I could before shoving the keys back into my pocket. I fell into step with Anderson as he led me back down the main road. The deserted city still gave me the creepy feeling that I was being watched by malevolent eyes, but it didn't seem to disturb Anderson in the least.

"What is this place?" I asked, hoping that breaking the silence would help me shake off the heebie-jeebies.

Anderson slanted a glance at me. "It's the City of the Dead. Well, one of them, anyway."

That didn't exactly tell me much. "Does that mean there are dead people hanging around here?"

But Anderson shook his head. "The city has been deserted for a long, long time. Ever since the gods abandoned Earth. The same is true, at least for the most part, of the entire Underworld."

I resisted the urge to ask him what he meant by "for the most part." I was pretty sure I didn't want to know.

Anderson led me back to the tunnel from which I'd come, and we left the City of the Dead behind. The hair on the back of my neck remained raised until the city disappeared from view. When we were back to the spot where I'd fallen through the portal— I recognized it by the splotch of Kerner's blood that marked the floor—Anderson reached over and took my hand.

"Hold on tight," he warned me. "Whatever you do, don't let go."

He took a step forward, and his foot landed on empty air, about eight inches from the ground. His next step was about eight inches higher than that, and I realized he was climbing stairs I couldn't see. He was also pulling on my hand, so I took a tentative step forward, lowering my foot until I felt something solid below. I glanced down just to be sure, but yes, my foot was resting on empty air.

Blowing out a deep breath, I squeezed Anderson's hand a little tighter and followed him upward into the impenetrable darkness.

TWENTY-FOUR

Life in the outside world had not come to a stop while I was in the Underworld, and by the time Anderson and I emerged from the portal into the cemetery, it was deserted.

"Are Jack and Jamaal all right?" I asked, ashamed of myself for not having asked earlier. I remembered Kerner's jackal chomping down on Jack's hand, and I remembered the blood I'd seen on Jamaal. That meant they were far from "all right," but I hoped what I'd seen had been the worst of it, that the jackals hadn't done any more damage when I'd run off in pursuit of Kerner.

Anderson waggled his hand in the universal gesture for so-so. "Jamaal was passed out when I came after you, but his wounds seemed to be healing. Jack was already starting to run a fever, but he'd only been bitten once, so it'll take a while for the infection to put him on his back. I sent them home while I went after you."

"You sent them home when Jamaal was unconscious and Jack was infected?" Jack was a lunatic driver under the best of circumstances, but with the super-rabies in his system . . .

Anderson shrugged. "It was either that or leave them lying in the graveyard for however long it took me to retrieve you. I thought it was the lesser of two evils."

"And what did you tell Jack when you created a portal to the Underworld?"

Anderson's people all assumed he was *Liberi,* but none of them knew who his divine ancestor was.

"I admitted that I'm descended from a death god," he said. "There was no harm in telling him that much, though I made it clear the discussion was going no further."

"And what are you going to say about Kerner?"

"We trapped him in the Underworld." His expression dared me to contradict him, but I wasn't about to. As long as he'd put Kerner out of his misery, I was happy to let him keep however many secrets he wanted.

I was following Anderson blindly, but when we came to the edge of the cemetery, I blinked and did a quick visual survey. Anderson turned left after stepping over the miniature fence that marked the cemetery's boundary.

"My car is that way," I told him with a jerk of my thumb toward the right. Another perk of my ancestry was an extremely good sense of direction.

Anderson kept walking. "Not anymore it isn't."

I hurried after him, frowning. "What do you mean?"

"I sent the boys home in it." He shot me a look that was almost apologetic. "It was closer than my car, and Jack and I had to carry Jamaal, who is not a feather-weight."

I narrowed my eyes at him suspiciously. How convenient that the car with my suitcase in it wasn't there and that I would therefore have to go back to the mansion after all. Then I shook my head.

"Wait a minute. How did you guys get keys to my car?" Jack had managed to pick my pocket earlier that evening, but I knew for certain the keys had been on my person when I jumped into the portal, seeing as they'd been the weapon I'd used to kill Kerner.

Anderson laughed. "Jack's a trickster, Nikki. Do you really think he doesn't know how to steal a car?"

I bit my tongue to prevent myself from saying anything unwise. Not only had Jack jeopardized our mission by calling Anderson, but he'd also monkeyed with my car. Sure, he'd probably saved all of our lives by ratting us out—even with Anderson's help, the jackals had done some serious damage—but it was the principle of the thing. I'd have loved to entertain myself with fantasies about getting revenge, but I wouldn't be around to carry them out.

The ride back to the mansion showed me just how exhausted I was. Within minutes of climbing into the passenger seat of Anderson's car, I was fast asleep with my head against the window. I'm sure I'd have slept all the way back if we hadn't hit a pothole that made my head bump painfully against said window. I sat up with a start, then promptly yawned so big my jaw made an alarming cracking sound.

"If you're still determined to leave," Anderson said, watching the road studiously, "you should at least wait until morning. You're worn out."

He was right about that, and my body begged me to agree. My eyelids felt like they weighed about ten pounds each, and my mind was all fuzzy around the edges. I wouldn't be the safest driver in the world, and I certainly wouldn't get far.

It was tempting, I won't lie. But I knew that if I spent the night at the mansion in my own bed—I wondered briefly when I had come to think of the bed in the mansion as "my own"—it would be even harder to get myself to leave.

"Please make sure Emma doesn't do anything to Steph when I'm gone," I said. "I know you don't really believe she'll do it, but look out for Steph anyway."

Anderson didn't answer, but the tightening around the corners of his eyes and mouth proved he'd heard me just fine. In the letters I'd left at the mansion, I'd asked both Anderson and Blake to keep their eyes on Steph and keep her safe, though I still hoped that was an unnecessary precaution, that Emma would have no interest in Steph if I wasn't around to be hurt by whatever she did.

My head was starting to inch back toward the window, my eyes almost closed, when Anderson spoke again.

"Jamaal needs you."

The words startled me enough to wake me up and make me feel almost alert. My throat tightened at the mention of Jamaal's name. There was no denying there was a connection between us, whether we wanted there to be or not. And despite his failure to ask me not to leave, I knew it would hurt him when I did, that some little part of him would see my departure as just one more abandonment. But he had the rest of Anderson's *Liberi* to help him through the tough times, and he'd figured out how to manifest his death magic in a way that might help him control it.

"He'll be fine," I said tightly, not truly believing my own words.

Anderson made a little snorting sound that bore no resemblance to agreement, but that was all he had to say on the subject.

I figured that despite the ungodly hour, there would be people up and about at the mansion, since Jack's and Jamaal's return would have caused a stir even if Anderson's departure hadn't. But I hadn't expected to see practically every window lit, nor had I expected the porch lights to be blazing. From the way Anderson stiffened beside me, I knew he hadn't expected that, either.

As we made our way down the long driveway, our headlights picked up an unfamiliar car parked in the circular drive. Anderson stepped on the gas a little harder. I tried to muster some alarm, but I was too exhausted, and my body seemed to have run out of adrenaline.

Instead of turning off toward the garage, Anderson pulled up beside the mysterious car, and that was when I saw a very unexpected tableau.

Emma, dressed in an elegant mink coat and stiletto heels, was sitting on the porch swing, a large suitcase at her side and a smile on her face that didn't match the fury in her eyes. Lounging against one of the columns that supported the porch stood Cyrus, holding a knife to Blake's throat. Blood trickled from a small cut on Blake's throat and also from a split and bleeding lip. Even so, he seemed remarkably . . . relaxed in Cyrus's grip. Of course, Cyrus couldn't kill him, but I doubted Blake would enjoy having his throat slashed.

Anderson was out of the car and at the base of the porch steps before I'd even managed to open my door.

"What the hell is going on here?" he demanded, looking back and forth between Cyrus and Emma.

Emma rose lazily to her feet as I fumbled my way out of the car, swaying from exhaustion. Anderson was right, I realized—there was no way I was making my great escape right now. I couldn't kill *myself* if I fell asleep at the wheel, but I could kill someone else, and I didn't want to take that chance.

Emma gave me a quick glance and a curl of her lip before fixing her eyes on Anderson.

"What's going on is I'm leaving you," Emma declared, raising her chin proudly.

Anderson tried to keep his face expressionless, but there was no missing the pain that punched through him at Emma's declaration. And there was no missing Emma's pleasure at his reaction. He hid his pain quickly, turning an icy look toward Cyrus.

"And what's *your* story?" he asked in a tone that would have made a wise man take a hasty step backward.

Cyrus smiled and adjusted his grip on Blake, pulling the other man tighter against him in something that looked almost like a lover's embrace—or at least it would have, without the knife. Blake rolled his eyes.

"Blake objected to the idea of my leaving with your wife," Cyrus said. "I figured I'd better control him before he had me performing unnatural acts with my car."

Anderson slowly climbed the stairs to the porch, eyes fixed on Cyrus.

"We have an agreement with Konstantin," Anderson grated. "Trust me, you don't want to break it."

"It only applies if I try to remove someone by force, but Emma's the one who called *me*. Isn't that right, my dear?"

I half expected Anderson to forget his whole disguise and go on a rampage when Emma smiled and nodded.

"You can't mean that!" Anderson said, his voice just below a shout. "You wanted me to let that monster roam free just so he could kill Konstantin, and now you're going to run off and become one of his Olympians?"

"Perhaps I should clarify," Cyrus said before

Emma could answer. "My father is not in charge anymore. *I* am."

A whole slew of expressions crossed Anderson's
face all at once, foremost of which was shock.

Cyrus smirked. "My father made a grave error
in judgment that could have resulted in the death of
every single Olympian in the world. You don't seriously think we're all going to keep following him after
that."

"So you killed him."

Cyrus shook his head. "He's not an idiot. He saw
the writing on the wall and went on the run. Took a
few of his best friends with him."

"But not you?" Anderson taunted. "His only son?
Living son, that is?"

The look on Cyrus's face didn't change. Anderson's
taunt had missed its mark. "I'm not an idiot, either,"
he said, and there was a hint of sadness in his voice. "I
know I've never been one of his nearest and dearest."

"I'm sure you cry about that every night," Blake
muttered under his breath. "You think you could put
the knife away now?"

Cyrus looked at Anderson. "I'm not here for any
nefarious purpose," he said. "I'm just giving Emma a
ride, if she wants it. If you'll tell Blake not to try any of
his tricks, I'll put the knife away."

Anderson looked like he was grinding his teeth,
but he gave a brief nod. Cyrus lifted the knife from
Blake's throat and retracted the blade. Blake pushed
away from him but without any obvious rancor. Then
he turned and gave Cyrus a dirty look, which seemed

like a pretty mild reaction to me, considering the blood that spotted his throat and face. Cyrus reached out and swept his thumb over the blood beneath Blake's swollen lip, smiling enigmatically.

"Sorry about that," he murmured.

I'm sure I wasn't the only one who noticed the bulge in Cyrus's tight pants, and I didn't think it was Blake's lust aura that was causing it. If I'd had any doubts before that they'd once been lovers, I was certain now.

Cyrus made his switchblade disappear—up his sleeve, I think, though I didn't see him do it—then headed for the stairs, brushing past Anderson.

"I'll wait in the car," he said, then stopped a moment. "And I will uphold my father's agreement with you," he added to Anderson. "I see no reason why your people and mine need to be at war with one another."

Anderson sighed. "No, of course you wouldn't."

Cyrus turned to Emma. "Join me when you're ready." He descended the last few steps and then got into his car, starting the engine.

Anderson had a brief staring match with Emma, but he lost, his eyes dropping to the floor as his shoulders hunched with pain. I wanted to be anywhere but here, but I'd have to walk past both of them to get away, and that wasn't going to happen.

"Send her away," Emma said, pointing at me without taking her eyes off Anderson. "If she goes, I'll stay."

I opened my mouth to tell Emma I was going

anyway, but Anderson silenced me with a look. The expression on his face hardened.

"If you'd rather be an Olympian than stay here with me, then I won't stop you."

Fury blazed in Emma's eyes—fury that she aimed equally at Anderson and me. But it would be a lot easier for her to hurt me than to hurt Anderson, so I knew I would bear the brunt of it should she decide to exact revenge.

"If you're an Olympian, then you have to abide by the Olympians' treaty," I said, unable to keep my mouth shut when I could so clearly read the threat in her eyes. "My sister and I are both off-limits to you."

Emma made a sound that reminded me of a snarling jackal, and I doubted the Olympians' treaty would keep me safe from her wrath. Not when it was so very, very personal. She reached into her mink coat and pulled out a handful of envelopes, dropping them haphazardly to the floor. I saw the names hand-printed on the fronts of those envelopes—and I also saw that they were open. Emma had been snooping in my room while I was gone, which explained why she was packed and ready to go. She knew I was breaking our agreement, and she wasn't as confident as she'd pretended to be. Better to leave Anderson in a huff than face the possibility that he might believe me over her.

It also meant that Emma had known I was already planning to leave when she demanded Anderson kick me out.

"The treaty won't protect you—or your family— unless you're living in the mansion," Emma said. "If you think I'm going to let bygones be bygones just because you've left town, you're sadly mistaken. *Please* leave town. Give me the opening I need. I know word of what I do will reach you one way or another, and I'll enjoy fantasizing about your reaction even if I can't see it."

Anderson looked at her like she was an alien. Maybe he was finally really seeing her for what she'd become. He looked so lost my heart ached for him, even as Emma's threat sent a bolt of terror through me.

Anderson was back to trying to hide his feelings, and his face was almost completely blank when he reached out to pick up Emma's suitcase.

"I'll carry this for you," he said, lugging it toward Cyrus's idling car.

I'm sure Emma had been expecting Anderson to protest more, to try harder to get her to stay. Hell, I'd been expecting it, too. But maybe Anderson had finally woken up to what she'd become.

With a last venomous look at me, she stomped down the stairs and got into the car without a backward glance. The trunk popped open, and Anderson hefted her suitcase inside, then slammed it closed. Cyrus tapped the horn a couple of times in a pseudo-friendly farewell, then worked his way past Anderson's car and onto the driveway.

Blake and I stood and watched the lights receding while Anderson stalked into the house and slammed the door behind him.

I was so exhausted I had to steady myself on the railing to get up the steps to the porch, and I wanted to follow Anderson into the house and retreat to my bedroom with every fiber of my being. And if Blake weren't dating my sister, I'd have done just that.

"Does Steph know about you and Cyrus?" I asked him.

It looked for a moment like Blake was going to deny there was anything between the two of them, but he must have seen from the look on my face that it would never work. He reached up and dabbed away the blood on his throat, and I saw that the wound had been so small it had already healed.

"She knows," Blake said. "Not about Cyrus specifically, but . . . She knows I've been with men, if that's what you're really asking. Not that it's any of your business."

"It's my business if it's something that's going to hurt Steph in the long run. And it's pretty obvious there's still something going on between you and Cyrus. I don't want you breaking Steph's heart over *anyone,* much less an Olympian scumbag."

"He's not—" Blake started indignantly, then his cheeks reddened as he realized how his instant defense sounded. He sighed. "Cyrus isn't a bad sort as long as he's not trying to impress Konstantin, but the only thing left between us is a bunch of regret. When I left the Olympians to join Anderson, I couldn't get Cyrus to come with me."

"But if he had, you two would still be together?"

Blake shook his head. "I'm not gay. Being descended from Eros gives me a lot more flexibility than your average straight guy, but I still have a strong preference for women. It's just . . ." He rubbed his eyes like this conversation was making him tired. "I can't sleep with a woman more than once. I can never have a real relationship with anyone, even Steph. I mean, there's only so long she's going to put up with me. But I don't have the same effect on men."

For the first time ever, I really thought about what it would be like to be in Blake's shoes. If he slept with a woman more than once, she would never be satisfied by a normal lover again. Which was fine, I suppose, if they were both willing to bet her future happiness that they would be together for the rest of her life, but even a starry-eyed optimist would have trouble gambling on that.

"So you can sleep with a guy multiple times without ruining his sex life forevermore?"

Blake nodded. "If I ever want a sexual relationship that lasts more than one night, it has to be with a guy, even if I'm not naturally wired that way. So even if Cyrus had left the Olympians with me, it wouldn't have lasted. Friends-with-benefits gets old when one of you wants more and the other can't give it."

"And Steph knows all this?"

"Cyrus would have dumped me eventually when he got tired of sex without love, and Steph is going to dump me when she gets tired of love without sex." He looked me square in the eye for the first time since we'd started talking. "It would be nice if you could cut me some slack every once in a while, let me enjoy what I have with Steph for the short time I have it without constantly having to defend myself to you."

I felt sorry for him, I really did. Living with his peculiar set of powers couldn't be easy. But as much compassion as I might have for him, the fact remained that he was not good for Steph. His conscience had so far kept him out of her bed, but I wasn't sure the loneliness inside him was going to give him the strength to let her go in the long run. Which would be all well and good if he and Steph were ready to commit to each other for the rest of Steph's life, but building that kind of relationship would take time. Time they might not have if Blake got too lonely to resist temptation.

And so I did the one thing I could to plant a seed of doubt in Blake's mind, doubt that he really would spend the rest of his life alone if he didn't forget his conscience and bind a woman to him.

"You're still in love with Cyrus," I told him, and I wasn't sure I was making that up. There had been a definite vibe between them every time I'd seen them together, and I didn't think it was all on Cyrus's side, despite what Blake thought.

"I was never in love with him," Blake countered, perhaps a little too fast. "I like him on the rare occasions when he's not acting like an Olympian, but it can never be more than that."

Maybe I was actually doing Blake a favor in my effort to protect Steph. Looking in from the outside, it seemed pretty clear to me that there was something more than friends-with-benefits going on between Blake and Cyrus. And if Blake had hopes that he could build a lasting relationship with someone other than Steph, he'd have a lot easier time letting her go.

"That's not what it looked like from where I stand," I said. "If you could have seen—"

Suddenly snarling, Blake gave my shoulder a push, hard enough to make me stagger but not fall down.

"You don't know what the hell you're talking about!" he spat. "Even if I could fall in love with a man, it wouldn't be Cyrus, not after the things he's done."

To my shock, there was a sheen of tears in Blake's eyes as he turned away from me and stormed through the front door, leaving me standing on the porch in a state of exhausted confusion. And curiosity.

Deciding it was past time for my brain to shut down for the night, I followed Blake's example and entered the house. Blake was nowhere to be seen, which was just as well. I was so tired I didn't want to tackle the stairs and instead spent the remainder of the night— actually, early morning—on the sofa in the den.

Epilogue

It's going to take quite a while to sort through all of the fallout from my hunt for Justin Kerner, and I know I'm going to be spending a lot of time second-guessing my decisions.

Jack was infected with the super-rabies and had to go through the same draconian cure that I had. When he revived afterward, there was a shadow in his eyes that didn't belong there, not in eyes that usually sparkled with mischief. As mercurial and capricious as he seemed, he'd been the true hero of that night, making the decision to call Anderson and tell all while we were en route and then jumping to Jamaal's defense when Jamaal zoned out. If it hadn't been for his actions and decisions, we might very well not have lived through that night.

Although Jamaal had been bitten more times than Jack, the bites healed normally, and he showed no signs that he'd been infected. He suspected that this had something to do with his death magic. He can create the tiger now at will, although he has difficulty controlling it—as Logan discovered one time when he interrupted one of Jamaal's self-training sessions. Jamaal reeled the tiger in before it tore Logan's throat out, but just barely. On the plus side, Jamaal's moods are evening out, and he no longer smokes like a chimney in a vain attempt to keep calm.

Leaving town is no longer an option, not with Emma's threat hanging over my head. I can't leave the Glasses and Steph vulnerable to her malice, especially not when she's got the Olympians backing her. Sometimes I feel a kind of guilty gratitude that Fate provided me with a reason to stay.

Konstantin and his cronies are still out there, in hiding somewhere. Right now, Anderson is too devastated about losing Emma to think about what that means, but I know that one day soon, he'll realize that he's now free to attack Konstantin without having to start a war with the Olympians and risk losing his people. How long will it be before he asks me to go on a new manhunt? Hunting Kerner to stop his killing spree was one thing, but hunting a man down for personal vengeance is another. I'm not sure how my conscience will swallow that when the time comes.

And then there are the Olympians themselves. To all appearances, Cyrus is by far a lesser evil than Konstantin. According to Blake, he will put a stop to the most egregious of the Olympians' actions—like killing Descendant children—but that doesn't make him one of the good guys. He still believes in the basic Olympian philosophy, which is that they are the pinnacle of creation and can do whatever they please, unfettered by the morality of mere humans. Blake has warned me to be very careful with Cyrus, who he's sure will want to recruit me as an Olympian just as his father had—but who will do so in a more subtle and insidious manner.

Personally, I'm not worried that Cyrus is going to sweet-talk me into joining him. I don't care how subtle or charming he can be; he's the enemy, and my mind is very clear about that. I just hope that once he realizes I can't be persuaded, he doesn't decide he needs to employ tactics like his father's to change my mind.

My heart—or maybe just my innate pessimism—tells me that eventually, I'm going to be forced to make myself disappear. Even if I somehow manage to make peace with Emma so I don't have to worry about her hurting my family, my power is unique and useful enough that I can't see the Olympians ever giving up hope of getting their claws into me. Hell, even a revenge-crazed madman like Kerner had wanted to bend me to his will. If I stayed out in the open long enough, someone would eventually find a way to crack me, and that was something I could never allow to happen.

But for now, for however long as I can, I will stay here with my fellow *Liberi* and bask in the feeling that I almost kind of belong.

For me, that's a big step in the right direction.

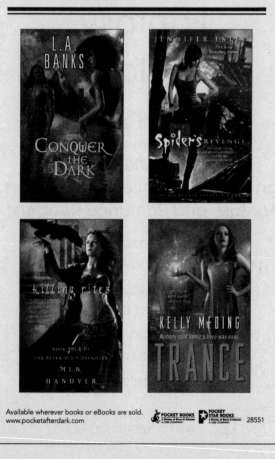

Walk these dark streets... if you dare.

Pick up a bestselling Urban Fantasy
from Pocket Books!